ESCAPE FROM THE ASYLUM

Written by
Jim Ricca

Discover other titles by Jim Ricca on Smashwords.com

ESCAPE FROM THE ASYLUM

CHAPTER ONE

"Mr. Nunzio, can you hear me?" A woman's voice, soft but persistent repeated, "Mr. Nunzio, can you hear me?"

My head felt like I'd been hit by a bus before it backed over me to make sure I was dead. I tried to answer her, but my mouth was dry as the Mojave and tasted like shit. She gave me a sip of water through a straw. I opened one eye to see a woman in nurse's whites staring at me.

"Where the hell am I and how did I get here?"

"Don't you remember anything from last night, Mr. Nunzio?"

I went to rub my aching head, but my arms were tied down. "Can you release my arms? My head is about to explode."

"I'll release your restraints if you promise to behave."

With my right arm freed, I gently massaged my face and scalp as I tried to recall the previous evening's events. "The last thing I recall is walking in the front door of my house to find my old lady standing there with a nasty sneer on her ugly face."

"Don't try to stand just yet," She remarked as she stood, "I'll be right back with something for your head injury."

I slowly and carefully rubbed my head with both hands to discover a sizeable lump on the back of my skull. The hair around it had been shaved off, and I could feel numerous sutures.

"Hey, dude, that was some show you put on last night." A man about 60 years of age with a long gray beard and hair tied back in a ponytail was leaning against the doorframe. He was grinning from ear to ear as he slowly entered the room with his hand held out. "Steve Hamm," he offered, "And who might you be?"

"Vince Nunzio," I replied, shaking his strong hand. "Where the hell am I and how did I get here?"

He knitted his eyebrows, slowly shook his head, and asked, "You don't know?"

"Would I be asking if I did?"

"You're in Crownsville State Hospital, the veterans' ward." He helped me sit upright, sat next to me, and added, "You were brought in last night by the state police and an ambulance crew. I must tell you, Vince, you did not go gently into the night. It took

6

four troopers and three EMTs to hold you down long enough to get a tranquilizer shot into your ass. And from what I overheard, the troopers said you put two of their men in the hospital, along with four EMTs..."

"Steven, if you don't mind; I'd like to administer his pain medication and begin recording his medical history," the nurse stated as she slid a chair next to my bed.

"Okay, Merri," Steve replied as he rose, turned to me and said, "I hate to say it, but welcome to Crownsville, Vince. Things here aren't as bad as you'd think, but we'll meet up later and I'll introduce you to the rest of the guys."

Merri handed me a little cup with two pills and a paper cup full of water, "Take these for your headache." She stared at me for a moment before stating, "You had a very violent encounter with the people assigned to bring you in for evaluation last evening, Mr. Nunzio."

"Call me Vince, Nurse Merri," I replied after swallowing the pills and water. "Like I told Steve; all I saw when I entered my house was the old lady giving me a sneer, and then someone hit me from behind. I don't remember anything after that."

"According to the report filed by the EMTs, you were presented with forcible commitment papers, and after reviewing them, you became very belligerent. It states they had to call the police to subdue you and get you into the ambulance."

"We're going through a divorce, and she probably thinks she'll be able to seize all my property and money if I'm committed here."

"She has somehow managed to secure power of attorney..."

"How the hell can she do that when I was, and I am, still quite sane?"

"I don't know how she did it in advance of your commitment and final diagnosis, but she did!" Merri handed me a sheet of paper and it clearly indicated the bitch now had power of attorney. "But all the legal issues will have to wait until you've been evaluated by our psychologists and psychiatrists." She smiled and added, "We also have legal specialists to help with any other non-medical issues that frequently arise from a forcible commitment."

"How soon can I use a phone? I need to call a few people to protect my assets and possibly facilitate my discharge from here."

"Not until the doctors give their approval, which might not be until next week."

"She can clean out all my accounts and be gone by then!"

"I'm sorry, but those are the rules, Mr. Nunzio."

We spent the next hour completing my medical history, and after she checked my vitals, I was free to use the bathroom and take a shower. At least the bitch sent along my duffel bag full of clothes and my toiletries. Feeling somewhat better, Merri led me to the nurse's station where Merri Wahl, RN, introduced me to the other nurses who seemed nice enough, but it was obvious they were a little wary of the man with a history of taking down cops and EMTs.

Shirley Davis, a psych nurse, laid down the rules of the ward in no uncertain terms. "No smoking indoors, no drugs-other than what we give you. There will be no fighting, loud arguments, and no arguing with the staff. You'll get out of bed by seven, be showered, and shaved by eight, and breakfast is from eight to nine. You'll have no weapons of any kind. The staff controls the TV, and if there's a particular show you'd like to watch, put in a request here at the nurse's station at least an hour in advance. There will be no loud music from your personal devices. You are restricted to the building and a small fenced in yard where you may smoke."

"Kinda like prison!" I laughed, shook my head, and asked, "How soon will I see the doctors?"

"You're scheduled to see Dr. Fitzpatrick tomorrow morning at nine." Nurse Davis smiled, "I know you're in a hurry to be evaluated and possibly secure your discharge, but these things take time and you won't be leaving anytime soon."

I knew enough not to explode in anger at the nurse, but I had to ask, "What did the whore claim I did to cause my commitment?"

Shirley slowly shook her head, "I'm not permitted to release information to a patient, but Dr. Fitzpatrick will review everything with you tomorrow." She smiled again, "Why don't you introduce yourself to the other veterans before we have lunch, which will be in one hour, Mr. Nunzio."

"Call me Vince, Nurse Davis. My father was Mr. Nunzio. He was a damn mean drunk, and I'd appreciate it if you didn't mix us up."

"I understand, Vince. Call me Shirley, and of course, you know to call Merri by her first name, too. We're very informal here since we're all veterans, and we do what we can to help each other. Some of the vets are particularly helpful during group therapy."

A familiar tall and very attractive black nurse entered the ward, stared at me for a few moments before she broke into a huge grin, and shouted, "Vincent Nunzio! I can't believe you've returned to us!" She rushed to me with open arms and as we hugged, I suddenly remembered, "Barbara Wilson! What a surprise to see you again! I thought you would have been promoted to head the health and mental hygiene department by now, especially since they closed down the main part of the hospital."

She leaned back, smiled, and gave me a brief kiss, "I've really missed you, Vinny! You were the best damn health and safety officer I've ever seen or even heard about. I thought you quit and moved back to Pennsylvania for a high paying job with some big manufacturing company. So, tell me how they got you back here."

"I did relocate for that job, but I was in the middle of a nasty divorce when the sneaky bitch had someone draw up forcible commitment papers. She had somebody club me over the back of the head before they brought me here."

Barb froze, her eyes went wide, and quickly glanced at Shirley for reassurance I was only kidding her. However, Shirley just nodded before Barb backed up, grabbed my hand, dragged me down the hall to an empty office, and closed the door behind us.

"Tell me everything," Barb gasped as she had me sit. "I'm the director of nursing here, and I'll do whatever I can to help you."

After relating what I could recall, I added, "She seems to think she deserves every penny we have in our joint accounts plus the house. So, she probably talked to her family, and they must have put her in touch with some scumbag lawyer. He managed to get her power of attorney, so she could seize all our assets."

Barb leaned forward and whispered, "You weren't treated for any mental problems since you worked here; were you?"

"Of course not; so, I have no idea where she got the evidence or documentation to have me committed."

"You always seemed to be the sanest person I've ever met, Vince. You had a wild and crazy sense of humor, but you are definitely sane and have no business being here."

"Barb, I need to use the phone to lock down my accounts before she empties them."

She pushed the desk phone in front of me before she got up and said, "I'll be right back, Vinny. I want to make sure your nurses know you're a close friend of mine, and you're treated properly while you're here. Go ahead and make your calls."

My stockbroker answered on the third ring, and after explaining what happened, he agreed to shift all but one share of each stock from the joint account, to a new account he'd establish for me. Dave promised to send the related paperwork to my new address at the hospital by next day air in care of Barb. He would have transferred the entire amount, but it was a joint account with the bitch. He'd just gone through a nasty divorce, so he was very sympathetic. Since I had my new brokerage account number, I called the bank and transferred the entire checking and savings accounts to my new brokerage account, except for ten dollars to keep the accounts open. The transfer would take effect in three days; in the meantime, the account would remain frozen.

I was about to call the firm holding my annuity when Barb, Merri, and Shirley entered the office, and stood there staring at me with wide eyes and gaping mouths. Barb held her hand toward me, "Merri, Shirley, meet Vince Nunzio! He who used to be our Health and Safety officer, in addition to our credentialing officer and a long list of other titles he held here back in the early nineties. Vinny was personally responsible for reducing our patient population from over five hundred to less than three hundred in only two months, in addition to firing four deadbeat doctors, at least twenty lazy and or drug- addicted nurses, and I couldn't count the number of direct care aides and maintenance people. And every damn one of those people got exactly what they deserved, and the hospital was much better off for his efforts."

Shirley gasped, "You fired civil service people?"

Barb answered, "Vinny was sharp, and he kept all kinds of documentation on those people, even though the Human Resources manager was too lazy and too damned scared of the unions to help him. Every one of those people filed grievances, and he beat every damn one of them. They even sued him for discrimination, and he beat them in court without using a state lawyer." She grabbed both their arms and said forcefully, "Vince is my close friend, and I want you to take very good care of him. Let him use the phone when he needs to and don't give him meds if they are prescribed. There's nothing wrong with him except he married a greedy, two-faced bitch of a wife. Of course, if he wants to see me, call right away, and let him have his visitors." Barb turned to me, "My extension is 4029, and feel free to call even if you just need to talk to someone."

I let her know to expect an overnight delivery for me tomorrow. Barb readily agreed to sign for it and bring it right over. I received a long embrace before she left, promising to have me released as soon as possible.

Merri gave me a warm smile before stating, "I'd love to hear about your time here, but let's get you introduced to the others before we have lunch."

Steve was the first to approach when we entered the day room. He threw an arm around my shoulder and called to the room, "Hey, everybody, we have a new inmate! Let me introduce Vince Nunzio to our little family of misfits." As he walked me toward the group of about twelve men, all of whom appeared to be about my age, he poked one stocky man in the gut and said, "This is Victor Smith, a former flyboy."

We shook hands as Vic remarked, "Sorry to see you here, Vince, but we'll do what we can to help you with whatever problems you've been having."

Then I met Tom Hewitt, "Tommy was in the Army, and his main claim to fame is that he spent thirty years in the army and never missed a meal!"

Tom shook hands and welcomed me to Crownsville before giving Steve a shot to the gut. Just as I started laughing, there was a sudden and horrendous screeching noise from the hallway. "What the fuck is that?" I began looking around for somewhere to hide, when Tom grabbed my arm, and walked me out to meet the source of the terrible cacophony.

"This is Ray Norsworthy, Vince," Tom said as Ray ceased his tortured wailing, smiled, and shook my hand.

"Nice to meet you, Vince," Ray said before he let out with another earsplitting screech. He was snapping his fingers and moving to music only he could hear.

"Ray was an Elvis impersonator," Steve interjected with a wink, "But one night he was performing at an outdoor concert and decided to do it on orange sunshine acid. He was in the middle of his third song when the acid kicked in, only a few minutes before multiple bolts of lightning nailed his ass."

"I guess it ruined his voice…"

Ray suddenly stopped, looked at Steve, Tom, and me then said, "Thank you; thank you very much!"

The rest of the vets introduced themselves as we walked to the dining room at the end of the hall. Most were friendly enough, except for one pot-bellied, red-faced man wearing a Marine Corps T-shirt who stated angrily, "You ain't never getting out of here, you fucking doggie. You're one sick motherfucker, and now we're going to have to put up with your ugly ass…"

"That's enough, Yates," Tom growled at the man. "We don't need any of your shit, so keep your fucking mouth shut before I put my fist in it." Steve shoved him away just before Merri called for me to sit with her and the other nurses.

The food was relatively tasteless, but it was filling. I ate while Merri reviewed my schedule for the rest of the week. "You'll meet with Dr. Fitzpatrick tomorrow morning at ten. Then I'll take you down to the clinic for your physical, which should take an hour at most. If you promise to be good, we'll have lunch at the staff dining room and take a quick trip to the library if you want something to read."

"How many evaluations will I have to go through before I'm declared sane and released?"

"You'll need to be seen by two psychologists and two psychiatrists, plus an MD before they meet to discuss your mental condition." Dawn gave me a weak smile, "But we're severely understaffed, even as small as we are; so, it could be at least two months before we can run you through the process."

"Can I bring in my own specialists to speed things up?"

Merri nodded her head, but replied, "You can bring in as many as you want. Their evaluations can, and will outweigh our doctors, but the credentialing process with the VA can take as long as six months or more, Vince. So why don't you just let the system take care of you, and with Barb pulling strings, I'm sure you'll be out of here in record time!"

"As you know, I used to work here and made a lot of friends among the staff. Are any of the MDs, psychologists, or psychiatrists from the early nineties still here?"

"There's a few nurses, housekeepers, and Dr. Kodibandalou, or Dr. K as we call him, who stayed on. Dr. K is head of Psychiatry, and you know Barb is now Director of Nursing. If you knew

Geraldine Potter from housekeeping; she's now head of housekeeping, and Dr. Sostre, who ran the geriatric or somatic ward is now Director of Medicine."

"Dr. K and I were good friends, but he must be at least 100 years old by now."

"I have no idea how old he is, but he's still sharp as hell and has a wicked sense of humor. Dr. Fitz doesn't approve of him, and I know they've had numerous battles over patient meds and therapies."

"From what I recall, Dr. K believes in using as little medication as possible. He relies heavily on various types of therapy to help people get better, and he was damn good at it."

"Fitz likes to keep patients drugged to the max so they'll be quiet, cooperative, and easier to handle, but I haven't seen much progress in anyone she's been treating." Merri slowly shook her head, "I've heard some amazing things about Dr. K and his therapies, and how they get the patients back home. However, the VA has a very rigid system and although he's technically her boss, Dr. K can't overrule Dr. Fitz's diagnosis, prognosis, or treatment regimen without first having a peer review, which can take at least six to eight months."

"Can I be transferred to his list of patients? I definitely don't want someone like Fitzpatrick determining my future."

"You came in on Fitz's rotation, but I'll see what I can do, Vince. Let's head back to my office, and I'll call Barb to let her know."

Steve grabbed my arm as I walked by his table, "See you out on the patio when you're done with Merri."

Merri's phone rang as soon as we entered her office, and after answering it, she replied, "He's right here!" She handed me the phone with a smile, "Word of your arrival got around fast, Vince."

A Urdu-accented voice shouted, "Vincente, I'll be right over with your medication! I'm prescribing 100 CCs of LSD every hour until this episode passes!" He hung up before I could say anything, but I knew it was Dr. K.

Ten minutes later, my old friend rushed into the ward with a huge smile on his gaunt face, and an old bicycle pump equipped with a long needle in his hand. After exchanging embraces and our recent histories, he asked for the exact details of my commitment. I told him what little I could before he opened my file, scanned through it, slammed it shut and remarked, "I'll do what I can to have you transferred to my care, Vince. It's obvious from reading your history, you were never thoroughly evaluated by a qualified psychiatrist or psychologist. This will be a simple matter of our refuting their diagnosis and discrediting their methods, if not their actual credentials. So, hang in there, cooperate with the staff, and I'll have you out of here before your hair turns gray."

"It's already gray, Doc…"

He laughed, shook my hand, and rose to leave. "I was just joking, Vince. I think we can you have discharged by the end of next year at the latest."

"Next year?"

"We're dealing with the VA and you've been forcibly committed, so it isn't like it was when the state ran this place. There's a huge bureaucracy to contend with, and they move just slightly slower than geologic time." He gave me a sad smile, "We'll take good care of you, Vince, but you and I have to play by the rules. As soon as Fitz turns you over to me, I'll get you released. Until then, I'll order you to have grounds privileges and occupational therapy in the health and safety department."

I thanked him for his help before he left for his office.

Steve and a few other men were on the patio catching a smoke. He introduced me to a man I hadn't met this morning.

"Nice meeting you Vince," Don Farmer stated with a grin as we shook hands. "Sorry to meet you here, but if you need help, this is the place to get it; if not from the shrinks, then you'll get plenty from the vets during our group meetings."

"Thanks, Don, but the only help I need is getting out of here."

"You were forcibly committed?"

"Yeah, Vinny was put here by his old lady so she could grab all his money," Steve replied. "But he used to work here and has a lot of good friends in key places that can help him."

I glanced around at the three men at our table, "Weren't you guys committed too?"

Don grinned, "I had myself committed to get my head straightened out again." He gave me a conspirator's grin, "I work for the University of Maryland, and I have one hell of an ignorant boss, but my department head is even worse! They've been trying to have my tenure rescinded because we don't see eye to eye on how athletes should be graded. I reviewed my contract to see if they could void my tenure, when I discovered our medical benefits allow for thirty days of in-patient mental health care every year. I asked the HR manager how I would apply for it; he told my department head, which is a violation of at least five university, state, and federal laws. Nevertheless, the department head threatened to fire me if I took a mental health leave." He grinned, pointed his finger at me, and stated, "His threat is considered retaliation, and I told the bastard, if fires me, I'll sue the university and retire early with a hefty sum of money in the bank, plus all benefits paid till I reach 95." He laughed, slapped the table, and roared, "The son of a bitch fired me, and my lawyer already filed several lawsuits against the university. As soon as I finish my R&R, I'm moving someplace warm with good fishing and retire from all the bullshit."

"You can leave any time you want?" I gasped at his revelation.

"Sure; as long as I don't hit anyone, I can leave any time I want, just like any of the other voluntary patients."

Steve winked, "Me, you, and Elvis are the only forcibly committed patients here, Vinny."

"How did you end up in here, Steve?"

"I'm bi-polar, which means I have two separate and distinct personalities. My alter ego got me arrested and convicted for theft, but I'm really not a thief." He winked, quickly glanced around the room, and whispered, "We'll talk later."

Supper was just as tasteless as lunch. After watching the news and a PBS show about killer penguins, I turned in for the night. A DCA advised I'd stay in a private room until declared safe to sleep in a room with other patients.

"I hope that never happens," I laughed at the direct care aide as he handed me fresh sheets and blankets. "I like sleeping alone and have a hard time falling asleep with others in the room."

"I'll tell the charge nurse know for you," He replied before closing, but not locking my door.

I fell asleep about an hour later, despite the worn mattress and strange surroundings.

CHAPTER TWO

I awoke before anyone came to rouse me, so I grabbed my toiletry bag, took a long hot shower and returned to my room. While dressing, Steve entered, introduced me to Jim Iovine, a tall dark-haired ex-marine, and they asked me to sit with them for breakfast.

"No problem," I replied, "I'm sure the breakfast is just as tasteless as the other meals prepared here."

"They cook everything in the dietary building and drive them up here," Jim stated. "If you have any dietary restriction, be sure to tell Merri and she'll pass it along to the head dietician. The food will be warm, the eggs tough, bacon hard as a rock, and the home fries a congealed mass of grease. If you can't handle it, let me know. I'll be calling out with breakfast orders as soon as we finish choking down what they serve here."

"You can call out?"

"Hell, yeah! My brother owns a diner down the street, and he'll deliver almost anything I order. I'll give you the menu, but you have to pay for the food."

"Does he take credit cards?"

"Yeah, and you can run a tab like the rest of us. We get our VA disability checks at the end of the month, and we square up with him then." He grinned, "He charges us a little less than he does at his diner; plus, his chow is a damn sight better than what we get here."

"I'm surprised they let you order out!"

"I'm not sure if it's against the rules of the hospital or the VA, but no one specifically said we can't do it, and besides, the staff almost always orders too."

We ambled downstairs to the dining room just in time to help the truck driver unload our food. Everyone had their own favorite seating, but Steve, Jim, and Don saved a seat for me at their table. As advertised, the breakfast was not only tasteless; it was barely lukewarm, greasy and smelled a lot like soap. I turned to Jim, "Can I see that menu, buddy?" He handed me a copy and after reading it, I began to give him my order.

"Hold up, Vinny," Jim laughed, "Just mark what you want on the menu and put your name on the top. I'll call it in as soon as we've had our coffee."

"I have a credit card in my wallet, but I don't know if she shut it off on me."

"Today's meals are on me, Vince," Steve said with a grin. "And I'll cover you until you get your finances together. I know what you're going through because I went through a nasty divorce two years ago, and my old lady tried to seize all my assets too. You seem like a nice person, and I think I can trust you for the money, so don't go hungry if you're worried about paying for the food."

I was thanking Steve for his generosity when Merri stopped by our table to remind me of my appointment with Dr. Fitzpatrick.

"It's at ten, but the Doc is always at least thirty minutes late, so you'll have more than enough time to eat your good breakfast!" She smiled, handed Jim her menu order before adding, "Just wait in the day room and someone will let you know when she's ready for you."

Don slapped his forehead, "Too bad, you got Dr. Fitz too! I don't want to prejudice your opinion before you meet, but that idiot went to the fountain of knowledge and only gargled."

Jim slowly shook his head, "I have a B.A. and master's in psychology from Hopkins, but I think Fitz got her PhD through a matchbook correspondence course. I swear to God, she's a Pollyanna, and hasn't come up with one good idea based on reality since I've been here. All she does is tell you things aren't that bad, and this is such a nice place to be, and then writes you a prescription for anti-depressants."

"If you have master's in psych, what the hell are you doing here?"

"I work for the Federal Aviation Administration as a traffic controller evaluator. I interview the air traffic controllers to determine how well they're handling the stress. Then again, if they put in for disability when they can't handle it anymore."

Steve interjected, "And their stress got to you?"

"No, I could handle their problems okay, but my boss was an unmitigated, micromanaging asshole. She was always breaking my balls about the number of people going out on disability and claiming the government couldn't afford it. She wanted me to find some way to prove they're malingering, so she could fire them."

"Sounds like a bitch I used to work for," I replied.

"She doesn't have a degree in psychology, but she kept trying to overrule my findings," He laughed, "Not a good idea for someone with a B.A. in Art History." He laughed again, "So, like Don, I checked our benefits package and discovered I can take thirty continuous days a year for mental health issues, and it won't affect my career or my annual leave accrual. So, one day while she was screaming at me because there was no toilet paper in the ladies' room, which wasn't my responsibility, I told her I needed a mental health break, dropped the form on her desk, and walked out."

"No shit! That's a great benefit, Jim!" I was staring at him in awe when he smiled and said, "I have two more weeks here if I want to stay, or I can ask to spend the rest of the time at home and come here on an outpatient basis."

Jim excused himself to call in our breakfast orders, and just as he left the dining room, Barb rushed in with two shopping bags in hand and a big smile on her beautiful face.

After exchanging embraces and greetings, she stated, "The FedEx man gave me a package for you, and I bought you some things to make your stay here a little more comfortable." She handed me two sets of pajamas, a set of bath towels, a box of laundry soap, several different types of candy, a carton of smokes, and a pair of slippers. "I know you didn't bring this stuff, but you don't want the hospital laundry to wash your clothing. They use a very strong detergent and it leaves your clothes smelling like a refinery, so you'll want to wash your own in the ward's laundry room."

"Thanks, Barb, it's very thoughtful of you. As soon as I get access to my money, I'll…"

"Don't even think about paying me back, Vinny," Barb growled, "I owe you so much for all the favors you did for me while you were here, I'll never be able to pay you back." Steve muttered something, and Barb shot back at him, "Shut up, you stinking thief! Vinny is an old and dear friend of mine who always put the needs of the patients before his own, and now I have a chance to pay him back!"

Jim returned to our table, glanced at Barb and said, "If you want anything to eat, let me know because I just called in our order, but if I call now, yours will just make the delivery." Barb politely refused his offer before Jim added, "It will be here in thirty minutes."

"Let me take this stuff up to my room, Barb, and I'll be right back," I remarked and moved toward the hall.

Barb grabbed one bag, "We need to talk in private, Vince." As we entered the empty stairwell she began, "Dr. Fitzpatrick was asked to transfer you to Dr. K yesterday afternoon at the staff meeting. She became very defensive and then angry with Dr. K. She thinks Dr. K doesn't trust her judgment and treatment methods. When she asked why, Dr. K told her you were an old friend and an ex-employee here, which only made her angrier, even after Dr. K said he was familiar with your history. So be very careful what you say to her or you'll never get out of here. She's more than willing to lie about her patients behind their backs and, she'll overmedicate you just to keep you compliant."

"Thanks, Barb, I appreciate the information. The guys told me a little about her, but they didn't say she was vindictive. Jim and Don said she was a Pollyanna and basically useless as a therapist."

"Vinny, if that woman were any dumber, we'd have to stand her in a corner and water her twice a week. She got her PhD from the University of California at Berkeley, and if you recall, we had two others from there while you worked here, and you fired them both!"

I thought back for a second, "Oh yeah! One dude signed in first thing in the morning, went to his office, and locked the door. He'd climb out through the window and spend the day at his private practice." I laughed, "He sure knew how to pencil-whip his daily reports to make it look like he was treating patients, at one hundred dollars an hour."

"But you found out he was going AWOL during the day while you conducted your inspections?"

"Yeah, I guess he didn't know I had keys to every door in this place. When I saw he wasn't in his office and everything was coated with dust, I got a little suspicious, so I checked the sign in sheet, and saw he came in that morning but hadn't signed out. I found the window's security screen was unlocked, so I relocked it with one of my locks, and then came back at four-fifteen to wait for him, because he always signed out at four-thirty."

Barb grinned, "I would have loved to see the look on his face when he couldn't open the screen."

"You should have seen the look on his face when he looked through the window to find me and the hospital administrator staring back at him." Smiling at the memory, I added, "He was fired on the spot, but he filed a discrimination complaint against me and Helen because he was Hispanic. I beat that one easily by showing the board all his sign in sheets and the list of patients he was supposed to have seen..."

Barb laughed aloud, "Oh yeah, I remember now! Most of the patients had been discharged or transferred, and others didn't even exist." She grinned, "And the other Looney-tune was placing heated rocks on patient's heads to draw out the negative vibes and energy..."

"Yeah, I found out what she was doing after she gave me a bag of rocks and asked to have them disposed as hazardous medical waste. I questioned her about the exact nature of their hazards, and when she told me they were full of negative energy, I sent her to explain it to Dr. K. I think he tried to have her committed, but she split for California before we could process the paperwork."

"And she's now a semi-famous TV parapsychologist out there in Lala land!" Barb shook her head slowly as she muttered, "I spent over sixty thousand dollars getting my PhD in psychiatric nursing, and all she needed to become a millionaire was a bag of rocks she probably picked up at the garden center..."

I signed off on the papers from my broker, slipped them inside the overnight mailer he included in the package, handed it to Barb, and asked if she'd drop it in the FedEx box outside the administration building.

"I'll drop it on my way back to my office, Vinny." She glanced at her watch, "I have a meeting in a few minutes, so I have to go, but you should expect a visit later today from Doc Sostre."

I just finished my delivered breakfast sandwich when Merri called, "Vince, Dr. Fitzpatrick has arrived. She wants to see you in thirty minutes in her office, room 102." Merri rolled her eyes, gave me a forlorn look, and whispered, "Be good, and mind your manners."

I had time, so I joined the rest of the patients on the patio where we finished our coffees and had a smoke. Steve and Don smiled before Don stated, "You're about to meet one of the true wonders of nature, Vinny. About ten minutes into your session with her, you'll be hard pressed to figure out how she can handle something as complicated as a ballpoint pen, let alone a car, a computer or even a doorknob."

Steve laughed, "Don is right, but whatever you do, no matter how obvious the question becomes, don't ask who ties her shoes. She'll get very upset and go off on one of her rants about who the doctor is, and who is locked up in a mental hospital."

Tom stopped me just as I was about to re-enter the building for my appointment. He grinned, handed me a small toad he found in the grassy area of the patio before whispering, "Swallow this whole, Vinny. After you do, you can rest assured nothing worse can possibly happen to you today."

The toad was a small one, but I wasn't about to eat the damn thing. "Thanks, Tom, I appreciate the advice, but I think I'll save it for later." I slipped the frog into my shirt pocket then strolled down the hall to room 102, knocked twice and let myself in.

Dr. Fitzpatrick, or at least I assumed it was Fitzpatrick, sat behind an old, beat up, gray metal Government Issue desk, and she didn't bother to look up when I entered and introduced myself. I assumed she was reading my file, and all I saw of her was a big head of red hair. It was too uniform in color to be natural, and judging from the size of the beehive hairdo, she must invest heavily in various aerosol adhesives and hairsprays. She ignored me for a solid five minutes, even after I coughed, cleared my throat a few times, and said, "Good morning, Doctor," to attract her attention, but to no avail. She hadn't turned a page, moved her head or hands the entire time, so I said quietly as I smiled, "Do you need help with the big words on the report, Doc?"

Her head instantly snapped up to reveal the scowling face of one very pissed-off woman. She appeared to be somewhat familiar, but before I could ask if we'd met before, she growled, "I see you're still the same smart-ass, son of a bitch you were before, Vinny Nunzio!"

I didn't know whether to shit or go blind, because the woman who held my immediate future in her bony fingers, was now extremely pissed over what I intended to be a joke. Then she gave me a very nasty glare, "Don't you remember me, you rotten bastard?"

I just stared at her while my brain feverishly tried to place her face, but before it rose from the depths of my imperfect memory, she growled with bared teeth, "I was Marie Kennedy before I married another loser from Father Judge named Sean Fitzpatrick."

I raised my eyebrows and hands as a signal for her to continue, because I still could not recall her.

"Don't tell me you forgot about the prom from hell, Nunzio; you rotten bastard!"

"I'm sorry, Doc, but that was fifty years ago and a lots happened since then. They drafted me and sent me to participate in the Southeast Asian War Games. I received a severe head wound along with several other souvenirs, so my memory isn't exactly what it should be, especially when it comes to my history prior to being wounded. Therefore, you'll have to excuse me if I can't recall the cause of your animosity. If you would be kind enough to provide your recollection of what occurred back then, I'll sincerely apologize for whatever I did. Plus, you might just help fill in some blanks in my memory of that era in my life."

Of course, I instantly remembered who she was as soon as the angry redhead mentioned my old drinking and dope-smoking buddy, Sean Francis "Fuzzy" Fitzpatrick, otherwise known as "The Great White Land Tuna." I had to bite my tongue hard to keep from smiling, as I fondly recalled how Fuzzy did not have the words, "excessive," "common sense" or "moderation" in his vocabulary. He could out-drink, out-run, out-smoke, out-eat, out-fight, and gross-out any man, woman or beast on the planet. He was funnier than hell, and no matter the situation; Fuzzy would always come up with an extremely inappropriate remark. If there was trouble anywhere in the Philadelphia area, he was usually in the center of it, and more than likely, the root cause.

I suddenly snapped back to the present when she slapped the desktop and shouted for me to pay attention. "Agreeing to go out with you was the worst mistake of my life, you rude, crude son of a bitch! And to make matters worse, like an idiot, I asked you to take me to the prom, which turned to be one of the worst nights of my life!"

"I'm sorry, but as I just told you, I can't recall much of anything that occurred before I was drafted." I was hoping to get a little sympathy, but she cut me off before I could continue."

"Let me remind you of that horrible nightmare, Mr. Nunzio." She gritted her teeth, gave me a glare that would have scorched concrete, but I was lucky it only gave me a first-degree burn. "First, you picked me up in that damn souped-up, green Volkswagen bug you loved so much, while everyone else drove to the prom in nice cars. Then you just had to drag race a guy on Roosevelt Boulevard on the way, and spent the next half-hour driving like a mad-man through the streets of Mayfair to lose the police when they tried to pull you over."

She slowly shook her head at the memory of the wild, high-speed ride through the Mayfair section of Northeast Philly. I tore down numerous streets, alleys, driveways and sped up and down one-way streets the wrong way, in addition to using sidewalks, yards, and shopping centers to shake off the dozen or so police cars trying to chase me down for a couple lousy traffic tickets. I'd installed a Porsche engine in my bug, along with chrome reverse wheels and ten-inch wide, Mickey Thompson wide-oval street-racing slicks for traction. My bug was the fastest VW in the city, and those tires allowed the bug to take turns no Detroit iron could even dream about.

"You scared me half to death during your suicidal run through the streets to avoid being stopped, and then we had to walk three blocks to the hall because you parked your car behind a gas station, so the police wouldn't see it. I should have gone home right then, but like an idiot, I thought the worst was over. However, I failed to consider what your crazy friends had in store for the rest of the night! Had I known that bastard Fuzzy spiked every punchbowl with a quart of pure grain alcohol, I would have called the police, but by the time anyone realized what had happened, it was too late. Then your other buddy, Ziggy-whatever his name was, had sprinkled some drug all over the pastries, which caused most of my classmates and their dates to lose all self-control!"

I bit down hard on my tongue as the scene flashed through my mind. Over one hundred high school seniors, boys and girls, along with half the chaperones danced wildly to the music as Ziggy's hash and Fuzzy's alcohol slowly but surely eliminated their inhibitions. Fuzzy, Ziggy, and their dates began shedding their tuxedos and prom gowns in a hilariously uncoordinated strip tease. A few moments later, half the dancers joined them, throwing bits and pieces of clothing across the dance floor. A few sober nuns and parents screamed for them to get dressed as they frantically ran around the ballroom grabbing teenage girls and boys, forcing them toward the bathrooms with various clothing items in their hands. However, as it turned out, many of the attendees had brought their own supply of alcohol, in addition to significant quantities of grass, which they freely shared in the bathrooms.

"I can see you're finally remembering now, you disgusting bastard," Marie screamed.

"As a matter of fact, it's all coming back, so thanks for helping to fill in the events of that night, Marie," I replied with what I hoped was a quizzical look on my face. "Yeah, I remember now, and definitely recall warning you not to touch the punch or the pastries, but you just laughed at me and knocked back five or six big glasses of punch before you pigged out on the chocolate cake."

Her face went blank for a few moments as I continued. "I remember you wore a blue dress with white and gold trim, or whatever you call that stuff. Moreover, it wasn't long after we arrived before you wandered away from our table with the McCafferty twins looking for some action, and a few minutes later, you three and a few others were up on the stage stripped down to your undies, trying to belly dance to the song, "Save the Last Dance for Me.""

"You're a lying son of a bitch, Vincent Nunzio!" Her eyes were as wide as dinner plates as her face flushed to the color of her hair. She was about to unload on me when the door burst open. Barb and Doctor K rushed in and pulled me from my chair.

"What the hell is going on in here?" Dr. K growled while staring angrily at Fitz and then me.

"We heard Dr. Fitz screaming and yelling," Merri interjected as she glared at Marie. "We didn't hear Vince saying anything, but we heard Dr. Fitz all the way down the hall only a few minutes after he went into her office. I was going to enter the room, but Barb told me to call you first since you're her supervisor."

Doc K stood back and seemed shocked at Marie's livid complexion, but he asked me, "What did you say or do to her, Vince?"

"In case you weren't aware of it," I held my hand out toward Dr. Fitz, "I used to date Marie Kennedy before she became Dr. Fitzpatrick, and she is still holding a considerable amount of animosity toward me for events that occurred over fifty years ago, even though most of them weren't my fault."

Dr. K grabbed a chair, sat, and asked me to recount everything from the time I entered the office. After completing my statement, he requested Dr. Fitz to do the same, and since our stories were almost identical, he gave me a raised eyebrow, nodded for Barb to sit, then said, "I'd like to hear the rest of the events of that night."

Since Marie was still silently steaming, I volunteered to go first. "Marie and three or four of her friends had imbibed a considerable amount of punch spiked with grain alcohol. In addition, she and her friends ate several helpings of chocolate cake sprinkled with hash shortly after we arrived at the prom, even though I warned her not to touch anything. I remained at our table while they wandered off and eventually ended up on the stage, stripped down to their skivvies and doing their best to perform belly dances. While they were embarrassing themselves, a fight broke out on the far side of the hall between a couple chaperones and a few of the kids. I was trying to decide if it would be better to get Marie off the stage or help break up the fight when the fire alarm went off and the sprinkler system let loose."

"You tripped that alarm, Nunzio!" Marie was foaming at the mouth as she made her accusation, but I held up my hand.

"I was standing right in front of you at the time and doing my best to get you off the stage, if you'll recall. I also had what I thought was your dress in my hand when the sprinkler system started flooding the hall."

She quieted as the memory slowly came back, but she was still extremely angry when she shouted, "It wasn't my dress, you idiot! That damn thing was three sizes too big!"

I looked at Barb and Dr. K, "Well, as I was saying; the sprinklers went off, probably because of all the marijuana smoke pouring out of the bathrooms. Then someone went into the kitchen and emptied several large bottles of dish soap on the floor, which soon coated everything and everybody." I gave a short chuckle at the memory of the scene. "I eventually pulled Marie from the stage, and with considerable effort, not to mention a lot of slipping, sliding and falling down, got her to the door, just as the fire department and police showed up in one hell of a rush. You see, the prom was held in her school's gym, so they were in a hell of a hurry to get there to save all the kids attending at the time."

Dr. Fitz had her head down, her face in her hands. Dr. K. was giving me an evil grin, while Barb was wide-eyed with amusement. "I dragged her out of the gym and held her against the wall while trying to get her dressed, but she kept yelling the prom wasn't over and she wasn't leaving until the last song was sung. So, I tossed her over my shoulder and was carrying her back to where my car was hidden when a dog ran up and took off with her dress, or at least the part that tore off while I was trying to hang onto it." I took a sip of her coffee and continued, noting my therapist was now quietly sobbing into her hands.

"I got us to the car without too much trouble, but when I tried to have her stand and don her dress, she was too drunk to do anything except vomit a couple times. Thankfully, she didn't get any on me or my car's new paint job. I eventually put her in the passenger seat and that was when I realized she'd puked all over herself, so I stopped at a do-it-yourself car wash and hosed her down, along with the passenger seat because she not only barfed all over herself but crapped in her undies, too!"

"I'm not listening to anymore of his shit," Fitz screamed before attempting to leave the room, but Barb stopped her as Dr. K. barked, "I need to hear everything that happened that evening, especially since you've managed to hold all this anger over an incident that occurred fifty years ago! Sit down and you'll have your chance to rebut his statements when he's done!" He waved his hand for me to continue with a wild grin on his face.

"I had to lean her back against the hood of my beetle to wash the puke and feces off her, before I tried to put her dress on, but the only part left was the upper section, and as she said, it was way too big and wouldn't stay up since it didn't have straps. I found a bungee cord in the back seat and hooked it in front and the back to hold it up over her boobs, but it was kinda short and didn't quite reach her waistline. Too bad the dog tore off the lower half because her underpants were soaked, and you could see right through them." I snickered quietly, "And that's when I found out she was a real red-head!"

Fitz threw a stapler at me, but her aim was so bad it missed me and struck Merri on the arm. After she calmed down, I continued, "I was driving her home when it suddenly struck me, "What the hell was I going to tell her parents? Not only was she half-naked and drunk as a skunk, but her prom gown was gone, and she was out cold! But just as I turned down her street, I began smelling shit, and it was really nasty, too! When I pulled over, it quickly became apparent she had the Hershey squirts again. It was oozing all over the passenger seat and running down on the floor of my car! If that wasn't bad enough, a Philly cop pulled in front of me, and as soon as he looked in the car, he knew something wasn't quite right."

Dr. K. was leaning forward in his chair, his eyes glistened with excitement, "Go on, Vinny; please continue!"

"I told the cop she had too much spiked punch at St. Hubert's prom, and I was taking her home. I explained I was stone cold sober and hadn't touched a drop of anything. In addition, after to pointing to her soaking wet hair and remnants of her dress, I described how the sprinklers went off, but while telling him about the dog making off with her gown, he yanked me out of the car and called for the paddy wagon." I couldn't help but laugh out loud at that point. "In the meantime, her parents must have seen my bug, the cop car with its overhead lights flashing and came running up the street to see what was going on. The old man took one look at his daughter and went ballistic, especially after he got a good whiff of her as he opened the door to help her get out. The cop tried to hold him back, and it turned into one a hell of a fight."

I took another sip of Marie's coffee before I summed up the night's events. "So, before everything was said and done, the cops needed two more paddy wagons to haul everyone off to the slammer, which included Marie, her old man, me, her mother, sister and some guys I knew from high school, who tried to protect me from her family. When we got to the station, the place was full of kids and chaperones from the prom, all drunker than hell, and fighting with each other and the cops. It wasn't until late the following morning before the police got everyone separated and their stories written down. I was lucky one of the nuns and a priest swore they saw me dragging Marie off the stage, and then try to get her dressed out in the parking lot. The police decided to let me go, and I was damn lucky they forgot about our high-speed chase the night before!"

Fitz slammed her hand down on the desk and screamed, "But I was charged with underage drinking, and my parents were charged with assaulting an officer; all because of you and your goddam friends!"

"I heard they dropped the underage drinking charges against you and the others after everyone swore, they didn't know the punch was spiked."

"That doesn't matter, you son of a bitch! I was still charged and had to appear in court…"

"And it took me two months to get the stink of your piss and shit out of my car, Marie, so let's call it even!" I winked and added, "But, I'd really like my bungee cord back, and to be honest, of all the girls on the stage that night, I think you did the best belly dance…"

Marie screamed, lunged across the desk for me, but Barb intercepted her, and with Dr. K. and Merri's help, restrained the overexcited shrink while I surreptitiously dropped the bullfrog in her big handbag, and then ran for the safety of the smoking patio and my new buddies.

"Sounds like you had a very productive session with Dr. Fitz, Vinny," Don laughed as everyone gathered around to hear the gory details.

They were still roaring with laughter when we gathered in the dining room for lunch.

CHAPTER THREE

Merri and Barb forced their chairs into our group as we ate, and one hostile glare from Barb was enough to convince Steve to eat his lunch elsewhere.

"Dr. Fitz cancelled all her appointments for this afternoon because she'll be tied up with Dr. K and several other members of the department," Barb reported with an evil grin. "Geez, Vinny, I had no idea you were such a romantic teenager!"

"Do you think Dr. K will be able to take me as a patient now?" I had my hopes up for a positive answer, but Barb and Merri just shook their heads.

"From now on, he wants to be in the room with you two to make sure she's honest and impartial with her diagnosis and prognosis. As it is, she prescribed several exceptionally strong psychotropic drugs for you, but Dr. K took one look at them and immediately tore up the script." Barb grinned, "He's watching out for you, Vince, just like he said he would."

We suddenly heard a man's voice from the other side of the dining room, "No shit! Vinny used to date Dr. Fitz? Hey, Vince; was she a swallower or a spitter?" The room burst out laughing until Merri stood, turned, and shouted, "Gregory, that was completely rude, crude, and uncouth, and I don't ever want to hear that kind of talk in here ever again! No grounds privileges for you for the next week!"

I could have sworn I heard Steve mutter, "I think she uses it to hold up her hair," but no one commented on his remark.

After we finished our lunches, Barb drove me to the clinic where I had a happy reunion with Dr. Sostre and her staff. She'd never examined me before and was suitably impressed with the scars I accumulated as souvenirs during my time in the Army, but she declared me to healthy enough to be a mental patient. We went to the administration building next, where I met a few of my old friends and after bringing them up to date on my recent history, we all went out to dinner at a local seafood restaurant. Barb and Dr. K asked me to relate my colorful history with Dr. Fitz and just as I finished, Barb announced it was time for me to return to the cottage, as it was almost nine PM.

"We wouldn't want our Vinny to be listed as missing and probably eloped, now would we?" She smiled at everyone, "And I'm going to tape his next session with Dr. Fitz, so he won't have to repeat himself."

Upon our return, the nightshift nurse gave me a hairy eyeball and stated, "Dr. Fitzpatrick called and ordered a prescription for Mr. Nunzio. The pharmacy was already closed..."

"Barb snapped, "What did she order?"

"She prescribed heavy doses of Lithium, Thorazine..."

Barb snatched the paper from the nurse's hand, "She was told by Dr. K, Vincent does not need a prescription, and he even tore up her scripts right in front of her. That bitch is going to be answering to a peer review if she keeps up her shit!" Barbara grabbed the nurse by her shoulder, "I am the director of nursing, Cathy, and I'm ordering you to contact me and Dr. K immediately if Dr. Fitzpatrick prescribes anything for this man; do you understand?"

"Sure, Barb, I understand. I've heard you two are old friends and Vince used to work here, but his chart says he has violent mood swings, is subject to vivid hallucinations, and is suffering from early onset Alzheimer's..."

"That's all a lie, Cathy. His soon-to-be ex-wife had some shyster lawyers and a couple quacks falsify the forcible commitment papers! He's to receive no meds unless he asks for aspirin or some other over the counter medication."

Cathy gave me a sympathetic look before asking if I needed anything to help me sleep.

"Thanks, Cathy, but I don't need anything." I gave Barb a goodnight hug and kiss before running upstairs to my room, where I found Don, Steve, Jimmy and a few others hanging around in the bathroom catching a smoke.

"Hey, man," Don laughed, "We all thought you went over the hill."

"Naw, I was just visiting with some of my old friends from here, and we went out to dinner at the seafood joint down the street."

Steve coughed, "Did they give you any meds?"

"That bitch tried to prescribe some, but Dr. K ripped up the script, and then she tried calling it in after hours, but Barb stopped that shit."

Steve reached around to his back pocket and handed me a slider of Crown Royal. "Have some muscle relaxer, buddy. You look like you can use it."

I took a snort, handed it back and raised my eyebrows.

"My brother sends me a bottle once or twice a week with my dinner or lunch order. No one checks the food they deliver, and unless I get caught with the bottle by the wrong person, it's no big deal."

Don took a short sip, handed it off to Jimmy, then asked, "What the hell is going to happen now you've embarrassed the shit out of Fitz?"

"I have no idea, buddy, but I have a sneaking suspicion I'm going to find out the hard way." After thanking Steve for the nightcap, I turned in and slept like a baby.

Merri sat with me during breakfast the following morning. "I just received a call from Dr. K. He said you're to take part in group therapy sessions from now on. He's afraid Dr. Fitz will get violent if you bring up any more embarrassing incidents from her past."

Jimmy was sitting next to me, and he grinned, "Maybe if we bring up enough embarrassing moments, she'll find another line of work, or at least peddle her drugs someplace else."

Tommy laughed, "And if she was dumb enough to date Vinny, I'm sure he has a long list of memorable moments for her to enjoy!"

Jimmy added, "In my humble opinion, Fitz has delusions of adequacy, but has yet to achieve anything like it. So, why don't we help her along the road to achieving peace with honor here at Crownsville?"

Merri smiled, coughed and said quietly, "Just don't do anything illegal, immoral, or unhealthy, boys."

The group session was scheduled for two this afternoon. Barb and Dr. K arrived promptly at two. While we waited for Fitz to arrive at her normal thirty-minute delay time, Barb pulled me into an office and after locking the door warned, "Vinny, you have to be careful! Fitzpatrick filed a complaint against you with the board. She claims you were exceptionally uncooperative and became extremely aggressive when she brought up your past."

"You told me she'd lie, but to lie so blatantly even when you were in the room with us is unbelievable! Did you and Dr. K file your own accounts of what occurred?"

"Yes, we did, this morning after we read her statement. Dr. K is requesting a peer review of her behavior and past practices, but it will be at least two months before one can be convened."

"What do you suggest I do?"

"Keep your mouth shut and don't say a damned thing unless you're asked a question, and then keep your answers as short as possible! Don't give that bitch a damned thing to hold against you! And now that I've seen her in action, I get the distinct impression the cheese slid off her cracker a long time ago."

I suddenly had a thought, "Is she a veteran, Barb?"

"Yes, she is. Fitz was a psychological evaluator in the Air Force for six years. She primarily tested pilots for the space program, but she got riffed when the Shuttle program was shit-canned."

"Those lucky bastards," I muttered under my breath just as Dr. Fitzpatrick entered the cottage in a rush. She stopped long enough to give me an angry, contemptuous stare then entered her office and slammed the door behind her.

"Hey, Barb, play along with me. I'm going to act like I took the drugs she called in last night. Make sure you tell Merri in case Fitz checks my meds record."

Barb just stared at me for a few moments before she ran to the nurse's station.

Merri was fully on board by the time she left her office with Barb. "I'll help you, Vinny," She whispered while helping me to my feet, and as I staggered into the day room, Fitz rushed past us with an evil grin on her face.

Dr. K was already in the room and having a quiet conversation with several vets when he glanced up at me. His eyes went wide with shock and dismay, as he thought I'd actually taken the drugs Fitz prescribed, but I gave him a quick wink and then sat on a chair between Don and Steve.

I put on my best doped up patient act; rolling my eyes, exhibited difficulty holding my head up, while maintaining a goofy smile and drooling. A quick glance at Fitz was all I needed to see she believed my Academy Award winning performance. I leaned heavily against Steve, resting my head on his shoulder for a few moments before doubling over at the waist and almost falling off my chair. Steve and Don grabbed me just before I hit the floor, sat me back on my chair, and then used their shoulders to pin me against the backrest.

"I thought I told you not to prescribe any meds for Vincent, Dr. Fitzpatrick!" Dr. K sounded rather angry.

"I'm his therapist and after the behavior he exhibited yesterday, I decided to prescribe meds to contain his over-aggressive personality and hallucinations!"

"We discussed his behavior, memories, and unique personality at length yesterday afternoon, and we both agreed they were well within norms…"

"I'd like to discuss this matter later, DOCTOR Kodibandalou! At the moment, I'm attempting to conduct a group therapy session for these men, and my time is very limited. So, if you don't mind, I'd like to begin." Fitz was obviously growing angry at Dr. Ks interference and questioning in front of her patients. She was just beginning to flush, the veins in her forehead growing more prominent.

Dr. K glanced at Barb who gave him just the slightest shake of her head, indicating he should let the matter drop, which he did with a sigh of reluctance.

"Okay, everyone! Now, with that unpleasant matter behind us, if I can have your attention," Fitz stated with a voice and hand motions one would normally use on kindergarten children. "I just want to take a moment to welcome Vincent Nunzio to our group therapy session. Vincent, if you'll just introduce yourself and describe some of the problems that brought you here; I'm sure some of our group members will be more than happy to relate their similar problems and recommend processes they learned in our group to alleviate those problems."

Tommy was sitting next to the shrink, and I noticed he kept glancing down at her oversized leather bag. Just as Don and Steve propped me up in my seat so I'd be sitting erect, Tom looked down again, leaned over just a bit then glanced at me with a conspirator's grin.

Since I was supposed to be heavily dosed with anti-depressants, psychotropic drugs and Lithium, I knew enough to slur my speech and mentally wander off subject. In order to do this right, I had to stand, so I struggled to get up until my two buddies got the hint. Steve held me from behind by the belt, while Don maintained a good grip on the back of my shirt collar. I flailed my arms around a little, rocked my head from side to side a few times to let the drool fly, and with the goofiest smile I could muster, began singing the opening words to The Band's old hit song, "The Weight."

"The Weight" was a song I knew she hated with every fiber in her body. It was the very same tune that repeatedly played on my VW's broken eight-track tape player the night of her senior prom. I sang loud enough to be heard by everyone in the room, while being careful not to slur the words too badly, *"I pulled into Nazareth, was feeling bout half-past dead. I just need some place, where I can lay my head..."* Before I started the next word, most of the men joined right in, *"Hey, mister can you tell me, where a man might find a bed? He just grinned, and shook my hand; no, was all he said..."*

By the time we all hit the chorus at max volume, *"Take a load off, Fanny..."* Fitz vaulted to her feet, ran across the room, seized me by the throat with both hands, and violently choked me with all her might. However, Don and Steve let me go to stop her and I immediately dropped to my knees then fell forward against her legs, breaking the insanely angry shrink's grip on my neck. Don, Steve, and a few others pulled Fitz back to her chair, and forced her to sit as Dr. K rose to help me into my chair. While he checked to make sure I wasn't injured, he whispered, "My God, man; that was absolutely brilliant!"

Fitz was still struggling to get at me as she screamed every swear word she'd ever heard before in her life. Barb was asking Merri for a restraint jacket when Dr. K turned to Jimmy, "Take him outside until we get Dr. Fitzpatrick under control."

I smiled and waved at Dr. Fitz as I staggered toward the door, but just as Jimmy opened the door, Fitz leaned over to grab her bag, and in a flash, the toad I dropped into it yesterday leapt out. It smacked her in the face, fell on her lap, croaked once or twice, and just as she realized what it was, the frog jumped straight at her overly large beehive hairdo, quickly burrowing into the mass of tangled hair.

I think Tommy and I were the only two people in the room to observe the amphibian's attack on Dr. Fitz, so when she began shrieking and clawing at her mass of hair, no one had the slightest idea what she was doing. They assumed she was throwing an exceptionally violent and self-destructive temper tantrum. Just as I turned to leave, Tommy snatched something from behind Fitz, dropped it in his shirt pocket, and then rushed to help Jimmy lead me out of the building.

"I picked up the toad when it jumped out of her hair, so they'll think she was hallucinating," Tom whispered before he broke down laughing.

Jimmy stopped to hold the door to the patio, and asked, "What's so funny, Tom?"

My buddy grinned, "Not only did Vinny put on a hell of a show in there with his song and dance routine, I think we finally have the last nail hammered into Fitz's career here." He went on to explain why she violently freaked out after being forced back into her chair.

We were still roaring with laughter a few minutes later when the rest of our group entered the patio, wide-eyed with wonder and hilarity. Tom thought it best not to reveal the cause for Fitz's second outburst just in case word got around to the wrong ears and mouths. Steve was still reenacting the doctor's attempt to choke me to death when everyone suddenly stopped what they were doing to watch Dr. K, Barb, and Merri lead Fitz out to Barb's car.

After they drove off, Don announced while poking me in the chest, "I think our group session has been brought to an abrupt end due to this sick bastard, and I think we should take a minute to properly show our disapproval of his behavior!"

Before I could say a word, someone handed me a lit joint, and at least five sliders of various types of booze refilled my coffee cup.

That evening during dinner, Merri and Barb entered the dining room and announced, "Dr. K and Dr. Malanai, our new psychiatrist, will henceforth see Dr. Fitzpatrick's patients."

"I want you men to be on your best behavior for Dr. Malanai," Barb growled and gave everyone a withering glare. "She's new to the VA and is probably one of the nicest people you'd ever want to meet. In addition, like Dr. K, she believes in administering the absolute minimal doses of any drug, and then only if absolutely necessary." She pointed her finger at me and then at the hallway before spinning on her heel and marching out of the dining hall.

While passing Merri, I received a hairy eyeball and, "We'll talk later!"

"What the hell was that song all about, you crazy bastard?" Barb was incredulous at the effect an old song would have on Dr. Fitzpatrick.

"The 8-track in my old VW bug was broken with the Band's tape stuck in it. I couldn't get the tape out, and I couldn't shut it off because the switch was broken. In addition, I had it wired into the ignition circuit, so I couldn't pull the fuse for it. It played the entire time she was in my car the night of her prom. I guess it triggered bad memories..."

"I want you to stop aggravating her, Vinny! It's one thing to get a few cheap shots, but now you're going to cause her serious mental trauma, if not PTSD. In addition, I'm beginning to think dating you back then was not exactly a romantic event."

"Okay, Barb, what do you want me to do next? I need to get the hell out of here as soon as possible..."

"You're being reassigned to Dr. Gul Malanai, so be on your best behavior. Dr. K said he'd speak with her and have her current on your situation as soon as possible." She glanced over my shoulder, grabbed my arm, and pulled me down the hall. "And I want you to stay the hell away from Steven Hamm. That man is a thief, a liar, a criminal, and a manipulative son of a bitch. Don't even talk to him if you can help it!"

"What did he do to wind up here, Barb? He seems nice enough to me..."

"That nice guy embezzled more than twenty million dollars from his employer and bankrupted the company, putting over fifty people out of work!" Her eyes narrowed to two mean slits as she added, "He worked for a ship's chandler company in the Port of Baltimore. They supplied all the ships coming to the port with things like laundry services, food, fuel and anything else they needed. However, your buddy decided to stash the money someplace and didn't pay any bills or taxes for almost two years. When they finally caught up to him, his damn lawyers said he was guilty but schizophrenic, and had four big name shrinks verify it. He claimed he didn't know where the money went. He wasn't flashing it around or living high off the hog. So, the courts ordered him here, and they're waiting for us to declare him sane enough to go back to prison where he belongs."

"He seems perfectly sane to me, Barb."

"He is sane, and his only mental problem is the son of a bitch is a greedy thief, and he's just waiting for his chance to get out of here long enough to grab his loot and split for someplace that doesn't have extradition treaties with the U.S. government for financial crimes."

"That would be Brazil, the Biminis, Laos, Cambodia, and if he's Jewish, Israel; but he'll have to buy immunity from extradition from the government there, and they'll want at least half of what he stole. Then there's a couple of the former Soviet bloc countries…"

Barb gave me a look that would blister concrete at a hundred yards before she growled, "You'd better keep your mouth shut about those places, Vinny."

"His lawyers probably already made contact with every one of those countries, so I don't know why they're waiting to get him out of here. After all, this is hardly a high security prison."

Barb quickly looked around before she whispered, "The FBI has at least two people here keeping an eye on him. As soon as he makes a move, they'll grab his skinny ass and throw him in the slammer where he belongs. He'll give up the money as soon as he meets up with a few of the amateur proctologists they have in the big house."

When we finished laughing, Barb gave me a quick hug and then turned to leave, but stopped short and said, "Oh, I almost forgot! You have an appointment with two lawyers tomorrow morning at ten. They must be your ex's attorneys because they seemed very arrogant and slimy."

"Yep, that's them!" I replied with a chuckle. "Ask Dr. K if he'll join me when I meet with them. Tell him he can play my attorney again, like he did when the Secret Service tried to have me locked up when I worked here before."

Barb almost fell over laughing, but she waved her hand in agreement, as she left the building.

CHAPTER FOUR

On my way to the patio for my last smoke of the day, I passed the shrink's office and saw the door was ajar. "I might as well call my buddy Gary to discover what the old lady has been doing," I remarked to myself, checked the hall and then quickly entered the office.

"What the fuck are you doing here?" The voice startled me, but I was even more surprised to see Elvis, or Ray Norsworthy sitting behind the desk with the phone's receiver cradled against his ear. He had a notepad out on the desk and a pen in his hand.

"I could ask you the same question, special agent…?"

"None of your damn business, Nunzio," He growled in return before muttering something into the phone, hung up and stood to face me. "I asked you a question, Nunzio, and I want an answer!"

"I stopped in to call my neighbor to see if the old lady put the house up for sale yet. However, you still haven't answered my question, special agent Elvis."

"What makes you think I'm a…"

"Come on, man! I'm not that stupid! I can spot a Fed a mile away, and I had you pegged as an FBI drone about ten minutes after I met you!" Actually, I was just guessing, but I doubted Elvis had permission to use the office phone this late at night, and his demeanor was a complete reversal of what I'd seen so far. Then I took another shot in the dark, "Let me guess; you guys have a housekeeper or DCA working here too?"

"It's none of your damn business, and if you know what's good for you, you'll keep your mouth shut about what you saw and heard here."

"What are you going to do? Put me in a nuthouse?" I didn't like being threatened, especially by this idiot and bully, but I had to be careful. "I know why you're here, so just do your fucking job and leave me alone. I need to make a call, so if you don't mind…" I waved my hand toward the door, and although I knew he wanted to say more, he just brushed past me as he left. "I'll settle up with you later," I muttered under my breath as I sat and dialed Gary's number.

I was pissed as hell after Gary told me the old lady not only had the house up for sale, but moved everything out of the house, shed and garage, including my supply of automotive and woodworking tools. He had no idea where she moved to, but she also had my cars towed. He did get the name and number of the towing company, and said he'd call them to find out where my 67 GTO, 67 Vette, and 71 Hemi GTX had been taken. They couldn't be sold without the titles, and I had the papers safely stashed in my safe deposit box at the bank. My two motorcycles were stored at the hangar with my Cessna Citation CJ3, and there was no way she could grab the bikes or the plane.

Registered to my consulting business, I rarely if ever flew in the Citation. I'd bought it after a series of trade-ups from my first plane, an old Cessna 172, and a number of exceedingly lucky breaks over the years. The most beneficial was when I discovered my favorite uncle, Serge, had passed away, and left me his collection of war birds. He'd bequeathed a P-51 Mustang in mint condition, a P-38 Lightning still in the original shipping crates, along with four Rolls-Royce Merlin engines, also in their original shipping crates. Since the bitch hated to fly, she had no idea what I owned, and I never found a reason to tell her.

The Citation was currently out on charter, but I could get it back with one call to the hangar or an e-mail to the flight crew. I saw no need to call them to pick me up for the time being; however, I called to find out where they were now and what their schedule was for the coming weeks, just in case.

I slept fairly well and woke up feeling refreshed and ready to take on all comers and would especially love to get my hands on the old lady to straighten out her greedy ass permanently. Dr. K called me to his office after breakfast to rehearse our meeting with the bitch's lawyers, and we finished just in time to sit down with the devil's advocates.

My part in the game was to keep my mouth shut and let Dr. K do all the talking, in Urdu, but the scumbags upset our plans. First, they tried to convince me they were really looking out for me and wanted to end all this unpleasantness as fast as possible. "If you'll just sign these papers, Mr. Nunzio, we can have the judge rule in your favor on the property settlement." The rat-faced bastard slid a thick pile of papers across the desk and handed me an expensive fountain pen before pointing to where I needed to sign.

I put the cap on the pen, dropped it inside my shirt while Dr. K snatched the papers off the table. He began reading them, or at least he appeared to be reading the documents while muttering something in his native language. When the scumbag lawyer held out his hand for his pen, Dr. K slapped it down and screamed, "You gave him that pen, and I am a witness! You have no right or reason to try to take it back from my client!"

"That's a Pilot 823 custom pen with an amber body! That pen cost over two hundred and fifty dollars, and I'll be damned if I'm going to let him steal it!" The shyster appeared ready to have a heart attack as he reached for me again, but I grabbed his hand, bent his fingers back almost to the point of breaking, and then shoved him back into his chair.

"If you attempt to touch my client again, I'll have you arrested for assault and battery!" K went into a long stream of Urdu curses before he ripped their document to shreds, tossed it back at them and screamed in English, "This is no agreement! It's no more than a blatant attempt to seize the rest of this poor man's property under the guise of false friendship!"

"Excuse me," The second asshole interrupted as he faced Dr K, "But I didn't get your name or your business card, or even your relationship to Nunzio."

Dr K suddenly rose to his full height of six-foot four inches, but the man couldn't possibly weigh more than one hundred sixty pounds; he was that skinny. But his large black eyes, long, thin white beard, and bald head made him appear to be the poster boy for, "save the evil mass murderer." He took a step towards the scumbag and hissed as he threw a long thin arm around my shoulders, "This man is my brother! He is my son! He is my client and my savior! This godly man is the alpha and the omega! I shall endeavor to persevere in my quest to see justice is done for him, while we vanquish the nasty witch who has so evilly sought to doom him to the dungeons of hopelessness and despair…"

Dr K was just getting started on his favorite rant when the first asshole reached for me again, but this time, I pulled the frog from my pocket and held it out to him as if it was a talisman that would ward off his evil. The lawyer's eyes went wide with shock a moment before Dr K shouted, "Open the gates of hell, and unleash the dogs of war!"

On cue, the office door burst open and in rushed two burly security officers, one of whom was an old friend from my period of employment there. Robbie, the larger of the two, grabbed me by the shoulders and lifted me from my chair, while his partner, Ralph wrapped his arms around Dr. K and shouted to the lawyers, "Get the hell out of here before they go completely berserk!"

The scumbags didn't need to be told twice. They shot out of the office, down the hall, out to the parking lot, and were several miles away before they remembered their briefcases. By the time they returned, we'd emptied them and carried off the contents, which included checkbooks, a nice collection of expensive Waterman pens, a wallet, and files from several other cases they were working on. Robbie promised to mail the files to the people they were suing. I handed the checkbooks and wallet, sans the cash it held, to Ralph. He promised to drop the wallet with its credit cards and the checkbook outside a college dorm, where the students would put the financial information to good use.

I used the cash to even up my account with Steve, after treating Dr K to a huge lunch at Outback Steakhouse. We made it back to the cottage just in time for our afternoon group session with the new shrink.

"Be nice to Dr Gul Malanai, Vinny," Dr. K cautioned. She's new to the VA and not used to dealing with evil, twisted bastards like you." He suddenly stopped in his tracks and stated, "Oh, I almost forgot. Dr. Fitz will also be in attendance today, but only as an advisor to Dr. Gul. She has no more privileges here except as an advisor or consultant. As a matter of fact, she's being seen for her rather severe PTSD later this afternoon, so be kind to her, too!"

Dr Gul was waiting in the day room when we arrived for our group therapy. She was a very pretty, tiny little raven-haired woman with beautiful large dark almond eyes. Dr. Fitz, seated next to Gul, was quick to point me out as she began frantically whispering to her. A few minutes later, we were arranged in a circle, and with coffees in hand, Dr. K had everyone introduce ourselves to the new doctor. Dr. Gul nodded and smiled at each of us before she gave us a brief description of her background and experience.

Only three of the men felt like discussing their combat history and associated problems. Their backgrounds were relatively similar: hard combat, lost friends, survivor's guilt, and difficulty adjusting to civilian life. The Vietnam vets had to deal with the hostility, harassment, and discrimination we received upon our return. The more recent vets developed problems accumulated during multiple deployments to two different war zones. However, the root cause of most of their problems, like ours, was the same: the sudden, bloody loss of close friends, excessive and extended periods of violence, terror, and frustration. Some people could handle it without suffering prolonged psychological effects, and others could not for any number of reasons. I had my own bouts with drug and alcohol abuse, but eventually overcame the demons haunting me and returned to sobriety seven years after my return.

After one of the vets of the Iraq war finished recounting his experiences, Dr. Gul sorted through a stack of files on her lap, opened one and looked at me with a smile. "Vincent, I understand your wife had you forcibly committed due to your behavior. Would you mind recalling an incident from your relationship that led her to believe you needed psychiatric help?"

Somewhat taken aback by her sudden question, I had to think a minute for an example, although she added, "If you're not ready to discuss it yet, I will understand."

Several of my new friends began coughing and shifting in their seats as they gave me conspirator's grins.

"Sure, Doctor Malanai; I don't mind talking about my past. Do you want to start at the beginning and work my way forward or work in reverse chronological order?"

She gave me a very understanding and sympathetic smile before Barb interjected, "There's nothing wrong with Vinny, Doctor. His wife is just a…"

Dr. Gul waved her hand at Barb to be quiet before she said, "Go ahead, Vincent."

I scratched my head and began. "I guess she just didn't have much of a sense of humor. You see, I joined the army reserves after I was discharged from the regular army, because I discovered the GI Bill didn't pay enough for anyone to go to college if they didn't have reasonably wealthy parents. I needed the Reserve money to pay for tuition, books, insurance, gas, rent, food, and everything else required to go to college full time since I was living on my own. My soon to be ex dated a few times when I had a little extra money, and I mean only a little money, so we didn't go anywhere fancy. Especially since the college I was attending at the time was in Erie, Pennsylvania and there isn't much up there in the way of fine dining by any stretch of the imagination. So, I'd take her to a movie and then out for a burger, but her curfew was eleven and there wasn't much time to do anything else."

I took a sip of coffee, gave Don a sly grin, and continued. "The reserve unit was an eight-inch self-propelled howitzer battalion with quite a few prior service vets in the unit and I made a few friends during my first drills. They were doing the same thing I was: supplementing their GI Bill with reserve pay to make ends meet, so we had quite a bit in common. One Friday evening in November, just as I was about to leave my dorm to take her out, I received a call from the battery commander. He asked if I'd help the gun crews with an emergency call. The Major said there was a ship in trouble out on Lake Erie and the Coast Guard needed illumination. It seems their star shells were defective, and their spotlights were inadequate for their rescue mission."

Another sip of coffee before I continued, but first had to explain what the eight-inch gun was, and how it would fire huge illumination rounds almost twenty miles. "Well, the Major said two of the guns were on the way to Presque Isle State Park, and the third was waiting for a driver before it could proceed. I told him I wouldn't have time to change if they needed me right away, because I was on my way out for a date. He told me to go as I was, and I could bring my date to show her how the unit does more than just meet on weekends. Since her home was on the way to the reserve center, I stopped by her place, and after telling her parents I was taking her on a demonstration by my reserve unit, I hustled her to the center. The gunner, a Staff Sergeant, laughed like hell when I told him what the Major told me. He had her sit in the assistant gunner's seat while I dropped in the driver's hatch, enclosed in the forward hull."

The Doc was giving me perplexed looks until one of the guys with a laptop showed her a picture of the self-propelled gun and pointed out the various seating positions. When she looked back at me to continue, I recalled, "At first, Cheryl thought it was a little strange to take what she called a tank, out on a date, in addition to having five GIs come along for the ride. But I didn't have time to explain, and I couldn't talk to her and neither could any of the other crewmen since my helmet microphone only communicated with the gunner, and his with me. The diesel engine was so damn loud, you'd have to scream in someone's ear to be heard, and you can't move around once the vehicle starts rolling. So, she sat there in the A-gunner's seat and held on for dear life while I drove as fast as I could through town with a police escort in front of us."

I laughed for a few seconds as I remembered driving the forty-ton tracked howitzer through the city streets, with civilians standing and pointing at us as I roared past. "The gunner told me, 'Your date looks scared half out of her mind, and she has both arms wrapped around part of the gun mount! Wait till she lets go and finds her coat covered with thick, black grease that won't wash out, Vinny!" I laughed again at the memory before continuing. "The other two guns were already set up in the parking lot at the far end of Presque Isle, and as I backed against a sand berm in preparation to setting and registering the gun, three ammo trucks pulled in and began unpacking the powder and illumination rounds. I climbed out of the driver's hatch and had to pry her arms from around the pedestal then half carry her to a police car, where I left her, so I could help lay and register the gun. I didn't have time to speak to her as we needed to lay the gun and start firing illumination rounds as fast as possible, so the Coast Guard could locate and rescue the crew of a sinking ship."

Dr. K leaned forward and said, "I recall something on the news about an army artillery unit helping the Coast Guard save the crew of a freighter on Lake Erie! Vinny, I can't believe that was you and your friends! How long ago was that?"

"It was way back in 1975, Doc. Long before the Coasties were issued all weather choppers and the big illumination flares for search and rescue." I grinned at Tommy Hewitt, winked, and continued my story. "So, Cheryl stood next to the police car crying about the big black smears of grease all over her pretty pink coat, but I was too damn busy laying the gun. Our first sergeant pulls up and yells for us to forget about the aiming stakes and all that shit, before he grabs the radio and starts discussing the problem with the Coasties. A minute later, he tells me to adjust the azimuth to 270 degrees, which is due west, and elevate the barrel to 45 degrees for maximum range. After we made the adjustments, he ordered us to set the fuse to detonate about 500 feet above the lake, then load it into the breach with the maximum charge to put the round out as far as possible."

"The Coasties will adjust range and deflection as soon as they see it! They said they're about 18 miles offshore, battling huge waves, so I hope like hell these illumination rounds will reach that far. We don't have time to be dicking around with the aiming circle and that shit right now! Get the guns loaded and ready to fire as fast as you can!" The highly experienced veteran artilleryman trotted between the three guns to direct the crews before he stopped at the police car to warn Cheryl, "Better stand back, missy; these things are not only the loudest damn things you'll ever hear, but the concussion will knock you down and bowl you over if you stand too close!"

"My future fiancé thought she knew everything and gave the top-kick a smart reply like, "I'll be fine right here!" The top didn't have time to argue with her and turned to see how far along we were loading the guns. We'd just finished ramming the illumination round and powder bags into the breach, when the gunner closed the breach block and set the blank into its position. I turned away from the gun, saw Cheryl standing about twenty feet off to the side and slightly in front of the barrel. I waved her back and shouted for her to get as far back as possible, but Cheryl pointed to the big black grease stains on her coat and began bitching, just as the Top yelled, "FIRE!" I turned to the rear and covered my ears, a split second before the gunner yanked the lanyard."

"Our 8-inchers fired two types of propellant charges; green bag and white bag. Green bag was for lower altitude trajectories and shorter ranges, but white bag was an extremely powerful charge for high trajectories and long ranges. We were using the maximum charge of white bag propellant, and when the charge went off, the noise, flash and concussion were extremely impressive, to say the least. As soon as the gun recoiled and the flash-bang was over, I turned to where I'd last seen Cheryl, but she wasn't there! I assumed she turned, ran, and crouched down behind the cop car to avoid the blast, but I didn't have time to check as I was required to help load the next round."

I finished my coffee before continuing. "Our gun can fire two rounds every three minutes, and although it sounds slow, you have to really hustle to keep up that rate of fire, especially when the crews are shorthanded like we were, and had to carry rounds weighing 145 pounds each. I think we fired six rounds between the three guns while the Coasties radioed back corrections until we were placing the rounds just upwind of the sinking freighter. At that point, we could slow down a little and while waiting to fire the next volley, I ran to where I thought Cheryl was, but didn't see her. Just as I was about to return to the gun, I saw something crawl out of the brush completely covered in mud. At first, I thought it was a small bear, but then it stood up on its hind legs and began cursing and swearing at me! Damned if it wasn't Cheryl, and I just couldn't help but laugh before I asked what the hell happened."

I laughed out loud for a few seconds as I recalled the sight of her and then went back to my story. "Before she could tell me what happened, I was called back to the guns. I yelled at her to either get inside the cop car or climb in the cab of a deuce-and-a-half parked well behind the cannons. About an hour later, the Coast Guard radioed they rescued the crew of the freighter, thanked us for our help and we immediately secured the guns, but I had to hang around to help burn the unused powder. Top told me to take his jeep and Cheryl back to the armory after we cooked off the powder charges. Cheryl was in the front seat of the deuce-and-a-half, shivering from the cold like a dog shitting razor blades. I helped her out and said I'd build a fire to warm her up before I drove her home. Since it was Erie, PA, our jeeps at least had cold weather side covers, so she would not be exposed to the cold wind like she was on the open gun carriage during the run to Presque Isle. After my buddy Jack and I carefully set out the left-over powder bags on the beach, and then made a long trail of propellant powder to the pile, I tossed a cigarette butt on the end before I turned and ran to Cheryl. I turned Cheryl away from pile before it all ignited, and when it did, it flared with tremendous heat, light, and noise. Of course, she had to stop, turn, and look at it while I was moving her to the jeep, in spite of my warning not to; and as she did, the radiated heat baked the grease and mud into her coat, hair, shoes and pants."

"Burning off the powder lasted about five minutes and she spent that time in the jeep, where the huge flare kept her and the jeep nice and toasty. After we checked to make sure all the powder burned, we left for her house. On the way back, she said I was mean to her because I didn't take her out to dinner and a movie like I promised. Then she bitched about freezing her ass off all the way to Presque Isle on the gun, and how scared she was because she only had a little metal seat to sit on, and it was out in the open and exposed to the cold wind. When I asked how she managed to get herself coated with mud and grease, she replied, "When the big gun went off, it knocked me over backward, right into a big puddle full of slush and mud! Then, when I went to get up, you fired the other one and it blew me into the bushes. My ears were ringing something awful, and just as I got up to run away from those cannons, they went off again and again, knocking me down and rolling me into every puddle there was! They finally stopped shooting those damn things just before you came around and told me to get into the police car, but it was locked, and I was afraid to go looking for the officer. I climbed into that big army truck, but it didn't have a heater and I froze my hiney off the entire time you were playing army and shooting those damn guns!"

"I told her our big noisy guns helped save the lives of forty men out on Lake Erie. Then I reminded Cheryl I had asked if she wanted to come along to watch us fire our cannons, but she'd be out in the cold the whole time, and she eagerly agreed. But she just kept bitching and whining all the way back to her house. I didn't walk her to the door since I had to get the jeep back to the armory before they locked the gates. The following week I saw her in school, and she was still pissed, but she admitted it was more her fault than mine because she should have known better than to accompany me on anything connected with the army. Her parents bitched about her ruined coat, pants, and shoes, in addition to the difficult time she had washing the reeking filth from her body and hair."

Dr. Gul knitted her eyebrows as she stated, "So, you did ask if she wanted to go with you, and you also warned her about the noise and cold she'd be exposed to, but she and her parents still blamed you to some extent."

"Yes, they did and still do, Doc," I replied, "But she had an older brother, about my age, and he was attending Penn State. The guy was a punk and a smart ass to boot; always making snide remarks about my being a vet and still serving in the reserves. The next time I went to take her out, he waited just outside the door until my back was turned before he jumped me and tried to put me in a chokehold, while screaming for me to get lost and never come back. I guess he never understood what it meant to be a military policeman, even though I'd told his family I'd originally trained as an MP and not as an artilleryman. My training instantly kicked in, and after I nailed him in the groin with a backstroke, I grabbed the arm he threw around my neck, tossed him over my shoulder and onto the driveway with a very satisfying thud. He was lucky I stopped feeding him knuckle sandwiches after the third or fourth one. The hippie punk should have felt fortunate he got off with only a dislocated shoulder, a broken nose, a cracked hip and broken jaw, because I was about to lay a proper beating on the coward when I remembered we had reservations at the restaurant, only 20 minutes later."

Dr. Gul appeared to be severely shocked over my actions. Dr. K was grinning from ear to ear. Doc Fitz was snarling at me, while the rest of the room cheered lustily as they rose to pat me on the back, shake my hand, and offer their congratulations. Dr. K called the meeting to an end before he told me to see Dr. Gul the following morning.

CHAPTER FIVE

Steve sent out for dinner since the dietary department was serving meatloaf, but only after the local starving homeless people refused it. While finishing our steak sandwiches, Steve leaned close and asked me to join him on the patio for a quiet talk.

"I noticed Elvis giving you the hairy eyeball all day," Steve stated as we lit our smokes. He glanced around to make sure we were alone before he added, "Of course you know that fucker isn't who he wants us to believe he is."

I raised my eyebrows and grinned, "I thought he was putting on an act for us. He seemed to be a little too inconsistent with his Elvis impersonation."

"He's a fucking FBI agent assigned to keep an eye on me, and there's another one, too! Do you know that Direct Care Aid, the one always hanging around wherever I am? If you haven't noticed, he's the only one who never speaks with the nurses and just stands around doing nothing!"

"Oh yeah; I know who you mean. He asks too many questions, particularly after he spots one of us talking to you. In addition, he drives a brand-new R/T Charger that costs over forty-five big ones, and I know the DCAs make somewhere south of fifteen an hour. So, he either has a wife with a real good job, or he's drawing another paycheck from a company that doesn't mind him working twelve and sixteen-hour days here."

"So why was Elvis giving you the evil eye today?"

"After I interrupted his top-secret telephone conversation last night, we exchanged some unfriendly words. He became very upset when I discovered he could do more than belch out oldies tunes, and the prick said he'd deal with me later."

"He and his buddy will have a whole new set of problems to deal with after my attorney makes a few phone calls, so I wouldn't worry about him, Vinny." Steve glanced around again and said softly, "If you want out of here, I can arrange it, but it will take a couple weeks."

"I know I'm going to get out of here, but I can't say how soon, buddy. What do you have in mind?"

"My attorney assures me he can get you out of here a lot faster than you can on your own, in spite of your connections here.

In addition, I'll cover his fees and pay top dollar to charter your Citation for a week."

"How do you even know I own a Citation?" I was shocked at his knowledge of my background and business.

"It's my business to learn as much as I can about certain people, especially when they may be critical to my survival, and I have a gut feeling you may be a key element to my enjoying a bright and shining future!"

"My own wife doesn't know about the Citation..."

"She doesn't have the resources I have to conduct a thorough investigation into someone's background. I bet she never thought you might be hiding assets, or even have assets to hide!"

"Are you trying to coerce me into helping you, Steve?"

He laughed briefly, "No way, man! I'm the last person in the world to try that, especially on someone as intelligent as you are! He looked me in the eyes, "Let's just say I'm offering a business proposition you'll find difficult to refuse, but not as a threat."

"And if I refuse?"

"We simply part company, and hopefully you'll keep this discussion to yourself. I'm taking a hell of a risk confiding in you, but you should understand you'll face very little if any risk if you accept my offer. I'll help you get out of here legally, and in return, you will allow me to charter your business jet for one or two weeks; no questions asked, in addition to the destruction or alteration of the pilot's logs."

"You probably know I can fly the Citation, but I will need a co-pilot, so that's only one person who will have to falsify their logs, plus fuel purchase records, flight plans, landing fees and all that. But if you want to fly someplace international, we have a whole new set of..."

"I'll let you know where and when after you've been sprung from here."

"What if I change my mind after I'm out?"

Steve shook his head, "I'll be very disappointed, but you'll have to pay my attorney's fees, which will be in the neighborhood of 10 big ones."

Just then, several vets walked out to the patio, laughing about something they saw on the news.

Steve leaned in close and whispered, "We'll talk later, but don't worry about being caught. It's all being arranged through several shell companies." He rose and walked back into the building a moment before Don, Tom and Jimmy sat with me.

"Well, Vinny, what's on our entertainment schedule for tomorrow?" Jimmy was grinning from ear-to-ear as he lit a smoke and then passed around a slider of vodka.

"I have to meet with Dr. Gul first thing in the morning, and I assume we'll partake in another group cluster-fuck in the afternoon."

"Fitz will be here for the afternoon follies, so it should be a good one," Don remarked before he and the rest of my friends broke up laughing.

The following morning, Barb and Merri sat with me during breakfast, and both warned me to be polite to Dr. Gul.

"I was nice to her yesterday, and I have no reason to be anything but polite and cooperative with her. She seems like a very professional and caring psychiatrist, with no axes to grind with me, so we should get along just fine."

Barb held my hand as she said, "Dr. Gul is very nice, and she even took the time to speak with us and Dr. K about you after the meeting. She seemed very concerned with your forcible commitment and even expressed her desire to see you discharged as soon as possible to make room for a really sick patient."

"Let's hope she can do it soon. I'm wasting time hanging around here while the old bitch is robbing me blind!"

Barb grinned, "I thought I'd let you know Dr. Fitz will be attending this afternoon's group therapy, so try to behave yourself."

I smiled, thanked them for their advice, and left for my appointment with Dr. Gul, standing at the door to the dining room and waving at me.

Dr. Gul didn't ask to review any past encounters with Dr. Fitz or my soon-to-be-ex. She asked numerous questions about my use of alcohol, drugs, and my job. She learned I'd ceased abusing illegal drugs back in the late 70s, and I was less than a social drinker. I didn't admit I'd started smoking grass again after being admitted here and probably drank more alcohol during the past few days than the previous ten years.

Satisfied I wasn't a mean drunk or a violent crackhead or junkie, the good doctor asked if I needed anything to help me sleep.

When I said a new, thicker mattress would be a big help, she laughed and promised to speak with housekeeping about it.

"You should know I spoke at length with a number of people who worked with you during your employment here, and the general impression they gave is that you are a well-adjusted man experiencing marital problems. The employees held and still hold you in very high regard due to your dedication to caring for the patients, and your willingness to remove abusive and non-performing staff. I was told you were so good at removing poor employees, they assaulted you on numerous occasions, in addition to an unsuccessful attempt to have you killed!"

I laughed for a few moments before replying, "Yes, they did try to ambush me several times, but I was always forewarned by other employees who appreciated what I was doing, so I was ready for them. And the ignorant, lazy bastards were dumb enough to hire an undercover state trooper to have me hit, but the stupid shits just ended up in prison for their efforts." I laughed again, "They even raised five thousand dollars to pay him, and then some of the co-conspirators who weren't initially arrested had the nerve to try to get their money back from the very same trooper! So, they joined their buddies in the slammer a short time later."

Dr. Gul sat in her chair and stared at me for quite some time before she pulled herself together, glanced at her watch and said, "We can talk again tomorrow about your time here. It sounds like you had a very interesting period of employment. For this afternoon's group therapy, I need you to explain why Dr. Fitz holds so much deep-seated animosity towards you."

"Isn't she going to be there, Doc?"

"Yes, she is, but she hasn't been very forthcoming with her history, so I'm relying on you to refresh her memory."

"Sure thing, Doc. I guess it would be best to start when she met my buddy, Fuzzy Fitzgerald, her ex-husband."

"That might be a big help, Vincent." She stood, shook my hand, and as she walked me to the door, "I'm looking forward to your contribution."

Steve sat with me during lunch and said quietly, "I called my attorney, and he'll file papers tomorrow morning to get you out of here. I at least expect you to keep your mouth shut about our conversations, and hopefully you'll cooperate when I need you to help me."

"I'll see what I can do, but I'll need to check my pilot's license. I think it's expired, and I'll need to get a flight physical…"

"I'm really not worried who flies the plane. I just need you to make sure I can charter it."

"Let me know when you'll need it, so I can block off those two weeks for you with my charter company, Steve." I glanced up and saw Elvis glaring at me while the DCA in question edged toward our table with a clipboard hand.

"I gotta hit the latrine, buddy," Steve rose and left the room.

Elvis rushed from his seat to sit next to me just as Jimmy, Don, and Tom sat with their trays. He did his best to stare down my friends, but they couldn't care less what he did and immediately struck up a conversation about our upcoming therapy session.

"Doc Gul asked me to recall more of my history with Doc Fitz, so it should be a session to remember for all eternity," I growled while staring back at Elvis.

Tommy asked, "Was she a swallower or a spitter, Vinny?"

"We never got that far, Tom. I only had a few dates with her before the prom disaster."

Jimmy noticed Elvis giving me the evil eye. He poked him in the chest and said, "Why don't you get the fuck out of here, you asshole? You're not fooling anyone with your phony Elvis impersonation, so go crawl back into whatever hole you came from."

Both men and the rest of us at the table instantly rose to our feet, ready to go at it with the bully when the DCA jumped between us, pushed his partner back away from the table as he stated, "Not here; not now, Ray. We'll settle up with these nut jobs later."

"Fuck you, too, asshole," Tom growled at the DCA. "Let's settle this shit right now!"

Just as the DCA turned to Tommy, Barb walked in, saw us about to riot and shouted, "Everyone settle down and grow up before I have you all put in restraints!" She gave us the evil eye until the two agents moved to the far side of the dining room. "Let's move to the community room for the afternoon therapy session! She pointed to the FBI men and growled, "But you two clowns better park your asses in my office right now!"

We were still a little tense as we arranged the chairs in a circle, and after a few minutes, Dr. Gul, Dr. K and Fitz strolled in, eyed each of us warily and then took their seats.

Dr. K sat next to me, slapped me on the back, and muttered, "They'll let anybody in here now-a-days!" He winked and said, "I blame the lousy screening they process they use in the admissions department."

Doc Gul asked for volunteers to speak about their problems, but no one felt up to it, especially since most of the guys had shared a few joints out on the patio before lunch and were doing their best to just stay awake.

"Vincent, would you like to relate some of your history with Dr. Fitzpatrick?" Dr. Gul gave me a warm smile and held out her hand for me to begin.

Heads popped up, eyes opened wide and anxious grins spread across the faces of the group as I coughed to clear my throat. "I guess I'd better start back when Marie met my buddy Fuzzy, or Sean Fitzpatrick for the first time. They never met before, even though he went to the senior prom at Hubert's and spiked the punch and salted the pastries that caused her so much trouble. I didn't see her again after the prom for obvious reasons, and a year later, Fuzzy and I were both drafted, approximately a month apart."

"I went into the army in March and he was drafted in April, so we occasionally ran into each other during basic training at Ft. Dix. I went into the Military Police and Fuzzy trained as a tanker, but we were sent to the same unit in Vietnam; the Big Red One, or First Infantry Division. They assigned me to an MP unit and Fuzzy as a tank driver. We got together a few times while there, until I was wounded and sent home early. About a month later, Fuzzy was sent home as part of the draw-down of troops from Nam, but he volunteered to work as a recruiter for a few months and then received an honorable discharge."

I sipped my coffee and continued as Dr. Fitz stared daggers at me and whispered something to Dr. Gul.

"Fuzzy drove me home from Valley Forge Army hospital after I was discharged, and on the way, we stopped at our favorite watering hole to celebrate surviving that stinking war. We were both in uniform and as we ate our dinner, Marie walked up to me, made some smart-ass remark about the army having low standards, before she saw Fuzzy and suddenly stopped her insults. She introduced herself, and being the gentleman, he was, Fuzzy invited her to sit with us. Marie ignored me during the entire meal and concentrated on trying to impress my old buddy. And Fuzzy, being eternally horny, never passed up an opportunity to get a little poontang." I laughed a little over the memory before I added, "You see, Marie never really met Fuzzy before and she was completely unaware he was the one who spiked the punch at her prom."

I glanced over at Fitz and couldn't help but laugh at how red her face had grown in such a short period of time. "Well, they hit it off right away and stayed together while Fuzzy and I went through four years of college, although we never, ever double dated. Moreover, like me, he came from a poor family, so he also joined the reserves to earn extra money to cover expenses. He went from Philly Community to LaSalle, while I made the mistake of going up to Erie and Mercyhurst for one semester after I graduated from Philly. Mercyhurst sucked as a college so I went back to Philly and attended LaSalle.

After we graduated with our bachelor's degrees, we decided to stay in the reserves due to the camaraderie among the vets in our unit: B Company, 1st Battalion, 315th Mechanized Infantry. We developed very close friendships with the men in the unit and we both felt our friendships and conversations about Vietnam really helped us with what is now known as PTSD. Fuzzy went to work as a maintenance supervisor for Amtrak, while I secured a job as a dock supervisor for a trucking company."

I glanced around the room to see everyone sitting on the edge of their chairs before I continued. "About a year after we graduated, Fuzzy asked me to be best man at his wedding. However, his fiancé, now known as Dr. Fitz, told him if I was going to be his best man, he'd end up marrying me! She screamed she wouldn't show up if I was even at the church, so he asked our buddy, Ziggy, or Bob Ziglenski, who was also at the prom, but again, she didn't know him very well. Zig enlisted in the Army as a medic to avoid the draft, and then joined our reserve unit for the same reasons we did."

Dr. Gul held up her hand, "Did you really find membership in a military organization helped to reduce the anxiety and other problems associated with your service in Vietnam? It would seem the familiar military atmosphere would have ignited flashbacks, nightmares and other problems."

"It did at first, but not as bad as you'd think." I added, "After a few drills and firing our weapons in a non-combat milieu, I began to relax a little before I began looking forward to the drills in order to blow off steam and release my pent-up aggression."

She nodded, made a few notes in my file, then indicated I should continue.

"You all have to remember how bad things were in the Army back in the late seventies. Most of the Vietnam combat vets got out and stayed out. The draft dodgers all took off and never came back after March of 73 when we pulled out of Vietnam. That wasn't a bad thing since I'd never want to go into combat with those cowards in my unit. Most of them would have split for Canada as soon as it became apparent, they were going to be mobilized. Many of the NCOs were reserve lifers as were the officers, and I definitely didn't trust them to lead us if a war broke out. However, a couple decent prior service officers and NCOs with combat experience eventually joined the unit. Since we were part of the second echelon of the rapid reaction force, we needed to keep every experienced man we had, even if we had to resort to unusual and possibly illegal means to do so."

I knocked back my coffee then explained. "Before one of the men in the unit married, we always questioned his future wife to see if she'd force her husband to quit the unit. Some said they were OK with his service for whatever reason, and some were very adamant about his getting out and spending his time with the family, rather than going away one weekend a month or more, and coming home stinking, filthy and hung over. So, we developed a plan to retain our veterans in addition to our unit's strength, and our efforts were approximately 75% effective."

Dr. Fitz began screaming at me, "You filthy bastard! Our wedding and reception cost me over $15,000.00, and it was all wasted because of you and your homosexual army cohorts!" Dr. K shouted for Fitz to shut up and after a few minutes, she calmed enough for me to recall that memorable event.

"We all knew Marie hated the army and the reserves with every fiber of her being, even though she was working for the Air Farts as a flight shrink at the time. Although Fuzzy was a big boy and really enjoyed our weekends and summer camps, we knew it would only be a matter of time before she wore him down and forced him to quit the unit. So according to our standard operating procedure, the night before his wedding, which was a Friday, we threw Fuzzy a huge bachelor party, complete with oceans of booze, tons of food and enough smoke to fog the city of London. Zig brought in a couple strippers, a good rock and roll band, along with some special meds to dump in Fuzzy's drinks to make sure he'd be out cold when the wedding started Saturday morning. We began the party at Zig's house, then moved to the local volunteer fire hall where things got out of control in one hell of a hurry. There were forty guys from our unit, plus a couple of Fuzzy's friends from the railroad and his brother Eddy, a former Marine fighter pilot who was even wilder than Fuzzy."

I laughed long and hard as scenes from the party flashed through my mind's eye. I managed to choke out, "Like I said, everyone pretty much behaved themselves at Ziggy's house, but after we relocated to the firehall and the strippers showed up, things went to hell in a big hurry. I was hitting the booze and hash pretty hard for a while there, before our commanding officer and executive officer showed up with cases of scotch, rye and bourbon before I blacked out. We must have had a wild night, because sometime during the festivities, we all moved to the reserve center, and that's where I woke up. Again, I don't recall exactly what happened, but I came to on top of an armored personnel carrier, with the track's treads all tangled up in about 100 yards of cyclone fencing. Another track was lying on its side, but it was on top of someone's car, with a completely crushed car right behind it."

I had to take a break and hit the latrine while everyone in the room roared with laughter. When I returned, several people were restraining Dr. Fitz while Dr. K administered a shot of sedative to the violently struggling woman.

"Go ahead, Vinny," Don shouted over the Fitz's screams, "I think you restored her memory of the era."

After the room quieted, I continued, "It took a while before I found anyone who was at least semi-coherent. Leo Mersberger, our supply sergeant had somehow ended up in the pond with just his head on the shore, and two Mallard ducks nestled in his arms. He was just waking up when I staggered past, and he suddenly said, "Hey, Vinny, we have to bail the rest of the guys out of the slammer."

I asked, "Who got arrested and why?"

"You don't want to know right now, but as soon as I cut away the fencing from the armored personnel carrier, we'll head over there and get them out."

"Why use a track, Leo?"

"Fuzzy and his brother tried to jump those cars with one of the APCs. They were so fucked up, Fuzzy and Eddie thought they were Evel Knievel or something. I guess they never studied stuff like physics while they were in college."

"Whose cars did they flatten?"

"The one they ran over belongs to the bail bondsman and the one under the track is a Bristol township police car."

"Holy shit!" I looked around and didn't see any other cars, so I asked; "How did we get here and why do we need the tracks?"

"Leo grunted; the guys used all the jeeps and trucks to get away before the State Police showed up. But let's get back to the party; I'll get to the rest later. After the cops showed up at the fire hall, we all beat feet over here thinking they wouldn't follow us in, but the gate was open, and the cops just drove in after us…"

"What about the bail bondsman? What the hell was he doing here?"

"The cops managed to get a couple guys cuffed before they hauled them off to the slammer. The judge gave them a grand bail and they called the bail bondsman. He drove them over here to seize Jake's car as collateral. Fuzzy, his brother, and you were drag racing the tracks when they arrived, and I heard Fuzzy calling you over the radio saying he was going to jump the two cars with his APC. Just after he ran over the bail guy's car, he sideswiped your track, forcing you into the fence, and it caused him to roll over on top of the cop car. We were damn lucky no one was in either car or we'd be in big trouble right now."

"Holy shit! We sure got into enough trouble for just one night!"

"Leo just stared at me before he suddenly stood and then waved at a couple military vehicles just emerging from the woods. Then he turned to me and laughed, "One night your ass! What day do you think this is?"

"It's Saturday, isn't it?"

"Hell no; it's Sunday! He glanced at his watch and stated, it's almost 16:30! Geez, Vinny, I can't believe you got so snockered you lost an entire day and half! You mean to tell me you don't remember taking the deuce and a half into Langhorne to pick up more booze and food, and then returned with a dozen women?"

"I have no recollection of the event at all. What happened to the women?"

"They're on their way here now. He pointed to a Deuce and several jeeps bouncing across the open field loaded with screaming and laughing people, all waving beer and liquor bottles over their heads."

"Shit, I can't believe I missed that!"

A jeep screeched to a halt next to me and two obviously drunk girls fell out just as the driver, Mickey Kopchinski handed me a beer and asked if the cops were coming back. Then he looked closely at my eyes and said, "Damn, Vinny, your eyes look like two piss holes in the snow!"

"If you think they look bad, you should see them from my side," I replied then knocked back the beer and watched as Ziggy, Ligget and Jake helped some very drunk and high girls from the back of the deuce. I didn't see Fuzzy, so I asked where our party boy was. Jake replied, "Fuzzy, his brother, and two girls went…"

ZOOOOOOMMM, a very low flying, twin-engine plane shot by no more than 50 feet off the ground. It did a couple victory rolls and then swung back for a second pass. Ligget yelled, "The sons of bitches found a plane!" They made one more pass before they flew off to the east, but not before they opened a door and dumped a dozen or so empty beer cans on us."

"It took Leo and me about an hour to cut away the chain link fencing tangled in the treads. In the meantime, Jake, Ligget, and Mickey used the deuce to pull the other APC upright and back onto its treads. The girls walked, crawled and staggered under a tree to watch us, but passed out in less than five minutes. After we cut away the fencing from the upper section of track, I climbed inside the APC to move it forward and noticed two more women out cold in the troop compartment. They didn't even wake up when I started the engine, so I left them there. Besides, one or both were covered with vomit and I really didn't want to touch them."

"I asked Leo why we needed the track to pick up the guys when we now had jeeps and a deuce. He said we might need something bulletproof if the cops wanted to argue the point. I opened the tailgate and the top hatch to air out the interior and Leo climbed in the driver's seat, while I dropped into the track commander's hatch, put on the TC's helmet, and plugged it into the commo set so we could talk. We were about halfway to the gate when the girls woke up and asked to be let out, so Leo stopped the track just long enough for them to crawl out. Then he stopped by the motor pool and used the hose to wash the puke and other unidentifiable body fluids from the troop compartment. We then went to arms room where we grabbed a .50 Caliber machinegun and mounted it before we hit the road."

Tom laughed like hell and asked, "Did you bring ammo too?"

"Naw, just the sight of that damn thing would be enough to scare the shit out of anyone. The police station was only about a mile or two up the road, and when we pulled into the parking lot, Leo decided to park it right in front of the building's entrance, so the desk sergeant could see us. My buddy hopped out and went into the station while I sat in the TC's hatch with the 50 pointed at the desk. I could see Leo arguing with an old fat cop sitting behind a desk before the cop picked up his phone. A few minutes later, six of our guys came staggering out of the building, and when they saw me and the track, they laughed their asses off. They wanted to stop at a bar on the way back, but the only place close enough that served beer was a Pizza Hut, so we pulled in there, picked up a dozen pizzas and a couple cases of beer."

Don asked, "Did you get them for free?"

"No, but they gave us a discount if we promised not to eat inside the restaurant where we'd disturb the other patrons. We all smelled pretty bad, especially Leo after he spent the night sleeping in the duck pond. By the time we returned to the armory, Fuzzy, his brother and the girls had returned, and they were using the big hose at the motor pool to wash everyone off with liquid dish soap from the mess hall. The entire parking lot was covered with soapsuds. The service pit, the mechanics used to work on the undersides of the vehicles had been turned into a big bathtub with everyone splashing around like a bunch of kids. Leo and our jailbirds joined them after we consumed our share of pizza and beer. About an hour later, Jake rinsed us off with the hose when I suddenly thought to ask Fuzzy; "Hey, man, weren't you supposed to be somewhere yesterday?"

"He just stared at me for the longest time with a blank look on his face before I saw the light come on. 'Geez, Vinny, I think I'm in a world of shit with Marie! Damn, Sam, why didn't somebody remind me?' Ziggy heard us talking, grabbed Fuzzy, handed him a bottle of vodka and said; 'As your platoon sergeant, I recommend you start drinking heavily, son!"

Dr. Gul appeared to be severely shocked by my story, but Fitz had quieted and was staring wide-eyed at me as if she'd just had an earth-shattering revelation.

I winked at her before continuing. "Fuzzy seemed exceptionally upset over missing his wedding and very possibly losing the affections of his inamorata, in addition to the painful death he'd suffer at her hands. He turned to Ziggy and then me and said, 'You two guys are the best bull-shitters I know! You've got to come up with an excuse she'll not only believe but keep her from killing me!' I knew they hadn't lived together before their scheduled marriage and were planning to move into an apartment when they returned from their two-week honeymoon, so I smiled and laid out one of the best bullshit stories ever devised by man."

"At this time, there were rumblings in the news media about the Communists gaining control of Central America, and the possible use of US troops to argue the point. I knew Marie was adamantly opposed to our involvement, and especially the possibility of Fuzzy's mobilization for the upcoming Central American war games, so I told him, 'Go put on your fatigues and muss them up a little.' I turned to Ziggy, 'You do the same, then drive Fuzzy to his apartment to pick up his field gear. After that, drive him to Marie's place, and Fuzzy; you tell her you've been activated for possible movement to San Salvador or Panama. You received notice Friday night at the party, when Ligget called for Ziggy to report in, but only after he notified the rest of his platoon. No one was permitted to call anyone because this is all top secret-code black, so make sure she understands not to say a word about this anyone. If she does and they find out, you'll be sent to the army's special security prison in the Aleutians until you turn blue, your pecker freezes solid and falls off.'"

Dr. Fitz began screaming, "You lying son of a bitch! I'm going to kill you! I thought he was really activated all these years..." Dr. K and Barb managed to quiet Fitz after injecting the highly agitated shrink with another dose of strong horse tranquilizer. The room exploded with derisive laughter after Fitz admitted she'd believed my outrageous story for almost 30 years.

"But to make it more believable, Fuzzy returned home two days later claiming the army decided not to activate our reserve unit because we were under-strength and they would instead use Special Forces units as advisors. And damn if it wasn't announced on the news a week later the Army was sending Special Forces down there!"

"And did they reschedule their wedding?" Dr. Gul gave me a strange look after glancing at her heavily drugged associate.

"Yes, they did, but they had to hold it at another church. Marie and Sean couldn't afford to pay for a second reception, so it was a very small affair, and she made sure Fuzzy spent the night before the wedding at his parents."

Dr. K ended the session, and with a huge evil grin, helped Fitz out to his car. Just as he reached the door, he stated, "We'll have another session tomorrow without Dr. Fitz."

Needless to say, the conversations among the vets were centered on my story for the rest of the day.

CHAPTER SIX

I just sat down to breakfast when Steve, Jimmy, Tom, and Don pulled up chairs and grinned at me. Steve slipped a menu to me and said, "I haven't seen Ray Norsworthy, also known as Elvis, and his buddy the DCA since Barb called them into her office yesterday."

Tom nodded, "He didn't sleep in his bed last night, and when I asked the night shift about him, they said he won't be back."

Steve smiled, "Breakfast is on me, boys. Order what you want but keep an eye open for any new admissions."

Merri waved for me to join her, and with a conspirator's grin she whispered, "That guy Norsworthy and the idiot DCA were FBI agents sent here to arrest Hamm if he tries to elope. Barb was fed up with their aggressive attitude and had them recalled by the FBI office in Annapolis. Of course, you know they'll send in at least two more undercover agents to keep an eye on Steve…"

"Yeah, you can count on that, Merri," I replied, "But I hope the next two are a little more subtle. You know Elvis and I almost came to blows the other night."

"Yes, I do. He came to me and demanded we relocate you out of here immediately." She shook her head slowly, "What an unmitigated ass for an undercover agent." She glanced around then said, "I thoroughly enjoyed your story about Fitz's fiancé and how he missed their wedding. How much of it was true?"

"All of it was true, but I left out the part about him spending the night with one of the bimbos I brought back to the reserve center. Plus, he had to borrow a pair of skivvy shorts because she put his on sometime during the night. And I also left out how he just barely missed being arrested for borrowing the plane he and his brother used to buzz the reserve center."

Merri shook her head, sighed, gave me a smile, and stated, "Dr. Gul and Dr. K will be leading today's group session, and both want some history on your relationship with your wife, so try to come up with something relevant." She rose, patted me on the head and as she walked away, remarked, "I'm sure your story will be very entertaining, Vinny."

The delivery man was just arriving with our breakfast. I returned to my friends' table where Steve handed me a large platter covered with foil. "I ordered a double for you, Vinny; enjoy it in good health!" Then he leaned in close, "My attorney is filing papers to have you discharged. You'll have to be examined by several other shrinks, but don't worry; they're the same ones who had me admitted here."

About an hour later, while we were enjoying a smoke out on the patio, two State Troopers came by to question me about the missing contents of two briefcases owned by a couple shyster lawyers. Fortunately, Dr. K was with me at the time and was able to convince the Troopers his patient was almost completely incoherent. My previously sharp memory was forever scrambled by certain psychotropic drugs required to control my violent outbursts. To lend credence to his statements, I slowly leaned forward, slid off my chair to the floor, then grabbed Tom's leg and tried to bite him. It was all I needed to convince the officers their suspect was not mentally competent to answer questions.

After lunch, we gathered in the day room for our group therapy session, now called, "The Fitz and Vinny Show."

Dr. K announced, "As you all know, Dr. Fitzpatrick has been experiencing some difficulties and won't be with us today, so Dr. Gul will take charge of your therapy sessions for the foreseeable future. I'm sure everyone will join me in wishing Dr. Fitz a swift and full recovery."

Don coughed, "I don't think that's going to happen until Vinny receives his discharge." The room burst out laughing until someone stated, "It seems our boy Vinny is hazardous to her mental health."

Dr. Gul glanced around the assembled Vets and asked for a volunteer to begin the session, but they all just shook their heads and pointed at me with evil grins. She shook her head slowly, raised her eyebrows and said, "Mr. Nunzio, perhaps we can delve into your relationship with your soon-to-be-ex. Would you be so kind as to relate events from your own wedding since you and your friends were instrumental in ruining Dr. Fitzpatrick's wedding?"

I smiled and replied, "Sure, Doc, but my wedding went off without a hitch, at least at first. You see, my fiancée wasn't disturbed by my service in the reserves. She had a job in retail and usually worked at least two or three weekends each month. Since she was management, she'd just schedule herself to work on my drill weekends and then take her vacations with her family, so my annual training never conflicted with her vacations. In addition, she appreciated the extra money the reserves paid because she liked to keep her closet full of new shoes and clothes."

"So, your army friends didn't kidnap you the night before your wedding?"

"No, they didn't need to, but Cheryl told me she didn't want them at the wedding or reception. She adamantly swore, 'None of those crazy, strange, drunken, army buddies of yours are coming to the reception,' but I convinced her they could come to the Church ceremony since there were no limits on the number of people we could have in the church. We did have a limit of 150 people for the reception, and she invited 100 of her friends, relatives, and co-workers, claiming most of my friend and relatives would not know how to behave. Therefore, I invited the boys in my unit to the wedding and said they could come to the reception, too, but we wouldn't have the seats to feed them all since the hall would be full. The first sergeant laughed, reminded me that my wedding was on a drill weekend, and scheduled for the reserve center, not at Ft. Dix where we normally went to maintain proficiency with our weapons."

After a sip of coffee, I smiled at Tommy and continued. "Please keep in mind the special bond between the men in my unit. Once the Vietnam War ended, the draft-dodgers who made up a large proportion of the Reserves just vanished. The threat of being punitively activated, and then sent to Vietnam for going AWOL had become moot. The Army really didn't care if they came back to drill or not; they weren't dependable and couldn't be trusted to fight if a general war broke out because they were basically cowards at heart. We prior-service veterans in B Company were glad to see them go. The Company shrank from 240 people down to 50 in less than three months. The 50 who remained were fighters; maybe not your best soldiers, but damn good fighters. Quite a few of the men's 201 files held awards for Silver Stars, Navy Crosses, Bronze Stars, and more Purple Hearts than you can count, in addition to more than a few Article 15s and Court Martials."

"The day of the wedding broke warm and sunny. Everyone from both families found the church okay and were seated on time, but as I stood in front of the altar, waiting for Cheryl and her dad to make the final stroll, I noticed there were no uniforms in the church. I thought the boys might not have received permission to come to the wedding, but I wasn't too upset over it; I had more distressing matters at hand."

Cheryl's brother, a Catholic priest, was marrying us, and he discreetly lifted his robe to show me he was packing a snub-nosed .38 pistol to make it understood I wouldn't make a break for the door. About halfway through the ceremony, during the quiet time of Communion, I thought I heard the rattle of small arms fire, but dismissed it as a flashback to the bad days of Vietnam brought on by the stress of the wedding.

The ceremony went as planned. I was doomed unto death as the rite goes. We then slowly walked down the aisle as her family looked on grimly and my family vainly tried to smother their hysterical laughter. As we exited the church, the families gathered to take our pictures and as the cameras clicked, I heard the unmistakable sounds of heavy automatic weapons fire again, this time from just up the street.

My experience in Vietnam made me flinch, and the men in our families with military experience quickly turned to see what was going on. The fire died down quickly. I clearly heard military diesel engines from the ubiquitous deuce-and-a-halfs racing in our direction. "Oh, no!" I thought. "Here they come!" They hit the wrong church! Moments later, two camouflage painted deuces: tarps down, packed full of fatigue-clad soldiers, came roaring up to the front of the church. Each man was carrying an M-16 with a banana clip full of blanks or an M-60 Machine gun, loaded with a long belt of blank ammo. My good buddy Ziggy was standing in the ring-mount on the front seat of the lead vehicle. He pointed at me and shouted in his loudest parade ground voice, "THERE THEY ARE BOYS, OPEN FIRE!"

"Now let me give you some background information on the town where I was married. Conshohocken, Pa. is a small town just west of Philadelphia. Conshy, as we called it, was heavily populated by three ethnic groups; the Polish, immigrants who came to work in the textile and steel mills; the Italian immigrants, who came to work as masons on the numerous stone structures in the area, and finally, the Irish/English immigrants, who also worked in the mills. However, although they were primarily Catholic, each group had to have their very own Catholic Church and school. Each group built their churches and schools within two blocks of each other, and all were on the same narrow, one-way street lined with row-homes."

"None of the guys in my unit knew Conshy all that well, and even though they had the address of the church, they didn't consider there would be more than one Catholic Church on the same street, so when they came to St. Matt's, the Irish/English church, they just assumed it was the right one. They arrived in front of the building just as a wedding party was exiting the church. Without looking to see who was standing on the steps, they gave the standard B Company, 1/315th Mechanized Infantry salute; all weapons set on full-automatic and fired in a sustained burst until their magazines were empty.

"I was told later, the people at St. Matt's had obviously never been under fire before and they reacted accordingly. People dove under cars, jumped over hedges, dropped straight to the ground, and generally ran around like chickens with their heads cut off. It wasn't until they'd emptied their magazines when the guys noticed I wasn't among the people standing, or running for their lives, which I wouldn't have done anyway. It was about that time when Leo; another good buddy, saw there was another church just down the street and advised Platoon Sergeant Ziggy of his discovery. Ziggy, being the decisive and born leader he was, ordered Leo to advance on the new church while the men reloaded."

"To take up where I left off; the men opened fire all at once and the noise was deafening in the narrow street. Especially when they began heaving grenade and artillery simulators, which sound like the real thing, and the concussions from explosions blew out the stained-glass windows on the front of the church. The effect on my wedding party was about the same as it was at the first church, except for a few people who saw them coming; one of which was my stepfather, Command Sergeant Major Luparelli, more affectionately known as Sergeant Major Potato Head. The sight of our guests scrambling across the lawn, diving behind and squeezing under parked cars and other embarrassing activities, did not amuse him in the least. But before he had a chance to note the vehicles numbers, the sound of approaching sirens signaled the men from B Company it was time to execute that classic military maneuver known as "Getting the hell out of here," and they departed the area full tilt boogey."

"It seems the local constabulary frowned upon people discharging automatic weapons early Saturday mornings, especially when they were otherwise heavily engaged in crime fighting at the local Dunkin Donuts. The boys made a clean getaway; how they did it in those big lumbering trucks I'll never know. However, they did make it to the reception later with their own supply of beer, whiskey, music, and chow that turned out to be better than what the caterer served us."

"Their appearance and 21-gun salute, in addition to their antics at the reception only added to the tensions between my in-laws and me over the next 25 years. I eventually had to leave the Reserves and my good friends due to my job some years later. However, as it happens too often, and sadly, we have fallen out of touch. Friends like them only come around once in a lifetime, if then. I really miss those guys."

"How in the hell did the simulators blow out the windows?" Jimmy asked with wide eyes.

"The road was one lane and one-way, so they had to throw them as high into the air as they could because they might hurt someone if they threw them on the ground. There was only a narrow sidewalk in front of the church, so they had nowhere else to toss them."

"That must have been one hell of a great wedding, man," Steve laughed.

"The reception was even better because they brought the field kitchen, two kegs of beer, about 100 pounds of venison, and a pig Jimmy Scarpetti rustled from a farm near his house in Jersey. The food they cooked was better than the reception hall's, and after they removed the DJ from his console, they played great rock and roll music that got everyone on their feet dancing."

"Was that man Fuzzy, Dr. Fitzpatrick's husband, there?" Dr. Gull asked.

"Yes, he was! He was the one throwing the grenade simulators because he had the best throwing arm. He also prepared the food and made sure the guys danced with all the single and older women, so they'd have a good time, too!"

"What did your in-laws have to say about it?" Dr. K inquired.

"My in-laws were a bunch of stuck-up snobs, and they really didn't appreciate Cheryl marrying an Italian, in addition to the fact I wasn't an engineer like her old man and brothers. Plus, when they saw my company show up the way they did, I thought they'd grab my wife and take her back to Erie. My family tried to be nice by sitting at their tables and to hold conversations, but they rudely turned their backs and refused to speak with anyone from my family."

"That was nasty," Don commented, "What did your family do?"

"They didn't do anything except return to their tables and enjoy the party, until my little sister asked Cheryl's younger brother to dance. The pizza-faced, pencil necked punk sneered at her and said, 'I don't dance with greasers!' Unfortunately, for him, my cousin Billy heard him, and after realizing the asshole was serious, he grabbed him by the neck, took him outside, and slapped the shit out of him for insulting my sister and Italians in general. I mean, it was very obvious there were two completely different ethnic groups at the reception. Her family looked like generic white bread, Anglo-Saxon geeks. My family; including my cousins from New York, were olive-skinned Italians, and if you ever saw our group pictures, you'd swear it was the wedding scene from *The Godfather* movie."

"We told everyone it would be an Italian wedding, which meant you don't give gifts of kitchen utensils and stuff like that, since we both had fully stocked apartments before we moved in together. You just put cash in an envelope and hand to the bride or groom during the first dance. Her family thought Italian wedding meant we'd have spaghetti for dinner, and they were disappointed when the hall served ham. But we at least held the wedding in an Italian church, complete with frescos on the ceiling. So, her family gave us toasters, knives, tableware and other unwanted gifts someone had given them. My friends and family gave us over two grand in envelopes they put in her purse, and that's not counting the grand in cash my friends stuffed in my shirt pocket."

Steve laughed, "Did you receive enough to pay for the wedding and reception?"

"We turned a thousand-dollar profit after the mailed gifts from my distant relatives arrived." I took a long drink of water and continued. "It was amazing how my cousins, aunts, and uncles all said the same thing about my wife. They'd get me aside to tell me, 'Hey Vinny, your inamorata isn't Sicilian, let alone Italian! What the hell is the matter with you? She's skinny as a rail and probably can't cook worth a damn! I hope like hell she'll learn how to cook from your mom and sisters or you're going to starve to death."

Jimmy asked, "Could she cook?"

"Hell no! Cheryl couldn't cook worth a shit! After a few months of choking down her tasteless slop, I got tired of asking her to spend Sundays at my mom's so she could learn to cook. She kept yelling she was using the same cookbook her mother used and there's nothing wrong with what she made. However, if we had an invite to eat at Mom's, she'd have the car started and ready to go before I even put my coat on. I gave up and put myself on second shift, so I wouldn't have to eat her food. I was lucky there was a maggot wagon that stopped by the terminal in the late afternoon, and the lady who ran it was a Sicilian. She made great spaghetti sauce, Italian sausage sandwiches and other Italian food."

"How long did you stay on second shift?" Dr. K asked as he shook his head.

"It was a good year before she asked if I could get a job working day shift, so she'd see me once in a while. I told her I'd change my shift after she learned to cook, but she just had to argue the point, claiming her family did just fine on the foods her mom cooked and so would we. I replied, 'You'll do fine eating that tasteless slop you make, and I'm doing just fine eating the food from Lucy's maggot wagon at work, so I'll be on second shift until you swallow your pride and admit you can't cook worth a shit and spend a few Sundays at my mother's to learn to cook right."

"Didn't you cook, Vinny?" Dr. K asked the obvious question.

"I didn't arrive home at a regular time in the evening due to the nature of my job. Cheryl was almost always home no later than five on days she worked the early shift at her store and could have dinner on the table no later than six, or she could put it in the fridge for me until I arrived. Besides that, I really don't like to cook, and I hated food shopping even more, so we never had the right ingredients on hand. I know it's a pretty ignorant way for me to be, but Cheryl always claimed she could cook and preferred to take charge of, her kitchen."

A couple of the men commented they preferred to do the cooking in their homes, but said every couple had to have their own agreement on such issues.

"After another two months, she finally admitted she couldn't cook and really preferred my mother's Italian meals to the crap she made herself. Cheryl arranged to spend the next four Sundays at my mother's learning to cook, and I'll tell you, by the time she finished, my mother and sisters were ready to kill her. You see, my ex couldn't cook to taste, which is how you prepare real Italian food. So, every time my mother or sisters would add something to the pot, Cheryl would grab their hand and empty it into a measuring cup and write down how much they were adding, which drove them nuts. They tried to explain how something should taste as you prepared it, but Cheryl had no idea what they were talking about, or how adding some oregano, salt or basil to the gravy would change the flavor. Not only that, she usually left out a few items in the process and her meals always tasted like something was missing. To make matters worse, if she didn't have an ingredient on hand while she was cooking, she'd just leave it out or substitute something else that would ruin the flavor completely."

Dr. Gul was staring at me as if I'd just admitted to raping the Pope.

"You gotta understand, Doc," I remarked with a grin, "I'm first generation Italian, and we Dagos value our food more than anything else in life."

Merri interjected, "I was married to a first-generation Italian, and that son of a bitch wouldn't let me in the kitchen! He could cook with the best of them, but every time I tried to cook anything for him, he'd take one bite, get up and dump his plate in the trash then cook something for himself."

"Did you divorce him, Merri?" Dr K asked with a grin.

"No, he died of a massive coronary ten years after we married. All the great food he cooked and ate, cemented his arteries closed, and it damn near killed me too! His death saved my life because I weighed 230 pounds when he keeled over at the stove one evening. Now I'm down to 140 with my cholesterol and blood pressure back where it's supposed to be."

Dr. K called our session to an end and then asked me to speak with him for a few minutes in his office. He closed the door and said with a big smile, "Dr. Gul told me she is going to move to have you discharged as soon as the admissions committee meets next week. She feels you have no business being here, and from what she's learned about you from the staff and your talks with her, you are no more than a victim of a conspiracy. She wants to call for a peer review of the two psychiatrists and the psychologist who submitted their diagnosis to the court as part of your forcible commitment." He slapped my shoulder, gave me a strong embrace, and said, "I just hope you'll stop by to see us more often after you're released."

"I most certainly will, Doc, and if you have some vacation time coming up, maybe we can do a little traveling to someplace tropical."

The good doctor threw an arm around my shoulders and whispered, "Have you and Mr. Hamm made plans for his escape and rendezvous with his money?"

"Nope, I am not going to help him escape from here, Doc. But I do own an executive jet charter business, and I think I deserve a few weeks in the Bahamas after the shit I've been through!"

"I think I should prescribe several weeks of saltwater therapy for you, Vinny. It will work wonders for your mental health and outlook, but I should accompany you as your personal physician to ensure your therapy proceeds as prescribed. In addition, I would be remiss if I didn't prescribe the initiation of a relationship with a lovely young lady, and possibly one for myself!" Doctor K gave me a huge hug, and then walked away signing, "Kokomo," by the Beach Boys.

CHAPTER SEVEN

Steve and Vic Caine sat with me during dinner because no one else could stand the smell of my dinner sandwich, liverwurst and onion on seeded Jewish rye with mustard. I guess there's no accounting for some people's lack of good taste.

"Listen up, Steve, Doc K told me Doctor Gul is pushing to have me discharged next week. She's also asking to convene a peer review for the quacks my wife's shysters hired to have me committed. I don't know if that throws a wrench in the works, but I thought I'd let you know before your lawyer starts running up a bill on you for my case."

"I just got off the phone with him," Steve grinned, "And he advised the alleged shrinks who had you committed aren't members of the American Psychiatric Association, and even better, there isn't any record of them having passed their medical or psychiatric boards, in addition to their not being licensed in the state of Maryland. He's sending a detective out tomorrow to check the addresses on the commitment papers, but he has a strong suspicion their addresses are vacant lots or just non-existent."

"I guess no one at the courthouse bothered to see if the shrinks even existed before they passed on the order to have me picked up and brought here. I always thought there was something hinky about this bullshit since no one ever spoke to me about anything before those pricks knocked me out."

Vic coughed, gave me a grin, and remarked, "Why are you even the slightest bit surprised? You were committed solely so your wife could loot your finances, and you thought she did it all above board and in the open? Wake up, Vinny, and smell the coffee, my good man. What's done is done, now we have to plan how we'll deal with our altered futures."

"Our futures?"

"Yes, you heard me correctly. It is now our futures, because I shall be released next week, too. You see, I was forcibly committed by my soon-to-be ex-wife, who is a psychiatrist, in partnership with her boyfriend, an attorney who specifically deals in family matters such as we have at hand."

"And she's looting your bank account?"

"In addition to the legacy left to me by my recently deceased father, which is considerable since he was a major shareholder in Exxon and owned extensive real estate holding in Manhattan and Washington, D.C. in addition to a number of other major cities in the U.S., Australia, and Europe."

Steve gave us a broad grin, "And both of you are now represented by my attorney's law firm in your battles with your exes, in exchange for your cooperation. After I part company with the VA mental health system and Crownsville Hospital, we shall have one hell of a party at a location with no extradition treaty with the U.S."

I had my doubts about Steve's honesty when it came to paying his lawyers to defend us, but I knew how to check his veracity and I'd make the call in the morning. We turned in for the night after we shared several nightcaps and a few tokes out on the patio.

The following morning, not more than ten minutes after we finished our breakfasts, the dining room was flooded with men and women in blue, FBI windbreakers.

Don yelled, "The fucking GOP finally passed a law making it illegal to use our VA benefits!"

Someone else shouted, "Up against the wall, you fucking moochers!"

The agents weren't armed, per hospital regulations, but they had us outnumbered two to one, and not one of the fuckers found any humor in our statements, especially after I called out, "This is no way to conduct a recruiting drive, you fucking pricks!"

The rest of the vets caught on and began shouting all kinds of insults, jokes and one guy even began singing an old sixties song, "I Fought the Law and the Law Won."

Barb, Dr. K, and Merri eventually shouted us down and announced, "These people are from the FBI and want to speak with each of you for a few minutes. They just need you to answer a few questions and then they'll leave us alone. No one here is under suspicion or anything like that, but you may have some important information for them. So please cooperate…"

Vic stood, held up his left hand, and stated forcefully, "I shot that fucker! I confess, but he needed killing after I came home from work early and caught him in bed with my Gertrude."

Jimmy remarked, "I thought your wife's name was Angie?"

"Fuck that filthy pig," Vic replied with a sneer. "Gertrude was my prize Blue Tick coon-hound. I had no idea she was…" He sat down sobbing into his hands as several guys at his table began consoling him.

Jimmy jumped to his feet, and with decent German accent, shouted, "I sank the *Lusitania*! My real identity is Captain Bendover Bumhumper, of the Krieg's Marine! And I had good intelligence the so-called passenger liner was transporting…"

"Jimmy, will you shut up and let these guys get to work so we can begin our group therapy!" Barb did not appear to be amused in the least, especially after a number of the men suddenly began confessing to various historical events, such as assassinating Lincoln, Kennedy, Tupac Shakur-whoever he was; Gandhi, abducting the Lindberg baby, and, of course, failing to kill Reagan. I then noticed two men leading Steve Hamm out of the room in cuffs. I glanced at Vic, and he slowly shook his head from side to side before he asked the agents standing next to him if we could step outside for a smoke while we waited for our interrogation to begin. The agent said he'd have to stay with us the entire time, so we rose and left the room for quick trip to the patio.

The Fed backed a distance away from us to avoid our cigarette smoke, before Vic whispered, "It seems our buddy will have a considerably more difficult time retrieving his loot now. I guess the security at Jessup jail or wherever they're taking him will be much more difficult to escape from…"

"Okay, you two," the Fed stated, "we can conduct your questioning right here as soon as you finish smoking." He shifted his jacket to show off the concealed pistol strapped to his belt in an effort to impress us, but all he received were a couple derisive snorts. Then Vic reminded him it was illegal to bring firearms into a patient area.

We sat at a picnic table and after he wrote down our names, began questioning my friend Vic. He seemed concerned about our relationship with Steve and wanted to know if he ever mentioned the money he embezzled. Vic was honest to a point, explaining, "Steve was friendly enough and spent most of the time with us recalling his life in the army. He never mentioned anything about money, except to say he had an alter ego who allegedly stole money from his employer." Vic answered more questions concerning what he may have heard, and what other people were saying about Steve, when

Dr. K wandered out to the patio, noticed me at the table, then gave me a wink and waved me over to another table.

I smiled at my old friend and whispered very quietly, "This Fed has no idea what he's doing. I learned a long time ago; you never interrogate people as a group. You always question them singly and in an isolated area, like an office, so no one can correlate their stories."

"Did you speak with him yet?" He grinned after I replied no, then the good doctor remarked, "I think you need to have an attorney present during your interrogation."

I smiled back, still whispering, "And an interpreter, too!"

Vic finished answering the agent's questions about fifteen minutes later, and the Fed immediately moved to our table. He stared at Dr. K, who was wearing a long-sleeve dress shirt and pants, rather than his well-worn hooded robe. He had shoes on his feet, instead of his ragged sandals, and even sported a bowtie. He had to appear in court later this afternoon and felt he'd look more respectable attired in western dress than what he wore in his native India.

"And who are you, sir?" The Fed stared at Dr. K before giving me a sideways glance.

Dr. K replied with a straight face, "I am Daneesh Kodibandalou, and I represent Mr. Nunzio in all matters, in addition to acting as his translator."

The Fed glanced through a file folder before replying, "I have no indication Mr. Nunzio requires a translator."

"Mr. Nunzio sustained a severe head injury during his apprehension prior to being transported here for treatment. He was bilingual previous to that time; speaking both English and an obscure Bengali-Hindi dialect used only in a very remote valley in the Eastern Himalayas. He was raised there in a Hindi monastery after his parents died tragically while conducting a census of Bengal tigers for the World Wildlife Federation."

The Fed stared at me with the strangest look as my friend continued. "The severe blows he sustained to the hippocampus and occipital regions of the brain caused a temporary loss of speech, similar to a stroke, but I have been able to assist him in regaining at least part of his…"

"Okay, Mr. Kandilope…"

"Kodibandalou, my good man! Please repeat after me until you can pronounce my name correctly! After all, it just common courtesy and good manners, so let us begin." Dr. K had the man repeat his name at least ten times before he had it right, although the Fed said it correctly after his fourth try. Just as the agent was about to start screaming, Doc K held up his hand and asked for the agent's first question. By this time Don, Tom, and Jimmy entered the patio, and sat next to Vic. He quietly brought them up to date on my "condition" before they smiled at me and waited for the fun to begin.

The agent stared at me for a moment before he asked, "Mr. Nunzio, can you tell me why you've been committed here?"

Dr. K growled, "I've already explained the circumstances of his commitment, Agent!"

The Fed replied, "I'm sorry, Doc. I'm Special Agent Koslowski." He whipped out his badge to show us, but Dr. K pushed his hand away, "I can buy one of those in the children's toy department. I want to see something with your photo, Agent Komorofski."

"That's Koslowski, Doc! He pulled his credentials and flashed them in front of the Doc's face, but not long enough to for him to read them, so Doc K snatched the bi-fold out of his hand and slowly read every line on the two means of ID in his native Urdu, so I would know what was going on. He suddenly added, "Vincent is illiterate," for the agent's benefit.

I took a good look at the photo ID and said, "Gondolara pingiofarben machupinny grofrenslagen," before I smiled at the Fed.

Dr. K turned to the surprised agent and remarked, "He wants to know if your picture was taken by an undertaker, because you look real natural!"

The Fed laughed for a moment then asked, "Did Mr. Nunzio spend much time with Steven Hamm since he's been here, and if so, did Hamm discuss the reason why he was committed here?"

Dr. K turned to me and began a long discourse in his own language, lasting at least two solid minutes before he raised his eyebrows to let me know he was finished. I replied with an equally long string of gibberish but added extensive and intricate hand and finger motions as if using sign language. Just as he thought I was finished, I threw in another long spiel in gibberish, but pointed at the floor and wall very emphatically to stress my words. A glance at the table where my friends were sitting revealed four very impressed gentlemen.

Dr. K then went into another long, long monologue, banging the table with his fists while kicking our table leg before I replied with a loud belch followed by a grunt. I nodded to the agent and watched as K took a deep breath, turned to the agent and just as he was about to reply, I slapped the table and gave him a solid five minutes of more nonsense. When I finished, K grinned, turned back to the Fed, who by now had both eyes wide open, his mouth hanging slack, and with pen and paper in hand, waited anxiously for my answer.

Doc K looked the Fed in the eye, "Vincent said he sat with him a few times during their meals, but he didn't say much about anything except how lousy the food was."

The fed snapped his head up and choked out, "After more than ten minutes of discussion, you mean to tell me that's all he said?"

"That's a pretty close approximation, but you have to keep in mind, this language is not as exacting as English. Moreover, as a good piece of advice, never ask for directions if you should travel to that part of the world. It can take all day just to get directions to a location only three blocks away."

"Holy shit! I hate to ask a more complicated question…"

I grinned at my friends and winked before I went into another long line of gibberish. When I finished, Dr. K gave me the hairy eyeball, turned to the agent, and said, "Vincent wants to know if you stole your shoes from a Goodwill box or did you have to chase down a homeless person for them?"

I stared deadpan at the Fed as he turned beet red with anger, but never one to leave well enough alone, I added another pile of bullshit for the Doc to ad-lib. The shrink shook his head slowly as he leaned in closer to whisper a few words of Urdu, as if he was warning me not to proceed, but I shook my head, pointed to the Fed and grunted.

"Vincent wants you to know deodorant isn't all that expensive, but if you can't afford it, he'll lend you a can until you get your next paycheck."

The people at the other table jumped from their chairs and ran for the entrance to the building, covering their mouths to keep from laughing aloud and blowing our game. I quickly turned back to

K, held my index finger out and made a noise, SSSSSSSS, and then pointed to the door, before I stood, entered the cottage, and ran for the men's room where I found my buddies roaring with laughter.

After I managed to gain control of myself and drained my bladder, Don barely choked out, "Give us a few minutes to pull ourselves together before you continue. I wouldn't miss this for all the money in the world!"

The agent was having a heated discussion with Dr. K as we returned to the patio. I sat down and was immediately confronted by the man, "You son of a bitch! I know you speak and understand English! You'd better knock off your bullshit before I drag your sorry ass out of here and toss you in jail for a few weeks where you'll learn to speak English real fast, you bastard!"

"You'd better to listen to me, you damn pencil-necked geek, FBI thug," Barb shouted while shoving the Fed away from our table and stepping in between us. "Mr. Nunzio is my patient and has been remanded to my hospital for treatment of a serious mental disorder, Post Traumatic Stress Syndrome, brought on by extensive, and prolonged combat experience while in the service of our country. I know for a fact he has difficulty with his language selection due to his recent head injury, and if you try to intimidate or threaten him one more time, I'll have hospital security haul your ass out of here! Plus, I'll file written complaints with the Justice Department, where my sister works as legal counsel for the Director of the FBI!"

Just as I was about to give Dr. K another round of gibberish, I saw Tom hold a four-foot by two-foot piece of plywood we use as a table extension above his head and then slam it flat on the ground, making a very loud bang in the process. Immediately, Jimmy, me, and Don all screamed, "INCOMING!" I dropped to the ground as they rushed past the shocked agent, while I low-crawled as fast as possible toward the door. Tommy grabbed my shirt, pulled me to my feet, and yelled, "TAKE COVER! Everyone run to the bunker before the next round kills us all!"

We ran screaming down the hall to the far stairwell, where we hunkered down in one mass of bodies under the stairs. We were trying hard to muffle our laughter when a few seconds later, Merri entered the stairwell wondering what the hell was going on. Our muffled and strangled laughter must have sounded like sobbing and crying due to the acoustics in the cinderblock enclosure, because she immediately shouted into the hallway for help from the nurses and

Dr. K. Then she screamed, "Anyone not a patient or staff must get the hell out of this building immediately! I don't care who the hell you are! You will leave right now, or I guarantee there will be hell to pay!"

Merri's comments only made us laugh harder, but someone was able to mutter, "There's certainly going to be hell to pay when she finds out what we're really doing here!"

Fifteen minutes later, after Dr. K and Barb recalled the events on the patio for Merri; we had to help the hysterically laughing nurse to her office. As we were leaving, Jimmy announced, "I think this calls for a celebration!"

We arrived back at the hospital late that night after a loud and rowdy dinner at the local steak house.

CHAPTER EIGHT

"Vincent, I want you to discuss more of your history with Dr. Fitzpatrick," Dr. K requested once our group were arranged properly in the day room.

We all turned to look at Dr. Fitz, who seemed quite serene compared to the last time we'd seen her. She gave us a weak smile before stating quietly, "I'm feeling much better now. Dr. K has been providing me with one-on-one counseling; so, go ahead Vinny, I can take it."

I stared at my old nemesis for a few moments as I tried to recall a particular incident from our past. Then I remembered her wedding day and began. "As you all know, Fuzzy, or Sean as the good doctor preferred to call him, was in my army reserve unit. Like the rest of us, he grew very frustrated with the way the Reagan administration treated us soldiers, and especially how he, Cheney, and the rest of the GOP kept cutting back our benefits. In addition, our new battalion and brigade commanders held our company in blatant contempt, even though we had more combat experience and medals for valor than the rest of the brigade combined."

I sipped my coffee and went on. "Fuzzy wasn't one to let bygones be bygones, and after the battalion commander forbade the veterans from wearing our CIBs, or combat infantrymen badges, along with our medals, he decided to let the bastard know how he felt. The battalion commander, a Lt. Colonel, had a helicopter assigned to him, and one day he flew out to the machine gun range to chew our asses out for something the unit on the adjoining range had done. While we were trying to convince him that we hadn't yet arrived at the range when the stupid ROTC fucks shot up a control tower, Fuzzy snuck over to his bird, lifted the seat cushion and left a huge turd under the co-pilot's seat, where the Lt. Colonel usually sat. The Colonel refused to admit he was wrong, even after range control officer told him he was on the wrong range. Therefore, the idiot threatened to have us all court marshaled and thrown out of the reserves before he strutted off to his chopper and flew off. He wasn't even out of sight before he turned around, landed at our range and literally exploded on us. He couldn't prove who did it, but he said he'd deny any and all promotions our Company that hit his desk for as long as he was in command."

After the room stopped laughing, I continued, "Most of us were pretty pissed because we knew he'd freeze our promotions. Even though we all knew Fuzzy shit in his chopper, no one held it against him. A few weeks later, Fuzzy quit the reserves over all the harassment and bullshit coming from Battalion and Brigade headquarters. We didn't hear much from him after that, since he and Doc Fitz moved out to California, so she could work for the Air Force. I ran into him a few years later at our high school reunion, when he said he'd moved back to the area because his wife was transferred to McGuire Air Force Base as a shrink. I'd thought about getting out too, but the guys convinced me to stay, claiming the battalion C.O. wouldn't be around much longer. To my surprise, he was relieved of command only two months later, after the State Police found several ounces of grass and some Quaaludes in his jeep. The police discovered the dope in his luggage while we were on a convoy to Indiantown Gap for a weekender. How and why they stopped him was beyond me, and how they knew to search his baggage was a mystery to everyone, but no one in my company missed the ignorant son of a bitch."

Don was giving me a conspirator's grin when I renewed my dialogue. "The next six or seven years in the reserves were relatively uneventful, in a way, until one particular summer camp. I was acting First Sargent and remained behind at the reserve center to prepare for an I.G. inspection. The phone rang, and Jim Scarpetti answered it. I distinctly heard him say, 'Fitzpatrick? Are you sure you have the right number? Sean Fitzpatrick hasn't been around for at least six years. He quit the reserves back in' 78 and we haven't seen him since!" Joe listened for a few minutes as the person on the other end screamed bloody murder. I picked up the line and heard his wife, Marie explaining their son had been hit by a car and was in the hospital. The kid wasn't critical, but his son was calling for his dad and Marie wanted Fuzzy there with him. I reluctantly told her Fuzzy quit the reserves six years ago and hasn't been seen or heard from since. Then she claimed her husband still left the house for "reserve meetings" one weekend a month and two weeks every summer. She added, 'The son of a bitch even polished his boots and ironed his uniforms before he left!' I suggested he may have joined another reserve unit, but she just hung up on me."

I had to wait for the laughter to die down before continuing, but Marie cut me off. "That son of a bitch was going out partying with his drinking and gambling buddies on his phony reserve weekends and spending his two weeks of annual training partying at a beach someplace with young girls he met! I knew he had a couple friends where he worked, plus his company needed to know where he was at all times in case of an emergency. So, I called his office and just told one of the managers I needed him home immediately because his son was in the hospital and hung up. He arrived late that night, and of course, he was in uniform, but he smelled like suntan lotion, beer and a trace of some woman's perfume in his hair. Then I saw the floor of his car covered with sand, and in the back seat were several wet beach towels and two pairs of flip-flops, but one pink pair was obviously a woman's."

Dr K asked, "So what happened then?"

Dr. Fitz glared at him before pointing to me, "During the divorce, I asked him if you had any part in his charade, but he admitted you and he hadn't seen each other for several years, so I have to apologize for initially accusing you of leading him astray. I'd completely forgotten you spoke to me when I called the reserve center." She shook her head and continued, "So I acted as if I was unaware of what he'd done and after he brought our son home from the hospital the next day, Fuzzy said he had to get back to summer camp with you and the rest of his unit. As soon as he pulled out of the drive, I called my brother, who is a great divorce lawyer. When that worthless bastard returned to the house a week and a half later, he discovered I'd taken everything, including the checkbook, and all our banking information. All he found was a copy of the divorce papers on a pile of his old uniforms in the middle of the living room floor."

The group laughed long and hard at her story before Dr. K and Dr. Gul smiled. They both gave me questioning glances, but all I could do in response was to throw up my hands and smile back. "I had no part in any of his escapades after he left the unit, and like I said, I rarely saw him after that."

Dr. Gul asked with a grim smile, "What adverse role did the army play in your marriage, Vincent?"

"I never did anything like Fuzzy, but there was one time when the old lady really freaked out on me. My unit had an agreement with a Special Forces unit in Pedricktown, New Jersey. They were chronically under strength and were in danger of being disbanded if they weren't up to minimal manpower standards when they went for annual training. We used to transfer back and forth between my company, which was mechanized infantry, and the Special Forces, depending on which unit had the better annual training lined up. The green beanies would transfer to our unit if we went some place interesting, like Korea, Germany, or California, and we'd transfer to their unit if they went someplace unique, like Norway, Japan, Spain or wherever. As soon as we returned home after the two-week training, we'd transfer back to our original company to maintain unit integrity. However, their C.O. screwed us royally when he called and said they were going to an island in the Caribbean for a special exercise sometime during the next five days."

Vic laughed and muttered, "This don't sound good!"

"You got that right, Vic," I responded ruefully. "He called us on Thursday evening and all the men in my unit who were going, agreed to meet at Pedricktown Friday afternoon, so I told the old lady and my boss I'd be back on Monday at the latest. We arrived at noon Friday and they immediately transported everyone to McGuire Air Force base. They swore us to secrecy and told everyone there was to be no contact with the outside world for any reason until the operation was over." I coughed and stated, "You have to remember, there were no cell phones back then, or at least ones we could afford, so we were all stuck with no way to update our families. Ziggy and the rest of the guys were discussing ways to sneak out to get beer when the C.O. walked in and ordered us to the ready hangar to draw parachutes and weapons."

"You mechanized infantry boys were all jump qualified?" Tom was staring at me with a really strange look until I replied, "None of us were jump qualified, so you can imagine the shit storm we kicked up after we heard that! But the Major said the army did a study back in the early 50s, and learned the injury rate for trained versus untrained parachute jumps was about the same, so we didn't have anything to worry about. We spent the rest of the day and night drawing equipment and getting shots and studying maps and sand tables of some fly-speck island called Grenada. The maps were no better than tourist brochures and left a lot of detail to be desired, especially our landing zones and designated objectives."

"I can't believe they'd drop a group of inexperienced troops into a combat zone like that," Jimmy laughed.

"You have to remember; according to the tables of organization, we were supposed to be experienced Special Forces troops and the real members of the group had already been through several in-depth briefings. I brought up your exact thoughts back then and all I heard in response was, 'Don't you worry your pretty little head about it, Vinny! We'll have fully briefed personnel with every squad, and if anything happens to them, just wing it and shoot anyone not wearing a U.S. uniform. However, be careful because there will be Navy Seals, Marine recon, and that's not to mention airborne troops and straight-leg infantry from the army and marines. So, be advised, those guys won't appreciate being nailed by friendly fire, plus they'll have naval gunfire and Tac-air support to smoke anyone who pisses them off!'

"Ziggy asked the obvious question, Will we have tac-air or naval gunfire support?' The C.O. replied with a grin, You won't need it because you'll have 60mm mortars dropped with you, so you can provide your own supporting fire."

"Everyone in the room groaned out loud before asking if it was too late to back out, but some colonel laughed and said we could back out anytime, as long as we didn't mind spending a few years in Leavenworth. I knew he was full of shit, but we all knew enough not to screw up the operation, and just agreed it would be best to play the game."

"Scarpetti made the understatement of the day when he asked, 'Just how bad could it be? There's only a handful of local yokels with maybe a company of Cubans, and I'll bet they'll shit themselves and throw away their weapons as soon as they see us coming."

I slowly shook my head from side to side remembering what we were told versus what actually occurred. "They loaded us on a C-5A in the middle of the night and as we were flying south, the jumpmaster stated there would be pathfinders on the ground with strobe lights to mark our landing zones. The only problem was, the island we saw wasn't blacked out, which would make our LZ stand out in the dark. The damn place was lit up like Times Square on New Year's Eve, and no one could make out our LZ with all the ambient light. The jumpmaster was talking to the pilot through the ship's intercom, and I guess the pilot was thinking like all Air Force pilots. They believed as long as we hit the ground, we'd be on target, so he gave us the green light and out we went in two long strings.

Most of us landed without injury, but we couldn't find our mortars and ammo, nor could we locate our machine guns and extra ammo in the dark."

"Were you anywhere near where you were supposed to be?" Vic was laughing like hell because he already knew the answer.

"We thought we landed on the opposite side of the island, but we didn't discover the really bad news until the sun came up the next morning after we bumped into a squad of Rangers, who were just as lost as we were. To make matters worse, half our team was nowhere to be found, and they had the radios and our maps. So, we set up an ambush on a road running east and west. After ten minutes, we stopped a truck loaded with locals, and luckily, for them, and us, they surrendered without a fight. They spoke Creole and we couldn't understand a word they were screaming at us, but they kept pointing to the south and waving in that direction. Then we noticed one hell of a lot of military air traffic flying to the south, but they were off to our west, along with dozens of navy ships. We found one person, that spoke a little English, who agreed to take us to his boss. After driving through cocoanut groves and farmland, we stopped in front of a police station and post office, where we not only scared the living shit out of the only cop on the island, but we learned we'd landed on the wrong island! He told us with a lot of laughter; we had conquered, the island of Carriacou, part of the Grenadines. The good-natured officer let us know we were only two islands, and about one hundred miles short of our target. Then he asked if a machine gun and its crate of ammo belonged to us. The load dropped right into his front yard the night before, but our mortars and ammo never turned up."

"That's air force accuracy and navigation for you, Vinny!" Dr. K and the rest of the group laughed heartily at his statement until I continued. "The police officer arranged transportation for us to Grenada after he discovered his overseas phone line was inoperable, probably due to our invasion. What was worse, the Rangers were unable to raise anyone on their radio because they were given the wrong frequencies before they left Fort Benning. Then, to add insult to injury, the only boat captain willing to take us to our destination was an old salt who claimed he served in the British navy during World War II. His trawler, *Ahab's Revenge*, looked like it had already sunk several times due to old age, wood rot, and years of neglect. The damn thing had a maximum speed of five knots, per

Captain Nelson, 'But a strong tail wind and following sea is required to attain speeds like that, me hearties!"

"So, like GI's everywhere with nothing else to do, we sat where we could, and those of us not chumming the waters or sleeping, engaged in the time-honored tradition of bullshitting each other until we were totally bored. However, we had a number of nervous young Rangers in our chat session who never saw combat before, in addition to being in the presence of a group of hard-core alcoholic vets for the first time. We broke out our supply of booze and grass, then brought each other up on events since our last drill."

"Scarpetti had some kind of job where he worked around fashion models, and he always dated at least one or two. He brought a particularly gorgeous blonde to our last big party so I asked, 'Hey, Joey, you still seeing that big titted blonde with the green eyes you brought to the party last month?' Joe gave us a stupid grin and replied, 'We were going at it hot and heavy a couple weeks ago in her place, and after she did an exceptional job of cleaning my pipes, she wanted me to return the favor. She spread her legs and rubbed her crotch to get me interested, so I slid down there and was about to start munching away when I saw what looked like cottage cheese on her twat. I knew what it was and wasn't too keen on acquiring something contagious, so I told her; 'Honey, you have a bad yeast infection and I'm on a low-carb diet, so I'll have to give it a pass. And that was the last time I saw her!' Then he told us about another beautiful model but discovered she hadn't accumulated enough money to complete his sex change. 'I just apologized for wasting his time and walked out of his apartment, but the dude kept calling me every day for over a month afterwards."

"We all laughed at Joe, before one of the Rangers, who'd been knocking back Ziggy's gin pretty hard, volunteered; 'I jerked off fifteen times in one day!' His buddy replied; 'Oh, that's nothing; I pissed in the big coffee urn in the mess hall every day for a week after you guys gave me that blanket party. I told you guys I wasn't the one who shit in the First Sargent's Hummer; it was Jacobs, but the fucker lied and blamed me for it, so I had to get even with you bastards.' Then another half-loaded Ranger added, 'I sucked a dick once when I was really drunk and lost a bet.'"

When the laughter died down, I went on, "Needless to say, before we landed on Grenada, one guy got his ass kicked. Another was told he'd better find another shelter-half because no one wanted to share a tent with him. Moreover, the masturbator discovered no one would shake his hand or let him touch anyone in his squad."

I needed a drink and a piss break, so we decided to adjourn for the next half-hour.

CHAPTER NINE

With everyone's fluid levels properly adjusted, I continued with the story.

"As we were slowly motoring toward our objective, I noticed we weren't moving away from the island and when I asked Nelson about it, he said we were running against the current and a ten-knot headwind. He was doing all he could just to keep from being blown back to our point of origin.

We were lucky when a navy helicopter spotted us and after he saw the tub was full of GIs, he called for a navy ship to pick us up. That was a real thrill, but they damn near killed us all. You have to remember, we were each carrying about a hundred pounds of gear and when the destroyer, or whatever it was pulled alongside, the navy guys just tossed a cargo net over the side and yelled for us to climb aboard. The two ships were bobbing up and down and rolling from side to side in the choppy sea. I watched as our wooden tub slammed against the steel hull of the destroyer and yelled for the navy to throw us a rope to have them haul our gear aboard first, because if anyone slipped off the cargo net, they'd go straight to the bottom. Some navy officer yelled they didn't have time to dick around with us, and if we couldn't scramble up the net, they'd take off and leave us there. I shouted back, why don't you tow us to Grenada? However, someone else on the destroyer must have been thinking because a minute later, a crane on the navy boat swung out and lowered another cargo net.

Not knowing we were supposed to toss our gear into the net and then climb up the side of the destroyer, six of my boys climbed into it and signaled to be taken aboard. Four lifts later, my men were standing along the rail and yelling obscenities to the rangers, who were now kinda drunk, and having problems climbing into the cargo net without falling down. They were eventually brought aboard before me and the Ranger's platoon sergeant took the last lift after making sure no American soldiers were left on the boat. Then, I realized we failed to take a headcount of our men."

"I was thanking a naval officer for picking us up when he grabbed my arm and asked, "I didn't know the Army allowed midgets to enlist!"

"Hey Major, Scarpetti may be a little on the short side, but five-foot-seven is hardly a midget!"

"He spun me around and pointed to someone I'd never seen before, and damn if it wasn't a midget. The little person was dressed in a camo uniform similar to the rangers, with a soft cap, pack, web gear, ammo pouches and he was packing an M-4 rifle with a scope. I turned to the Ranger's platoon sergeant. as I pointed out the little person, who was now handing out joints and passing around a bottle of Jack Daniels.

"I thought he was one of your guys, but I didn't notice him until we were on the boat," The ranger replied. "I heard you reserve units would take anyone with two arms, two legs and could piss a hole in the snow."

"We had the stranger follow us inside the ship to their mess hall, where the navy fed us a hot lunch. The abbreviated soldier, who asked us to call him Trevor, stated, 'I'm a scout sniper in the Grenadine Self Defense Force. I have orders to assist you and your men evict the Cubans from Grenada."

"I knew the guy was full of shit and so did the ranger, but we had to cut the man break after he spent all his money on weapons and uniforms. This would be his only chance to live his dream, so the ranger asked, 'Have you ever been to Grenada?"

"I used to live there until I knocked up my girlfriend, and her father exiled me to that shit hole two weeks ago. He reached into his pack and pulled out several satellite photos of Grenada, on which he'd painstakingly marked all the roads and prominent features, which was a hell of a lot better than anything we had. After comparing our maps to his, we decided to appoint him as our scout sniper, especially after he described our objective in detail and noted where the Cubans positioned their heavy weapons."

"The ship's captain sat with us and stated our lost squads were on the way to Grenada via navy helicopters. 'They couldn't make radio contact with anyone, so they used the public telephone in a restaurant they liberated. One of the men called your armory, who in turn called the Pentagon, and after numerous transfers, someone contacted one of our assault ships. They sent a couple big choppers to pick them up and get them into the fight. I also contacted the operational commander, and he told me to drop you off on a pier where you can just walk off my ship. Then I'm to loiter in the area to provide gunfire support."

"That sounds like a good idea, Captain; did they happen to say where the rest of my men were dropped off?"

"They'll be waiting for you at the pier, and they have the details of your new mission since your original target has been overtaken by events."

"The destroyer anchored at the end of a long rickety wooden pier where we began offloading, with the destroyer's radio frequency written on everyone's hands after we performed a radio check to be sure. Half the rangers were so drunk they were unable to walk without assistance. When we eventually reached the road at the end of the pier, the rest of our unruly company, in addition to a news crew, met us with jeers and shouted questions from the reporters. Then an army major stepped out of the crowd grabbed me by the arm and started bitching me out. He complained my platoon was not only drunk and insubordinate, but they threatened to shoot him after he said he'd have them all court-marshaled."

"Major, they may be drunk, rowdy, and insubordinate, but the air farts dropped us on the wrong fucking island, where we discovered the radio frequencies provided were wrong! So, you're damn lucky they didn't shoot you just on general principles. Now give me our new... I had to interrupt our conversation to shout at our men who formed a line and were singing and dancing for the cameras. Now, Major, what's our mission? I have to get these people in the fight before they get completely out of control."

"The man just stared at my rank tabs for a second before asking, 'Where are your officers, sergeant?"

"I have no idea, Major. They were on the plane when we took off, but I haven't seen or heard from them since."

"He pointed up the road toward a mountain peak, 'There's a Cuban radio transmeetter on top of daht hill. Take your men up there and eliminate it as fast as posseeble. Intelligence thinks they're transmeetting information to Cuba and the Cubans are using the information to prepare a counterstrike against our land and sea forces."

"How many men and what kind of weapons do they have up there?"

"The usual complement, Sergeant; didn't you pay attention to the intelligence briefing, or were you too drunk to remember?"

"So, you have no idea, Major, but you're willing to send us up there unprepared."

"Get moving or I'll end your career right here and now!"

"Well thanks, Major; I'd appreciate your help in getting me the hell out of the big green cluster-fuck! I glanced at his uniform and noticed he was wearing a patch from the 101st Airborne Division, but nothing on the other shoulder. He also didn't have jump wings on his left breast, plus he had no CIB, which meant he'd never been in combat. Then I looked down to find he was wearing low-quarter shoes with his fatigues, which was a blatant uniform violation, not to mention extremely bad taste. I listened more carefully as he began chewing me out and I noticed just a hint of Eastern European throatiness to his speech, but his nametag said, "Smith." Something wasn't right about this guy and I had to ask a couple questions to satisfy my curiosity. Major, where is your jeep or Humvee, and where are the rest of your men?"

He hesitated just a second too long before replying, "I was dropped here by heelicopter to intercept your unit and direct you to your destination."

"Where are you from in the States, sir?"

"Pheeladelphia, Pennsylvania; home of the Liberty Bell and the Eagles," He answered with a smile, but he screwed himself by pronouncing Pennsylvania with a W instead of the Vee, so he called it PennsylWania. I had the fucker, but to be sure, I stated, "I'm from Philly, too. I grew up in the Northeast side, at Broad and 14th streets."

"My old stomping grounds were on the south side near the Navy yard."

Nobody from Philly called the neighborhoods, "side" and Broad Street does not intersect with any numbered streets. They run in the same direction, and to top off his error, there is no 14th street because Broad would be 14th street. This guy had to be a plant; probably East-German or Russian, and I now knew he was sending us into an ambush. I asked him to hold on a second while I had my second in command listen to his briefing. I called Ziggy over and met him halfway, just out of earshot of the double agent. 'Hey Zig, I'm pretty sure this fucker is an East German planted here to send us into an ambush. Listen real careful, and as we walk away, speak German or Russian to him. If he responds, we'll grab him and turn him over to the intelligence people."

"Tell you what, Major, since we seemed to have lost our officers, why don't you lead the way? And while we're discussing our current status, where is your unit and why are you here alone?"

"The rest of my unit is at the airport fighting the Cubans, and like I told you before, I was dropped here to meet with you and your men!"

"Ziggy asked, 'How are you going to get back? You don't have a radio!"

"They're coming to retrieve me in an hour, but your men have to take care of that radio transmeetter as soon as possible."

"He rolled his R and pronounced transmitter, 'trahnsmeeter.'" Ziggy gave me a quick glance, used his index finger to push his nose to one side, nodded, and walked back to our group. I shouted after him, 'Get our new scout sniper and meet me at the corner store! Then I turned to the major, 'Lead the way, sir; we'll be honored to have you mit uns."

"He stammered, looked over my shoulder at the men as they formed up in two columns and began spacing themselves out while loading their weapons. He failed to note I used the German "mit uns", instead of the English "with us", when I invited him to take the lead."

"I must wait for the heleecopter. I would love to join you, but I have other duties to attend to this afternoon."

"Ziggy, Leo, and Bohan, a German immigrant, trotted up to us and just as I jacked a round into the chamber of my rifle. Bohan shouted something in German and the Major fucked up royally by answering him in German. He suddenly realized his fatal mistake, but as he reached for his pistol, I leveled my rifle at his face and said, 'Resistance is futile, comrade! Raise your hands above your head and don't move a muscle or you'll be dead before you hit the ground!'"

"Bohan laughed as he removed the man's pistol and belt, then said, 'The Gestapo was bad, but the Stazi, or Communist secret police, are even worse! He answered me; "Watch your mouth or you'll spend the rest of your life in a Gulag!"'"

"Our scout sniper walked over, stared at our prisoner, and laughed, 'Well, if it isn't our favorite neighborhood East-German spy! How are you doing, Dietrich? Not so good today, I see.'

"We all stared at Trevor for a moment before Leo pulled out a length of commo wire and began trussing up our prisoner. Trevor grinned and said, 'I've had run-ins with this prick before. He used to tell me his old regime in the Fatherland would have euthanized me shortly after birth to keep me from polluting their gene pool.'

"The TV reporter and his camera operator rushed over and fired questions at us concerning our treatment of an American officer. Ziggy replied, "We were assigned to apprehend this guy because he cheated on his high school English final.' He shook his head slowly, 'We have a really tough Catholic school system in Philly, and this guy is in a heap of trouble.' He poked the prisoner in the chest and growled, 'Just wait till Sister Mary Ballbuster gets her hands on you; you sorry son of a bitch!"

"I called for the destroyer to pick up Dietrich before we gathered in the local bar to eat lunch and plan our next move. I checked the phone behind the counter and was surprised to hear a dial tone. After several tries, I got an overseas operator and called the house. The wife did not pick up, so I left a message on the answering machine. 'Hey honey, I don't have time to call you at work, but turn on the national news or CNN as soon as you can, and you'll learn where the stinking army sent me. I'll be home as soon as possible, but don't hold dinner or wait up for me.'

"Trevor took off to see if he could locate the ambush site and returned an hour later in a rush and out of breath. 'They have an "L" shaped ambush set up about a mile up the road where it turns to the left and runs up the mountain.'

"We stared at him for a long moment before he added, 'They have about thirty or more men with two heavy and four light machineguns, sited here and here,' he stated while pointing to the locations on one of his maps. 'They also have the road mined and the Russian equivalent of your claymores along this side of the road and up in these trees.' He glanced around at us before he added, 'Since you don't have mortars or heavy machine guns or armor for supporting fire, I suggest you call for naval gunfire to hit those fuckers and tell them not to spare the ammo. Those fuckers mean to kill you guys and any Americans using the road!'

"Lead us to a point where I can see those bastards. I'll call in artillery to smoke those assholes,' I stated while strapping on my web gear and hefting my rifle. 'Leo, grab the radio, two of our men, a couple sober Rangers and follow us.'

"Trevor grabbed my arm, 'I have a truck we can use to get to this little rise where we can see them. It has lots of cover and a clear view of the ambush area.'

"While we were piling onto the old Dodge flatbed, the reporter asked if he and his cameraman could accompany us. 'There isn't enough room in the truck, but you can follow us if you have wheels.'

"He waved for his cameraman to take a position in front of me while asking if I'd give him a brief interview to explain what we were going to do. I told the camera, 'We have a report of a large Cuban ambush ready to kill American forces about a mile up the road. We're going out there to teach those Communist bastards that you don't fuck with the U.S. Army without us arguing the point!"

"The reporter then asked, 'Do you have anything you'd like to say to the folks back home?'

"I grinned at the camera as I slapped on my steel pot, jacked a round in the chamber of my rifle, and said, 'Don't hold dinner or wait up for me, honey. I'll be home as soon as we smoke those Commie bastards!'

"Someone on the truck behind me shouted, 'Let's go kill a Commie for mommy! Then I heard Trevor yell, 'Remember the Bay of Pigs!' A split second later, Leo, Bohan, and Ziggy began singing, 'Deutschland Uber Alles'. I immediately jumped in the driver's seat and drove off in a cloud of thick, stinking exhaust smoke.

"Less than a mile down the road, Trevor had me pull into a grove of trees and shut down the engine. He signaled for everyone to be quiet before cautiously leading us up a small dirt path until we were just short of the crest. Holding his index finger to his lips, he pointed to a space under a thick bush, nodded, then slowly crawled into it before he waved me up to him. When I was alongside, he again let me know to be silent and then slowly and carefully parted a few branches. The small man nudged me with his elbow, and then held two fingers under his eyes and then pointed forward.

"I already had my binoculars out and as I adjusted them, I was surprised to see a large group of soldiers wearing strange camo uniforms, black berets, and carrying AK-47s. What was even more surprising, they were walking in our direction from about 700 meters away. The troops were out in the open and obviously in no hurry to go anywhere, but their numbers and direction of travel dictated I needed to do something to rain on their parade as fast as possible. After carefully crawling out of our hide, I grabbed Leo who had a radio.

'Did you triangulate our position yet?'

'Yeah, I also followed on the map and I have the destroyer on the horn. They said there's a cruiser there with them if we need more firepower.' Leo had a grin on his face as he asked, 'Our call sign is Bravo two-niner. Are we going to light them up?'

"I took the radio mike, called the destroyer, gave them our location, and then the approximate location of where the Cubans would be in a few minutes. 'We have a large group of enemy infantry in the open and moving in our direction.

"The ships gunnery officer replied, 'Roger, Bravo two-niner, wait one. Approximately a minute later he called,' Bravo, marking round on the way. Shot out!'

"I quickly returned to the hide and arrived just in time to hear the round whistling overhead several seconds before it detonated halfway between my position and the approaching enemy. Recalling my position in relation to the ships, I radioed back to the ship as the infantry froze in place wondering where the round came from. 'Add 300 and fire for effect!

"'Roger, Bravo, add 300 and fire for effect!' Ten seconds later, I heard, 'Bravo, on the way!'

"I turned to Trevor, 'Use your rifle to shoot anyone running to either side or toward us but stay down because hell is on the way.'

"He nodded his acknowledgement before going fully prone and sighted through his scope just as multiple rounds whistled overhead. Four rounds detonated almost simultaneously in the midst of the Cubans before they could take cover or hit the ground. Stunned at the accuracy of the naval gunfire, I just lay there and watched body parts fly as salvo after salvo tore the Cubans to shreds.

"There were two enemy soldiers running for all they were worth toward the road, and I had to shoot them myself because Trevor had his head down with his hands over his ears to lessen the concussions and noise. I knew some Cubans would be out of range of the barrage, so I called the gunnery officer and added 200 meters to their range. The artillery let up for just a short time before it began to rain hot steel on a dozen or so men running toward the tree line where their ambush was set up. Just as I turned to call up the rest of my men, they ran through the brush, knelt or went prone before opening fire on the fleeing men.

"Leo shouted he sent one of the Rangers back to get the rest of our men before he blazed away with his M-60. At least two dozen rounds had impacted since my last correction, so I had the

Navy drop their rounds on the tree line and along the road where the ambush was waiting for us. Hearing a diesel engine approaching, I turned to find another, larger, flatbed truck pull up and disgorge the rest of our unit and the TV crew.

"The reporter ran up to me and shouted, 'I heard the shells exploding and paid a dude to take us up here, so we wouldn't miss the action!' He went wide-eyed as a salvo exploded in the tree line then stated, 'You owe me an interview, Sarge.'

"I replied, 'You'll get one as soon as we're done with those guys but stay out of the way because we're going over there to root the sons of bitches out of their positions.' Just then, a burst of heavy machine gun fire tore through the trees to our right. The fire was high and off target, but it was enough for my guys to take cover and scream we were being targeted by a 51-caliber machine gun. Ziggy crawled over, pulled the reporter off his feet, and reported the gun was a little farther up the hill from the impact zone. While adjusting the naval gunfire, another louder voice came over the radio.

"'Bravo two-niner, this is Jolly Roger flight three-three. We heard you might have use for a flight of four fast-movers loaded with seven-fifty HE earth shakers.'

"'Roger that, Jolly Roger!' 'I almost laughed at the thought of having an overabundance of firepower. 'If you have eyes on the impact zone, I need you to seed the area to the immediate northwest, just a little farther up the hill. But be advised we're taking fire from a heavy MG.'

"'Bravo, wait one for the navy to check fire before we take out that target for you, over.'

"The navy controller replied, 'Jolly Rogers, we need to allow our barrels to cool for a few minutes, so you can begin your run in to target as soon as you see the white smoke rounds.' The navy's announcement was followed a few seconds later by several white phosphorous rounds detonating in the trees, indicating they were taking a break. As soon as the smoke billowed upwards, several of our guys shouted to the Cubans, 'Willie Pete will cook your meat, you fucking bastards!'

"The A-6 Intruders came in fast and low; the roar of their engines drowning out all other sounds until their 750-pound, high explosive rounds erupted on the side of the hill like so many mini-volcanoes. Ziggy stood next to me and commented excitedly, 'They laid those snake rounds right on top of that heavy MG! Why don't you have them plaster the top of the hill while we have Tac-air support? There's no sense in us going up there and have our asses shot up, when we have an opportunity to smoke them first.'

"I had to agree with Zig, but then remembered why we were there in the first place. That German sent us out here to be ambushed. 'Do you think there's really a transmitter up there, Zig?'

"He took the binoculars, eyed the hilltop carefully for a minute or two, and said, 'I don't see any antennae or structures, so there may not be anything up there.'

"Trevor held out his hand for the glasses, scoped out the hill, laughed, and stated, 'This road is the only one to the top of the hill. There's no other way up there, and it turns into a goat path just above the area where the fighters dropped their bombs. I doubt the Cubans or locals had the energy or motivation to climb all the way up there carrying heavy equipment on their backs. I'd drop a few rounds on top just on general principles and then call it a day after we mop up what's left of the ambush.'

"The fighters dropped their loads and headed back to their carrier, but the destroyer and cruiser agreed to put a few salvos on the mountain top. Since they could see it from where they were on the sea, my help wasn't needed.

"Let's get the men formed into a combat diamond and move out to the ambush zone, Zig,' I ordered while waving my arm forward. With everyone in formation, we began slowly walking across the open field toward the hill, careful to watch where we placed our feet in case the Cubans mined the area. The reporter stayed right with me, and his cameraman-maintained position on my opposite side as the reporter asked some really stupid questions. I tried to answer him without sounding too sarcastic, but I eventually had to ask him to stay back a little as we reached the area where the naval gunfire destroyed the Cuban infantry. We saw blood pools, smoking chunks of unidentifiable meat and various body parts strewn over the area, in addition to pieces of weapons and field gear. My men and the Rangers were maintaining field discipline by remaining in formation and checking for intelligence material plus operable weapons and ammo."

We reached the formerly wooded area occupied by the Cubans where we found many corpses in various stages of dismemberment by the artillery. I knelt to inspect an almost whole corpse when I heard a frantic voice come from the radio speaker.

'Bravo, short round! I repeat, Bravo, short round!' I immediately shouted, 'Short round! Take cover, take cover!' I hit the ground as the men screamed the warning to each other as we all hit the ground. A split second later, a hissing and whooping sound assaulted our ears as the naval round wobbled low overhead. It detonated close enough for the blast wave to lift us off the ground and throw us back in the direction from where we came.

"Stunned at the suddenness and extreme violence of the explosion, I lost all situational awareness and couldn't hear a damn thing through the extremely loud ringing in my ears. Any attempt at movement brought waves of pain through my entire body. After several deep breaths and a few moments to gather my wits about me, I remembered what happened and called for everyone to sound off, but all that came out was a strangled cry of anguish. I opened my eyes, looked around for my men, and was somewhat relieved to see most of them moving about searching for wounded. Ziggy and I made eye contact and he immediately screamed for the medic and a dust-off as he ran to me.

"'Holy shit, Vinny, you look like you took a direct hit from that fucking short round!' Ziggy pulled out his canteen and began pouring water over my face as the Ranger medic and Jimmy Inglesby, our own medic, rushed over and began shouting questions.

"'How many were hit?' I groaned, but they just kept asking where I was hit, and if I could move my arms and legs. I asked again, and Ziggy replied, 'Scarp has a few scratches but nothing the docs can't handle. One of the Rangers lost a piece of his butt, but it's only superficial.'

"Leo leaned over, looked me up and down then turned and vomited on the cameraman. If the sight of my wounds made a Navy Cross holder toss his cookies, my wounds must be horrific, so I asked, 'How bad am I hit?'

"Ziggy was as white as a ghost, and he couldn't hold eye contact with me. 'You're covered with blood and guts, Vinny. We'll know more as soon as they cut away your uniform and wash off the worst of it.'

"'I can't move my arms and legs, Zig. If I'm going to be paralyzed, kill me now. I can't go through life a cripple, so do me this one last favor, buddy.'"

"The Ranger medic drew his pistol, pointed it at Ziggy, and told him to move away. 'We don't know enough about his condition yet, so nobody is going to kill anyone!'

"Leo knelt next to my head, 'The choppers on the way, Vinny. It will be here in less than five minutes, so hang in there, buddy. They're taking you to a hospital ship, so you'll get the best care there is!' Someone lifted my head to remove my helmet and I was briefly able to see my body. I almost blew my lunch when I saw nothing but blood, intestines, what looked like macerated organs, bone, and strips of burnt flesh.

"Everyone turned at the sound of approaching diesel engines. A Ranger shouted, 'Here comes the Cavalry, or the Marines or somebody from our side!' Another voice muttered, 'It's about fucking time, too!'

Many men suddenly shaded me as they stared down at my body while calling for their medics. Ziggy grabbed my hand, 'The chopper is here, Vinny. I'm going with you if they'll let me since we have the same blood type.'

"Thanks, Ziggy, and don't forget to see me out if my condition..."

"The crowd parted as two men wearing gray-blue flight suits and flight helmets knelt and asked about my wounds. While the Ranger medic and my friends were describing what happened, I looked up to see the fucking cameraman just backing away from the crowd with his camera on his shoulder. Strong hands lifted me gently onto a stretcher and then carefully strapped me down as the medics continued asking questions.

"'Are you in pain, Sarge?' The dust-off medic was staring into my eyes with real concern on his face.

"Yeah, I hurt all over, Doc. Can you give me something to at least take the edge off the pain?' He stuck a needle in my arm, and I was out before they loaded me on the med-evac bird."

Doc Gul asked, "Could your wounds have caused you to exhibit violent behavior later, Vincent? And how did this affect your marriage?"

I was about to answer her when Merri stated it was time for lunch, and for me to continue the story after we ate.

CHAPTER TEN

We were about halfway through lunch when Steve Hamm strolled in with a huge smile. "Howdy, boys! Anything interesting happen while I was a guest of the FBI?" he asked with a laugh.

"What the hell happened to you, Steve?" Jimmy shook his hand and pointed to me, "Vinny was just telling us about his adventures during the Grenada cluster-fuck."

"Vinny will pick up where he left off, Hamm," Barb stated, "So leave him alone until we resume the group session."

Steve pulled up a chair at my table, winked, and said quietly, "It seems our old buddy, Elvis, or Ray Norsworthy, is an undercover agent for the FBI, and his bosses wanted to know why his bank account suddenly expanded from two grand to fifty big ones in less than a week. Can you imagine they even suspected me of bribing him?"

"The nerve of some people, Steve," I replied. "I guess they don't trust anyone nowadays, and to suspect an honorably discharged veteran suffering from PTSD is just shameful!"

"My attorney convinced them to allow me to continue my rehabilitation, since they had no evidence I was involved in the man's penchant for accepting bribes."

"Do they know where the money came from?"

"They initially thought I paid him off, but they have no proof. However, he was previously involved in a political corruption investigation that ended up going south because the evidence had been tampered with." He snickered, winked, and turned to the suspect DCA standing right behind him, "Get lost, you idiot! I had nothing to do with your buddy's bribe money."

Steve regaled us with stories about how he and his attorney proved the FBI was fabricating evidence and then had to return him to our humble abode with an apology. What they were going to do to Norsworthy was still up in the air. Vic offered, "Since they have no evidence to prove where it came from and why he received it by way of a direct deposit from unknown sources, there isn't much they can do to him unless he confesses to some nefarious dealings with the criminal element. In the meantime, they'll probably reassign Elvis to a desk in the basement of a federal building; someplace cold, dark, and foreboding."

Just as we were finishing our meal, Merri called to me. "Vinny, there's a lawyer here to see you. He claims to be representing you in your divorce, in addition to having your commitment overturned."

If sleaze could be personified, the man who greeted me was everything you wouldn't want to see in an attorney, used car salesman, or politician. He held out his hand and introduced himself, "Hi, Vincent. I'm Jay Levin and I've been retained by a third party, who shall remain nameless, to represent you in your divorce and to counter your forcible commitment here."

His hand was damp, soft, and limp as a wet noodle. He emitted a strong aroma of boiled cabbage, and his breath was as rancid as rotten eggs. Thankfully, he kept his interview short and to the point.

"I have a psychologist and psychiatrist coming to interview you next week to refute the statements by the quacks who claim you needed to be committed. I have also filed motions with the court to contest the terms of your divorce settlement."

I was doing my best to keep from gagging over his breath. He handed me a small bundle of papers, "Read these over the weekend, and sign where indicated. I'll be back on Monday to pick them up. I should have you out of here no later than next Friday at the earliest, or the following Monday at the latest." He didn't offer me his hand before he turned to leave, but remarked as he walked from the room, "Don't worry about my fee; it's been taken care of by a third party."

The man was nothing if not brief and to the point, but his various aromas seemed to linger in the room after he left, so I tucked the papers under my arm and rushed out to find some fresh air.

I found Steve and our group on the patio. "Hey, buddy, that lawyer you use seems to have a problem with his…"

"Yeah, I know," Steve, replied quickly as he glanced around. "I gave him a toothbrush, toothpaste, and aftershave to use, but he claims he's extremely sensitive to anything that touches his skin or gums."

"He should at least be more careful about what he eats and how he washes his clothes. Man, his breath, and body odor could chase a maggot off a dead corpse."

"I didn't hire him for his personal hygiene, Vinny," Steve laughed, "He's the best criminal defense lawyer in the state, not to mention one of the best divorce attorneys in the area. Just the fact that he managed to have me committed here speaks volumes about his abilities, and the way he handled my divorce is the stuff of legend." He grinned while poking me in the chest, "Just wait till he gets involved in your divorce settlement. He'll not only clean her out, but that bitch will end up paying you support!"

Merri called us back to the day room, so I could continue with my story. After we were seated with drinks in hand, I had to take a second to recall where I'd left off.

"Oh yeah; I was taken aboard a Navy hospital ship," I laughed as the group shook their heads and Doc Gul asked, "Is your story going to go on for the rest of the afternoon or should I schedule meetings for the weekend, too?"

"I'm almost done, Doc. I was out cold when they carried me into the ship's OR, so I had no idea how bad I'd been hit. But when I woke up, I discovered they'd cleaned me up and laid me out on a regular cot with no IVs or anything else. I stopped a medic walking by, and he called for someone to speak with me since he worked in the pharmacy.

"A very pretty nurse came by, smiled and said, 'Get the hell out of bed, soldier. There isn't a damn thing wrong with you except for a concussion!'

"I looked down at my body and saw I was dressed in a hospital gown, so I lifted it up and couldn't see any of the blood or gore that was there after I'd been hit. There were a few black and blue marks and a few lacerations covered with bandages, but nothing else.

"The nurse laughed and stated, 'That's right Sergeant Nunzio; you weren't really wounded as bad as everyone thought. It seems all the blood and viscera belonged to someone else. According to your friend, Sgt. Ziglenski, the artillery round must have landed in a pile of dead Cubans and their body parts slammed into you, so you're okay, and as soon as the quartermaster brings a uniform for you, you'll be on your way back to your unit.'

"I was stunned over her good news to say the least, and I was also the happiest man on earth to not only be alive, but also have full control of my body. I shuddered to recall I'd asked Zig to blow me away out of fear of being a quadriplegic. I got off the cot, bummed a smoke off a marine, and while I was enjoying it, a sailor approached with an armload of camo clothing. They were a size too big, but I still had my boots, so it didn't matter. The sailor told me to head over to the helicopter-landing pad where I could catch a ride back to the island. An hour later, the pilot left me at the pier where the Navy originally dropped us, and damn if my boys weren't sitting around drinking and smoking up a storm.

"'Celebrating the recent opening of the E-8 position in the company boys?'

"Leo stood, slapped me on the back, handed me a bottle of rum and said with a big grin, 'Welcome back, Vinny! It's good to have you back with us!' Zig caught a chopper back as soon as he heard you were okay and gave us all the bad news."

"Trevor staggered over, gave me a long embrace and sobbed, 'I'm really glad you weren't hurt, Sgt. Nutzio. I was really worried about you, my friend.'

"He held on to me while I had a long pull on the rum, then replied and gave him a pat on the back, 'It's okay, Trevor. It takes more than a stinking 5-inch naval round to kill me.' I glanced up at the top of the hill, and saw it was still burning from the naval bombardment. 'Anyone bother to recon that hilltop for intelligence or a damage assessment?'

"Trevor, still holding me with all his might, responded, 'I took a few Rangers up there and found what could have been radio parts, pieces of vehicles, and scattered body parts. The Rangers claimed the Cubans also had an anti-aircraft gun, but they never used it. We couldn't figure out why.'

"'They probably thought if they used it on those jets, they'd get blown up by the navy, or the jets would bomb the shit out of them off as soon as they opened fire.' Leo held up the radio receiver for me. I tried to separate myself from Trevor, but the sucker was stronger than he looked, so I took the horn and heard our illustrious CO calling. 'Where the hell are you?'

"We're on the east end of the island, where we just finished wiping out a company of Cubans! Where the hell are you, and why didn't you jump with us?' The man may have been a captain, but I was in no mood for any shit; protocol, and military etiquette be damned.

"The captain told me he was up in the cockpit of the plane arguing with the pilot about the location of the drop zone, but the bastard hit the green light for us to jump before he could stop him.

He saw no reason to jump because by the time they got down to the cargo hold, we were gone, and they were flying over the fucking ocean. Ligget and Jake decided to stay with the plane, and now they're stuck at Eglin Air Farts base because the plane developed engine problems.

"'Well, ain't that the saddest fucking story I ever heard! What in the hell are we going to do now? We wiped out the Cubans who were going to wipe us out, eliminated a radio relay station, and captured an East German spy, so I guess we earned our pay for the day. And to top it off, I was almost blown to shit by a short round from the fucking navy…'

"Jake laughed, 'Ziggy told me all about it, Vinny. Get back to the armory any way you can. Head down to the airport and jump on any empty plane headed north. We'll catch up and complete your after-action report when you make it back to the armory. Good luck, and well done, Vinny; this is bravo two-six actual, out."

"The men in my immediate vicinity heard everything said between the CO and me. They just shook their heads before we piled into the two trucks. On the way to the airport, we stopped at a resort of some sort and liberated their supply of beer."

"By the time we arrived at the airport, it was absolute chaos and damn few people knew what the hell was going on. We heard the Navy Seals tragically lost some men when they were dropped in the ocean instead of their LZ, and the other special forces units also took some casualties, but overall, deaths were minimal considering just how fucked up the operation was from the onset. The Rangers went off looking for their unit, while the men from B Company decided to just bag the entire deal and let the regular Army and Marines have their fun."

"A C-5 was almost finished unloading, so I asked where the plane was headed after it emptied. An Air Force sergeant said they were going back to McGuire in Jersey after they refueled. Thankfully, he agreed to let us fly back on his plane after some of my men offered bloody Russian and Cuban helmets and uniform pieces in trade. As soon as the plane lifted off, we spread ourselves on the deck of the cavernous transport and fell fast asleep. I was shaken awake hours later by a rather surprised Air Force captain, who turned out to be the pilot. It quickly became obvious his loadmaster didn't bother to tell him he was carrying passengers back to the States, and heavily armed ones at that! The cargo doors were wide open, and I could see we were home. I quietly told the captain we were on a top-secret Special Forces and CIA mission, while I put on my Green Beret. 'We'll need transport back to Grenada as soon as we debrief and pick up some top-secret equipment. Don't go anywhere until you hear from my HQ. They use the call sign, Afghanistan Banana Stand, but don't mention it to anyone else or you can end up in a shitload of trouble.'

"Just as we entered the nearest hangar, I heard a familiar voice ask out loud, 'Can someone give me a lift to the Somerton section of Philadelphia? I have a cousin there I can stay with until things calm down back home.' I turned to see Trevor walking alongside Jimmy Inglesby with a big smile.

"'Trevor, you know we have government departments like immigration and the border patrol to limit who enters the country. Do you have a passport or a visa?'

'I have my passport, but I really don't need any of that stuff,' he replied with a laugh. 'No one thinks to question us little people, even if they can spot us.'

"'Where are you going to store your weapons and souvenirs?'

"You can hold them for me, Vinny." He handed me his custom M-4, two grenades and a block of C-4.

"Jimmy volunteered, 'I'll drop you off after we turn in our weapons, Trevor. I live in the area, so it won't be a problem.'

"Leo called the armory and they sent a Deuce and a half to pick us up. We went straight to Pedricktown, turned in our weapons, but I kept Trevor's rifle and explosives. I told the CQ we'd be back the following weekend to file our reports. We were too damn tired and hung over to do anything except go home. It was almost eight in the evening when I arrived at my house, but I couldn't pull in the driveway. It was full of strange cars and every damn light in house was on, so I parked in the back yard, staggered to the house and surprisingly, found it empty. I thought the old lady and her friends must have gone out partying, and her drinking buddies left their cars there, so they could ride together. Too tired to give a shit, I took a hot shower and crawled into bed where I immediately fell sound asleep.

"'That must have given you a few hours of peace and quiet before the old lady came home' Vic laughed. 'I'm sure she was pissed as hell over your disappearing like that.'

"I actually had a good night's sleep, Vic. You see, I can't sleep with someone else in the room, especially someone who snores as loud as that bitch, so we had separate bedrooms on opposite sides of the house. I didn't wake up until ten the following morning, and when I went to the kitchen, I saw she'd already left for work. I cooked myself a big breakfast, then called the office to let them know I'd return the following Monday. It was Thursday and I didn't feel like dealing with the assholes who worked with me until I was fully rested. I thought I'd left the message on my boss's voicemail, hung up, checked the mail, washed my uniforms, and went back to bed for a nap. Just as I was about to fall asleep, someone knocked hard on the door, and although I was tempted to ignore it, I opened it to find a deliveryman from the local flower shop with a huge bouquet of various flowers, and right behind him, stood Trevor. I sat the flowers on the kitchen table and turned to my new recruit."

"My cousin moved out last week and didn't leave a forwarding address,' he laughed as Leo dropped a bag at my feet.

"He spent the night with us, but with five kids, sleeping accommodations are a little tight, Vinny, so I thought you'd have room for him here until he can make arrangements to stay with his other relatives,' Leo gave me a grin, 'especially since you have this big house and no kids!'

"I showed Trevor to the guest bedroom upstairs and told him I was going to catch a few Zs and then scrounge something to eat for supper. Trevor muttered something about being a gourmet chef, but I didn't hear the rest. I searched through the flowers and found a card, "Please accept our deepest sympathies on your loss." The people where the old lady worked sent it, so I thought one of her relatives must have bit the dust. I wasn't about to shed a tear over it. I didn't like anyone in her family, and they sure as hell didn't like me. It explained the gathering last night, and the strange cars in the drive probably belonged to her friends."

"I woke two hours later, hungry for something good to eat. Thinking I'd take Trevor up on his offer of a gourmet meal, I dressed and while walking to the kitchen, I heard the old lady arguing with two male voices. 'Why can't the Army just give me check for his life insurance since you have proof he died from the TV news? It was obvious he died from those horrific wounds! Geez; all his intestines and internal organs were blown all over him, plus the newsman on the scene said he would die from his wounds!'

"A man's voice answered, 'I'm sorry Mrs. Nunzio, but the army doesn't operate that way. His death benefit is handled by another agency, and they usually take at least thirty days to verify a soldier's death before they cut the check...'

"'But he's dead! She was shouting angrily and banging the table. 'I want that money and I want it as soon as possible! He left us in debt and there will be expenses to bury him...'

"I was thinking how we didn't have any debt at all when another man's voice spoke, but this guy sounded awful familiar and he was obviously pissed. 'Listen, Mrs. Nunzio, these things take time and we're only here to help with funeral arrangements. Since Vincente died in the line of duty, he can be buried in Arlington National Cemetery at no cost to you. All we need to know is if you have a preference for another burial site.'

"Cheryl snapped back, 'I told him not to stay in the army, but he insisted on going out and playing army with his drunken friends. Now that you people managed to get him killed, you can bury him wherever you want, but I want his insurance money...' She stopped short and a split second later let out a loud scream before she shouted, 'Who the hell are you and how did you get in my house?'

"I entered the kitchen to see Trevor, wearing his camo trousers and no shirt, standing by the other door with wide eyes and gaping mouth. The bitch was sitting with her back to me, and seated across from her was Big Mac, our battalion sergeant major and next to him was a major from brigade HQ. Mac looked up at me and turned white.

"The major didn't know me, but he gave me a very strange look before he turned to Mac. 'Who is this guy?' Mac grinned, jumped from his chair, and rushed to give me a mighty embrace. 'Son of a bitch; we all thought you were dead, Vinny! We even saw it on the news! Man, if you didn't look like a goner, no one did...'

"While he went on about my condition, I turned to the wife and said, 'I ain't dead yet, bitch! However, you don't have to worry about collecting my insurance because I'm leaving it all to St. Jude's' Hospital. I changed the beneficiary to my SGLI insurance two years ago when I realized what a sneaky, lying, backstabbing thief you are!'

"She replied angrily, 'But we saw you on TV and you were dying for sure! The newsman said you'd never survive those wounds!'

"Just then, Trevor spoke up, 'It takes more than a naval artillery round and a few minor scratches to kill my buddy Vinny. I was there and saw the whole damn thing. I even helped put his guts back together again and then sewed him up as good as new!'

"Everyone turned and stared at Trevor with a mixture of awe and disbelief, before they figured he was full of shit. Big Mac spoke first, 'Who the fuck are you?'

"I'm Vinnie's personal aide-de-camp, bodyguard, chef, and valet.' Trevor said it with a straight face and then added, 'I was right next to him on Grenada when that naval round fell short.' The news was on the TV and just then they ran film of the action on Grenada. The scene looked familiar to Trevor and me, so we pointed to the screen and said, 'Watch and see for yourselves!'

"The camera moved from filming the hill being shelled, to a shot of my men slowly moving across the field before someone screamed, 'Short round!' The explosion appeared to be massive due to its close proximity, and it did look like it hit just in front of a tall lanky soldier, throwing him violently head over heels at least thirty feet away from the impact. The camera lost focus for a few moments before it settled on a mass of blood and guts lying amidst unidentified body parts. It refocused just as Zig emptied his canteen on of all things, my face! Trevor was kneeling next to me, holding my hand as he screamed for a medic. The cameraman slowly scanned the worried faces of my men as they muttered to each other, 'It might be better to pump Vinny full of morphine, so he won't suffer.' I distinctly heard Scarpetti state quietly, 'He'll be lucky to live long enough for the dust-off to get here. Ain't no way in hell they're going to put Vinny back together after taking a hit like that!'

"Just as the talking head exclaimed, 'We're witnessing the death of a brave Green Beret; Master Sergeant Vincent Nunzio, a veteran of the Vietnam war who survived the intense fighting there only to lose his life to friendly fire on some god-forsaken island in the Caribbean. Only God knows if it was worth it.'

"See! You're supposed to be dead!' The old lady screamed at me, pointing at the screen.

The doorbell rang. Trevor answered it, and after a few moments, he returned to the kitchen with a huge floral display. 'I think this is for you, Vinny.'

"The flowers came from my employer. I was surprised they hadn't checked the voice mail, but then I suddenly recalled I'd dialed my own office number, so I left the message on my phone! I was about to call them when the old lady began screaming; I cheated her out of my insurance money, especially after the policy I had from work and the one she took out on me refused to pay since I was involved in an act of war. 'You cost me over two hundred and fifty thousand dollars, you rotten bastard!'

"She tromped into her bedroom and returned not more than a minute later with two packed suitcases. 'I'm going to stay with my sister! At least she and her family are normal and don't get their loved one's hopes up by faking their deaths on TV!'

"Mac and the Major said their goodbyes and gave me their sympathies over the behavior of my wife while Trevor wandered into the bitch's bedroom. He returned a minute later with a handful of color brochures. "It seems your wife was planning to assuage her sorrow on a beach in the South Pacific, Vinny!' He handed me four travel brochures for resorts in Tahiti. I opened one to find an itinerary Cheryl had written. It had all the times, airlines, flight numbers and cities where she'd change planes en-route to Tahiti. In addition, it had the name of the resort where she'd made reservations for the next two weeks, starting the day after tomorrow. A call to the airline revealed she'd already paid for it with her credit card and it was too late for a refund or substitution."

"I asked Trevor, 'If you have a passport and credit card, we can celebrate my survival in Tahiti for the next two weeks!' He had both, and we had a hell of a good time celebrating on the old lady's credit card, since we charged everything to our, or rather, her room.

Vic asked with a grin, 'How was your reception when you arrived home?"

"I thought she was going to have a stroke when I walked in the door, all tanned, and rested, with a two-week beard and wearing a Hawaiian shirt. I even thanked her for the vacation in Tahiti. But the kicker was; we had our own bank accounts and charge cards, so she couldn't get the money from me."

After everyone ceased laughing, we ended the session and had an enjoyable dinner. Steve sat with me during dessert and whispered he wanted a meeting on the patio. Once we were alone, he said, "You're getting released next Friday. I'm getting out on Monday morning, early. Can you check the availability of your plane?" He handed me a cell phone, which he was not supposed to have. A few minutes later, the dispatcher advised the plane is at the

Salisbury, Maryland airport for routine maintenance. It would remain there for another week while the crew received their physicals and attended training on the new GPS/navigation system and flight rules established by the FAA.

I told the man, "Make sure the plane is fully fueled and ready for an international flight by the Monday morning after they finish with the servicing."

CHAPTER ELEVEN

The VA treated us Vets to a movie that evening, and some special chow for Saturday supper, courtesy of the local Vo-Tech culinary arts class. Almost all of us agreed the kids would have a brilliant future in food preparation at the prison of their choice. Up until that meal, I'd been constipated, but whatever they fed us cured me about an hour later. And I wasn't the only one suffering from their generosity. The continuous thunder from the latrine kept me and quite a few others awake that night.

We normally didn't have therapy scheduled for Saturdays, but Dr. Gul and Fitz thought it would be a good idea since they felt it really improved our morale, or to put it in other words; she and our group found my stories quite entertaining. However, my contributions to the group must have loosened up a few of the people because Jim, one of Fitz's patients, volunteered to take the lead as soon as we gathered.

"My wife and I are avid bird watchers and we maintain numerous bird feeders to keep our avian friends around the house. As anyone who feeds birds will know, you not only feed birds, but also other unwanted fauna, such as bear, deer, coons, and of course, squirrels. The squirrels seem by far to be the worst offenders at the feeders. They not only eat all the sunflower seeds, but they also destroy the feeders just for spite.

"We waged non-violent actions on these uninvited guests with various weapons. We used allegedly squirrel-proof feeders and have had some success with hot chili pepper, but the little tree rats either figured out how to bypass the guards or they've developed a taste for Mexican food. Therefore, in exasperation, I broke out the BB gun and started popping them. We discovered killing the squirrels is a lot like the death penalty for criminals. While it does prevent repeat offenses, it does not act as a deterrent to other tree rodents, who are very happy to fill the void left by their departed brethren.

"Lucy initially would not shoot them; she left that part to me. Whenever she or I would spot a squirrel at a feeder, I'd get the BB gun, open the sliding glass door and nail it. The squirrels eventually learned, if the big human came to the door, one of them was going to die, so they posted lookouts to determine when I was around. I think the little buggers figured out which car was mine, because as soon as I would leave, they would all rush to the Sunflower Seed Diners.

"Lucy, being the gentle person she is, would just rattle the window screens, shout, clap her hands, or go out and chase them away. After a short while, they determined Lucy wasn't a threat, so they became relaxed to her presence. They would merely move to a slightly higher perch if she came out to chase them. Eventually, the squirrels grew used to her non-violent methods; they didn't even bother to look up when she left the house to roust them. A few of the nasty little buggers would even scold her. However, one day, a contemptuous, overconfident adult male gray squirrel, stood on his hind legs and whizzed at her from a tree branch while mocking her with his front paws."

BAD MOVE!

"Lucy told me about it that night at dinner, and after I stopped laughing, she asked me how to work the BB gun. I told her I was aghast!! St. Francis of Assisi's female counterpart was now planning the violent demise of cute, furry little creatures! She let me know she was in no mood to hear it. "Well, she learned real quick how to load and pump the rifle. She already knew how to aim.

"What a bloody mess she created once she started on the squirrels. Hell knows no fury like that of a woman insulted by rodents. It was so bad I had to rake the dead squirrels off the lawn before I could mow it! I wasn't sure if she actually enjoyed the blood bath she created, until one day over lunch, she asked if I thought a BB gun would kill a deer. She was tired of spending all her time, effort, and money, working to make beautiful flowerbeds only to have the deer treat them like salad bars.

"Now, I've nailed a few deer in the butt with the BB gun to chase them out of the garden, but I know for a fact, you can't kill a deer with a BB gun, and I told her so. She didn't seem convinced, but I let it go, thinking Lucy might have been able to bring herself to eliminate a few squirrels, but there was no way she'd kill a big deer. That would be like the Pope joining the Taliban. No more was said about it, and I thought the issue was dead.

"About a week later, I was digging in my horseradish patch when I heard rustling in the brush. I turned and saw a nice big buck, an 8-pointer, emerging from the woods, and he was looking right at me. I wasn't afraid of him and he sure wasn't afraid of me, so I said,

"Hey, buddy, you can have all the grass you want, just stay out of the old lady's garden…" CRACK!

"A small spot of blood instantly appeared on his forehead, right between his eyes. The big buck went cross-eyed and collapsed in dead heap. I spun and looked behind me; there was Lucy, by the garage door, lowering the BB gun from her shoulder with a big grin growing on her face.

"'I thought you said I couldn't kill a deer with a BB gun?'

"I was in shock! I couldn't believe she'd do something like that! There was just nothing for me to say about her behavior, I was at a complete loss for words! My gentle, loving wife had turned into a killer! After a few moments, I overcame my shock and I told her, 'You killed it, you clean it!'

"Yeah, yeah," she said. "I'll have it cleaned before dinner." She went over to the deer, straddled it across the shoulders, and pulled up the head to get a look at its magnificent rack."

"'Get the camera, Toots, I have to have pictures of this. No one is going to believe I got a deer with the BB gun, especially a big one like this! Holy Cow! No one is going to believe I killed a deer, PERIOD!'

"I was just about to tell her about certain laws this state has concerning killing deer and hunting licenses, when the damn deer's eyes opened, and it suddenly stood up with Lucy still straddling its shoulders like a horse!'

"She had only knocked it out temporarily with the BB! I don't know who was more surprised, Lucy, because the deer wasn't dead, the deer because it now had a rider, or me, because they both looked so natural. Just picture this in your mind's eye for a moment, a big Pennsylvania Whitetail Buck, about five feet high at the shoulder, a great rack of antlers on his head. Then imagine Lucy, sitting astride the beautiful animal's shoulders, both hands death-gripped tightly around the main branches of his rack. Both had very wide, frightened eyes, and both badly wanting to be rid of the other, but neither knowing exactly how to go about doing it. Both were so surprised; they didn't know whether to shit or go blind!

"I quietly told Lucy, 'Just hold it right there, I GOTTA get the camera, Ain't NOBODY gonna believe this!'

"Nevertheless, the deer finally pulled himself together sufficiently to do what deer normally do when they get scared; they run like a bat out of hell! And right into the woods they went as if the hammers of hell were chasing them!

"I yelled to Lucy, "Steer him around this way in about a minute or so, honey, and I'll go get a real gun!' All I heard in response from Lucy was a strangled, high-pitched cry sounding sort of like Goofy in Walt Disney cartoons, YAaaAAAHHHHHOOOOOOOEEEEEYY!

"I suddenly realized how funny it was and began laughing uncontrollably as I went into the house to get my .45 automatic. No sooner had I picked it up, when I realized a .45 automatic wasn't much of a hunting pistol. Thinking I'd better go borrow my neighbor Ed's, 7-millimeter Mauser, I left the house and while crossing the street, I heard a commotion a few houses down and saw a bunch of kids, dogs, and adults tear out of their backyard in a panic. Following close on their heels was Lucy, still riding that deer. Both were wide-eyed with fear and still moving at a good clip too!

"I yelled at her again, 'I gotta get Ed's gun dear, just keep circling the neighborhood!' She was still putting out that awful scream, so I yelled, 'Try not to scream like that' honey, it probably annoys the deer!'

"Pounding on Ed's door until he opened it; I quickly explained why I needed his Mauser, but all I received in reply was a very skeptical look. Luckily, Lucy came galloping by on the buck. Ed's eyes got so big; I thought they'd fall out!

"'Holy Shit!' he exclaimed. He spun on his heel and ran back in the house. He came out a moment later with his Mauser, a 357 Magnum and a 12-gauge slug gun. 'One of these ought to do it,' he claimed, as he handed me the Mauser. We ran out into the street and just caught sight of Lucy on her venison steed as they hung a hard-right turn into my friend Luciano's driveway. Luciano had just returned from the airport with his cousin Guido. Lou knew us for five years, and by now is ready for anything, so he yells for Lucy to come back and meet his cousin. His cousin, thinking this is the way Americans welcome strangers to this country, starts applauding and shouting, 'Bravo, Bravo!'

"In the meantime, Ed stops, grabs me and says, 'We can't shoot the deer with Lucy on it! When it falls, it might break the rack!'

"I agreed and asked, 'How else can we stop it? He didn't know, but we had some time to think, since they were now running through the woods behind Luciano's house. We were still scratching our heads when we saw them coming at us from behind Ed's house. They were moving a lot slower now, the deer probably tired from carrying all her weight.

"Lucy yelled to us,' I can get it to turn by pulling on one side of his antlers, but I can't get him to stop!'

"Ed yelled, try pulling on both at once!"

"She did, and the animal stopped right in front of us as if it had power brakes.

"Ed and I quickly grabbed an antler as I told Lucy to get off easy, so as not to spook it again. She eased herself to the ground gently, and then ran for the house, shouting over her shoulder, 'I gotta go to the bathroom, real bad!'

"I looked at the deer, which appeared to be about half dead from its charge through the neighborhood."

"Ed was eyeing it also and said we ought to just let it go. 'After all it's been through today, killing it wouldn't be fair.'

"I agreed and we both let go of the animal. I expected it to bolt for the woods, full tilt boogie, but it just wandered back to Lucy's garden as if in a daze."

"I didn't have the heart to chase it away, so I went into the house to check on Lucy. She was just leaving the bathroom when I entered. I asked how she was. She said she wasn't hurt or anything, just shook up. So, I asked, 'Now that you've ridden a big wild deer, how does it compare to your broom? Then, I saw her fist headed toward my face just before the lights went out."

After the group finished laughing, Doctors Gul and Fitz both stared at Jimmy for a long moment before Gul asked, "And how did this incident contribute to your PTSD?"

Jim smiled, "It really didn't, but I thought everyone would get a laugh out of it."

Gul didn't bother to respond but instead asked the group, "Does anyone have something to relate that would help your fellow vets deal with their problems?"

Don Farmer raised his hand. Dr K pointed to him and said, "Why don't you take a few moments to enlighten us, Don."

Don grinned at me, winked, and began. "This goes back to when I was stationed in Alaska. My First Sgt told me I had a call from the big boss and when I picked up the phone, I heard the voice of the Command Sergeant Major. I knew it could only mean trouble; really big trouble! I was assigned to the Command Group of U.S. Army Alaska as a protocol bodyguard for visiting VIPs, since I was temporarily on assignment between my tour in Vietnam and discharge just three months away. This was a spit and polish job, and it required all the military bearing I could scrounge. I soon discovered from hobnobbing with the brass, there was an ongoing rivalry between the Commanding General and the Command Sergeant Major that centered on their hunting and shooting skills."

Don took a sip of his coffee, laughed a little, and then continued. "A little history is called for here. Alaska has always been a sportsman's paradise, with the best hunting and fishing in the world, but when you inject two extremely competitive people into the state, it reverts to a sportsman's battleground. Unfortunately, I got caught in the crossfire between two of my military superiors. Both were rabid bird hunters, and either could send me back to Vietnam in a heartbeat. The battle shaped up something like this."

"The only bird up there worth hunting is the Arctic, or Willow Ptarmigan; a small quail sized bird that is extremely smart. In winter, they have a snow-white coloration, which makes them extremely difficult to see. In the short summers, their brown feathers match perfectly with the muskeg. The only way to successfully shoot them is with a dog smart enough to creep up on them and flush them into taking flight. Their color contrasts against the sky and therefore enables the hunter to shoot them; otherwise, they just run along the ground, relying on their very effective camouflage to protect them from being seen.

"My immediate boss, the Sergeant Major, had called to ask me if I had a really good dog for him. He had just gone out hunting with the General and his mutt, as the SGM called it. The Smadge complained the General paid a small fortune for this bird dog and had it shipped all the way to Alaska from its trainer/seller in Alabama, where the General calls home. His dog gave the General the edge in their hunts and the Sarge wasn't going to take a back seat to any Alabama boy, especially since the SGM was from Texas.

"He called me because I was an MP dog handler and had trained some hunting dogs for a few friends we had in common. I was no expert trainer, but I could get the canines to obey voice commands and retrieve a bird or rabbit without eating it on the way back to the hunter.

"I told the Sarge he was in luck, because I did have a really good one; probably better than anything those rednecks could produce. He told me if the dog wasn't better than the general's, I would soon find myself on a one-way trip back to Vietnam. I replied we could take Sooner, (what I named the dog) out for a test hunt and if he didn't like him, then I'd get him another. Well, I found Sooner, an exceptionally smart puppy a couple of weeks prior to the call. It was a Malamute, who took to his training, like a hooker to the Fleet. The dog was an impressive hunting dog, but I also discovered by accident, he hunted best with a snoot full of Bourbon.

"We went out that weekend. On the way to an area I knew to be infested with Ptarmigan, I had to give Sooner a couple snorts of his 'medicine' as I explained to the Sarge. The boss told me he didn't care if he had to feed the dog colonels to get him to work, just so long as the damn dog outperformed the generals' mutt. We took to the field, and I gave Sooner the "Get a Bird" order. He took off over the hill.

"The SGM turned to me once the dog was out of sight and said, 'This is for you in case your drunken mutt doesn't live up to your promises.' He reached into his coat and handed me a bundle of papers, which after a quick scan, turned out to be my travel orders to Vietnam. 'All I have to do is sign the originals and you and that mutt, will be walking patrols on the DMZ in 48 hours,' he laughed viciously."

"Before I could respond, Sooner came running back. He stopped in front of us and barked twice. I told the SGM he found two birds, so we best get a move on. The SGM told me I was full of shit, but he followed me and Sooner to where he had taken up a point. I told Sooner to "Flush 'em", which he did, and two Ptarmigan took to the wing, their snowy white color contrasting beautifully against the sky.

"The SGM looked at me and said, 'It was just dumb luck, no dog could count like that!' I smiled at him then told the dog to "get a bird" again and off he went, happily running through the muskeg. He came back a few minutes later. He sat in front of me, barked three times, and looked over to his left. I told the SGM he found three birds this time, but we should approach from the left.

The SGM said I was as crazy as the dog, but again, he followed me and Sooner, probably just out of curiosity. When we took up our shooting positions, Sooner flushed up three birds. The

SGM was shocked; he threw down his shotgun, whipped out his checkbook, and asked how much I wanted for him. I said $1,000.00, which was what I thought the dog was worth; he readily agreed, handing me the check.

"'Let's see him do it one more time,' he requested. I sent the dog out again, but this time it was a good ten minutes before he came back. While we were waiting, I kept having flash-forwards of the jungles, little yellow guys pointing AK-47s at me and big nasty snakes. When Sooner finally did return, I almost had a heart attack.

"He was barking like crazy and carrying a stick in his mouth. He ran up to me, shaking the stick back and forth; then jumped up and began humping my leg. He dropped the stick, and still barking like crazy, jumped onto the SGM and humped his leg too. Sooner picked up the stick again, barking his head off, and started shaking the stick back and forth. The SGM looked at me as if I had grown a second nose and said, 'Your stinking dog has gone nuts.' He claimed I would be humping a 16 in the jungles of Vietnam within a week and he also wanted his check back.

"I told the Smadge, the dog is just showing you how smart he is! I told him, the dog is telling us he found more birds out there, than you can shake a fucking stick at!

"The Sergeant Major didn't even bother to check what the dog found. The SGM pointed his shotgun at me and repeated his demand for the check, so I handed it over."

"Three days later, I was very fortunate in finding my best friend from basic training, Pete, working as a personnel assignment clerk while in-processing at Da Nang. Pete asked me, 'What the hell are you doing back here, Donny?"

"I told him the story about the Sergeant Major and Sooner. When he stopped laughing, he blurted out, 'At least, this time the pooch screwed you, instead of the other way around!'

"'Yeah,' I agreed, laughing at the craziness of the whole situation.

"'Well, buddy, there's only one thing I can say about that rotten lifer,' he grinned at me, "Fuck him if he can't take a joke!"

"I laughed again with my old friend, as he tore up my travel orders.

"Guess what, Don?"

"'What, Pete?' I answered, looking at him in bewilderment as he just destroyed my orders and was feeding some forms into his typewriter.

"'I'm changing your orders. You have less than three months left in the Army. According to the regs, you can't be sent to Vietnam unless you have at least a full twelve months left in the Army before you ETS.'

"My heart skipped a beat. I raised my eyebrows, as far they would go, and said in shock, 'You're shitting me?'

"'Nope! Tell that asshole lifer to read 'em and weep. I'm assigning you to my unit for the next 24 hours, then we're both going home, buddy! My last day in this job is today; I rotate back to the world tomorrow at 0600 hours. I'll have your new orders and your discharge papers done in about ten minutes, then my buddy in transport will cut you a set of travel authorizations all the way back to Philly International'

"I couldn't say anything. I was at a complete loss for words; but Pete was good to his word and the very next day, we were on the Freedom Bird, winging our way back to the World."

"The 707 had to take the northern route back, due to a Pacific cyclone along the direct route to the U.S.A. We had to refuel in Anchorage, but we were unable to take off right away because of some mechanical problem with the plane. The flight crew said it would be at least 8 to 12 hours before we could leave, so I decided to take advantage of this opportunity Lady Luck dropped in my lap and pulled Pete from the plane for a special favor."

"We took a cab to Ft. Richardson, my old home base, where I was stationed only a week before. I had the cabby pull into the Headquarters Building driveway and stop in front of the Sergeant Majors' office window, which was on the first floor, almost level with the driveway. Pete was kind enough to toss a few snowballs at the Lifers' window just to get his attention. When the rotten bastard looked to see who had the guts to throw snowballs at his window, I got out of the cab, smiled and waved to him with my middle finger. His eyes bulged out so far, I thought he would lose them both. His face turned a brilliant scarlet, and his mouth was working a mile a minute. I calmly got back into the cab, rolled down the window, yanked down my G.I. trousers, and mooned him as the cab drove off for the airport and home."

"And that incident somehow contributed to your current problems, Donald?" Dr K was laughing too hard to comment, but Dr. Gul wanted an answer.

"Yes, it did," Don replied with a grin. "I keep having nightmares that somehow, the army will find an error in my paperwork and send me back to Vietnam." We all laughed at Don's explanation because everyone knew he was full of shit.

Fitz had heard enough and started screaming we should take these sessions more seriously or we'd be stuck here for the rest of our miserable lives. Dr. K calmed her down, then turned to us and asked for just one more contribution before we broke for lunch.

I raised my hand, and with a huge grin stated, "I have one incident to recall…" Dr Fitz went ballistic as soon as I raised my hand and charged across the room at me, but Don and Steve cut her off and held her down while Doc K gave her a shot of a strong tranquilizer. After she relaxed, Doc K turned to me, "Okay, Vinny, let's take a short break before you start your story."

While refilling my coffee cup, Merri told me to take a call in the office.

"Vinny, this is George, your lead pilot. I need to know where we're going internationally, so I can file the paperwork and flight plans. You know we can't just take off and fly into another country…"

I asked him to wait while I stepped out in the hall and yelled for Steve. "Hey, dude, my pilot needs a destination if we're flying internationally, and he needs it today, so he can file the flight plan."

Steve didn't blink an eye before he stated, "Brownsville, Texas, then Mexico City, Acapulco, Panama City, Panama; then terminate the flight in Recife, Brazil."

George didn't say a word as he wrote it all down. Just as I was about to ask if he had any questions, he stated, "Make sure they have current passports and updated vaccinations." He added, "Also, is this round trip or one way? I need to know so I can check for return fares en route to cut back on empty miles, boss."

"It's one way, and I'll be command pilot."

"I have nothing better to do, so I'll co-pilot for you, Vinny. This sounds like it should be a very long, strange and interesting trip. Call me when you have their itinerary nailed down and I'll have the plane and crew ready." He hung up without another word.

CHAPTER TWELVE

Doc Fitz was placed back in her chair and after everyone quieted, I began. "Back in early winter of 2000, the old lady and I, after enduring several weeks of sub-zero and near zero temperatures, along with a couple of nasty snow and ice storms, decided to give ourselves a week in the sun to thaw out and recharge our batteries. Since we had a nice experience at the Bluff House, on Green Turtle Cay in the Bahamas two years before, we thought we'd go back there rather than take a chance on another resort."

"The island had sustained serious damage from Hurricane Floyd the previous fall. There were still many trees down and damaged houses on the island six months after the storm had passed. Some of the houses were completely blown away. We saw nature can produce some really amazing devastation, but the resort suffered minimal damage."

"The Bluff House is on an island inhabited by 200 honest souls that proudly boast of no crime. They don't even have locks on the doors, simply because they're not needed. I was skeptical at first, but after our first visit, I was convinced. Our cabin was right on the beach. You fell asleep and awoke to the sounds of the gentle ocean surf and the songs of tropical birds."

"On our first full day, we chartered a boat for Bone Fishing. We caught a couple each, and true to their reputation, the fish put up a tremendous fight. That night, we were dead tired from fishing all day, along with a few extra drinks at dinner, and we slept like logs; except for what I thought was a weird dream. I dreamt four big guys crept into my room, chloroformed me and carried me away."

"I awoke the next day to find myself in a different room than the one where I had fallen asleep. A squad of huge, mean looking Cuban Commandos was standing around my bed with big grins on their bearded faces."

"Holy Sheep Shit! I hadn't dreamt about what happened the previous night! I tried to get up to fight my way out of there, but they had me securely tied to the bed."

"Where the hell am I and what the hell is going on here?" I demanded. "And where is my wife?"

"Senor," The ranking officer said in good, but accented English, "Your wife is still in the Bahamas. We did not abduct her. However, your government has refused to allow Elian Gonzalez to return to his homeland. They have even stooped so low as to try to brainwash him with expensive toys, gifts, and food, along with trips to that capitalist fantasyland, Disneyworld. So, my government has decided to retaliate by doing the same to an Americano. You will be treated the same way as our poor Elian, with hope we can convince you to forget your capitalist masters and realize the dream of our great leader, Fidel Castro!"

"NEVER!" I shouted in his face. "I am an American Army Veteran and have sworn to die rather than succumb to Communist propaganda and lies. I will fight you to my dying breath. I will never give up! My father fought the Nazis! I fought you Communist bastards in Vietnam, and I will never give in, NEVER! Kill me now, so at least I won't die tired."

"He started to ask me questions about my background, but all I would give him was my name, my old rank and serial number. He tried to convince me, hopelessly, that we would become friends. I spit in his eye to show what I thought of his friendship."

"I was about to tell this Commie Pig where to go and what he can do to himself when he gets there, when he jammed a hand rolled Romeo and Juliet, Cuban cigar in my mouth. In spite of my muffled protestations, he lit it and forced me to smoke it, while pouring a cup of 100% Colombian Coffee down my throat. This was quickly followed by an enormous breakfast, washed down with several glasses of fresh-squeezed orange juice. I tried my best to fight them off, but it's hard to argue with a squad of AK-47s on full rock and roll pointed right at your face."

"As soon as the breakfast dishes and cigar butts were cleared away, they untied me with the understanding I would not try to escape. It was hard to argue with a man holding an assault rifle against your head. They then had a procession of people enter the room bearing gifts, which they feebly hoped would turn me against my home country."

"First offered on the altar of weak wishes, was a new 10-speed bike. 'HA!' I retorted. 'That's for a kid, not an old man like me,' I scoffed at the Commie Pig. Then they produced three spanking new Penn Rod and Reel deep sea fishing combos. 'Just like Papa Hemingway's,' the senior officer said with pride. I choked a little on that one. Then it was a fully stocked tackle box, the size of a split-level.

"They led me outside and there on the front lawn, was a mint condition '57 Chevy. 'This was Fidel's' pride and joy, Meester Vinny. We spent a lot of time and money keeping it like new for him. As you know, we haven't had any new Detroit iron imported since 1960. However, Fidel feels the sacrifice of his own favorite car is the least he can do to show America what Cuba is really about.'

"I was really impressed now. I walked to the car on shaky legs, unable to believe my eyes. The paint gleamed. The interior sported a Hurst 4-speed. The engine rumbled with that distinctive, deep-throated purr you only get from a worked 327 with a 4-barrel and dual glass-packs. 'Ooooooohhh,' I murmured.

"The officer opened the driver's door for me. 'Get in Vincente; let's go see your next gift.'

"I must have put down forty feet of rubber burning out of there before I noticed my prison was actually an enormous beach-front hacienda. 'Crafty Communist Bastards,' I thought to myself, as Raoul, my Cuban host, directed me several miles down the road to a small marina.

"Parked alongside the pier sat a 62-foot, Chris-Craft, custom wood cabin cruiser, painted in the same color scheme as the '57. Raoul told me with just a hint of pride, 'It used to belong to Papa Hemingway. Fidel has had us preserve this in original condition too! By the way, it comes with a crew of Cuba's best fishing guides. They are the sons of the guides used by...'.

"'Don't tell me,' I cried, 'Papa Hemingway!'

"'Yes, yes, Vinny!' Raoul answered, lighting another cigar for me. I figured I better play along with these guys for a while, at least until I can make a break for it, as we left the dock to troll for some monster Marlin in the Gulf Stream.

"Raoul and I were exhausted after Marlin fishing the next two days. In addition, we both had vicious hangovers from all the Cuban rum we drank while celebrating our catch, an 18-foot, 2,400 lb. Marlin that will surely make the record books. If that wasn't bad enough, I felt very sluggish from eating too much prime rib and fresh seafood. I thought discretion might be the better part of valor at this time. I'd wait for just the right moment, before I make a break for it; recalling the escape and evasion training the Army gave me as we returned to the Hacienda. Later that night, I discreetly noticed the weather was turning cloudy while my personal maid helped me into the Jacuzzi. I put off any thoughts of making a run for it until the weather improved.

"After two nights and days of partying hard in an unsuccessful attempt to wear down the Cubans, I was teaching my guards and maids how to dance to Motown music. Chico, (Raoul's nickname) told me they had thought of grabbing my wife, Cheryl too. However, they found out she had a serious lobster addiction, and they didn't want to endanger the island's shellfish population trying to satisfy her. He said they would get word to her that I was OK, and he would see to it I'd videotape a message to reassure her.

"I knew this video would have to look coerced. No way was I going to help my country's enemies. Nevertheless, I agreed on the condition he would wait until my suntan faded and I could lose a little of the weight I gained.

"'No problem, Jimbo, we can do it in black and white. As a matter of fact, with the right light, we can make you look starved!"

"'OK, but no propaganda statements!'

"'I wouldn't think of it, Vinny. Besides, you haven't been properly indoctrinated yet,' Chico yelled as he attempted to throw a split during a Four Tops song.

"'Poor Chico,' I thought, 'he's never going to walk right again after that one.'

"Chico's aide, Fredo, said we would start filming tomorrow, right after we get back from surf fishing. He suggested it would be a good idea if we got some sleep since we'd be leaving right at the crack of noon.

"I noticed there was a full moon while I climbed into my king-size waterbed. Unfortunately, there was too much moonlight to make an escape attempt, so I tried to fall asleep. Tossing and turning, I dismissed brief, but terrible feelings of self–pity, caused by the poor chances of escape the Cubans and weather have afforded me. No sooner had I started to drift off into a nice surf-fishing dream, when a hand clamped firmly over my mouth. As I began to fight, a voice whispered in my ear, 'Mr. Nunzio, we're Navy SEALs, and we're here to get you out!'

"Turning my head, I could only see a dark form. I had to act now! They finally came for me, I thought excitedly. My country had not forgotten me! Cheryl must have gotten word to the right people, and they sent a team of America's best to rescue me from the Cubans. Now was my chance, I thought desperately, I had to act now! The iron was hot, and I had to strike! "I had to think and act fast! As he eased his hand off my mouth, I whispered back, 'No Habla English, Senor. My name is Habib.'

The SEAL's eyes opened wide with shock and surprise! He froze.

"'Hablas espaniol, senor?' I said in my best Spanish, remembering my surf-fishing appointment the next morning.

The Seal backed away from my bed and spoke into his throat microphone, 'We're in the wrong room! We've got the wrong guy!'

"'WAIT A MINUTE!' An all-too-familiar female voice said out loud, 'That's him! What are you trying to pull here, Toots? Get out of that bed and let's go home! You have to go back to work sooner or later, and your boss isn't going to hold your job forever! No way are you staying here! Now get up!' My too familiar wife's voice thundered in the room."

"'What the hell are you doing here?' I asked, resisting and overwhelming an urge to run for the guard's quarters.

"'I didn't have any pictures of you with me, so these guys said it would be a good idea if I came along to identify you,' my damn wife replied, 'and it's a good thing I did, too!"

"'AAAW SHIT!!' I screamed. 'NNNNOOOOOOOOOOOOOOO! CHICOOOO! HELLLLLPPPPP!!' I screamed as four big SEALs and Cheryl wrestled me to the floor, trussed me up like a pig and hustled me to a zodiac inflatable boat. 'NNOOOOOOOOOOOOOOOOOO,' I screamed continuously as they dropped me unceremoniously headfirst down the hatch of a sub waiting offshore.

"Once the sub submerged, the Seal team leader asked why I was being so difficult to save. I told him, 'Since I am an Army vet, I was really hoping to be rescued by the Green Berets.' I spent the rest of the trip to Miami stuffed in a torpedo tube."

"The room laughed for a few minutes while a couple men asked me questions about the fishing in Cuba. Then Merri called for an end to the session so we could eat lunch before Doc K stated we'd have just one more contribution from the group for the afternoon. He glanced at me and stated, 'Try to restrict your recollections to incidents that contributed to your commitment here or to anything that may have helped you overcome your PTSD.'

This caused the room to break out laughing; however, for the life of me, I couldn't think of anything pertinent, so I just let go with the first thing to come to mind. "I worked for a large quarry and paving company and was making good money for a while, but a huge construction corporation bought out my company and unfortunately; they already had six human resources managers and at least fifteen safety managers. They let me go, so I couldn't play with explosives or big trucks anymore. Bummer! I guess you could say I failed in my goal of becoming filthy, dirty rich, but I guess two out of three ain't bad. With the loss of my income, we decided to try to save some money on heat and added more insulation to the attic. Unfortunately, my soon-to-be ex, Cheryl, who happened to be one of the most uncoordinated and clumsy people I've ever met, wanted to help. In spite of my instructions, she continuously tried to stand on the ceiling drywall instead of the joists, and she dropped right to the first floor…at least five or six times. If anyone came to visit us, I had to warn them not to say anything about the holes in the ceiling; better yet, they shouldn't even look up. She was pretty sore about the whole thing for a long time."

After the laughter died down, I continued. "She was pretty damn jealous and suspicious of any woman I came in contact with. I had a colonoscopy just a few months ago and although the results were excellent, the two nurses assisting the doctor were old friends from high school, and I found out later they'd developed a nasty sense of humor. They asked if I had brought someone to drive me home since I was receiving a general anesthetic. I told them my wife was waiting for me. They had to check before they could begin the procedure, and afterward I heard them whispering to each other that Cheryl looked like the jealous type. When I got home, I needed to take a shower and while getting undressed, I saw in the mirror the nurses had written some obscene messages about me on my rear end while I was under anesthesia. If the old lady saw the writing, I'd go to sleep and never wake up again, so I've been careful to only undress in the dark or when she isn't around to see it. It took about a week of hard scrubbing to get their graffiti off my ass."

Doc K laughed shook his head, looked to Doc Gul and held out his hands. She just shook her head, covered her face with her hands, and muttered, "He's on a roll; just let him continue."

"The bitch came from Iowa corn farmer stock, and the farmer genes took over one spring. She wanted to fill in the swale along the road and make another flower garden, so we ordered a big dump truck full of topsoil for the fill, and I rented a skid-steer Bobcat to move the dirt. Now, I've run 980G front-end loaders and D-4 dozers, which are the biggest in the business with no trouble, but the controls of these little Bobcats are really touchy. Well, the bugger got away from me a few times while I was running it, and I ended up with a "B" shaped driveway, a new entrance to the living room, a couple of "Lawn Circles," where the grass won't grow and a pick-up truck with a long ugly gouge down the side. However, at least she had her new flower garden."

Everyone was shaking their heads and muttering side comments to their friends when I added, "Three or four winters back, my snow thrower acted up during our first real snow of the winter. After asking our company's crack mechanic, "Speed" to fix it, he recommended I just change the engine since it had nine years on it and it really wasn't worth the expense of a rebuild. Moreover, he just happened to have a spare engine I could use. It required quite a bit of engineering and welding to make it fit on the snow thrower frame, but I can tell you, a snow thrower with a 1200 cc Harley-Davidson engine is a sight to behold...and hear…and handle. It seems we failed to hook up the throttle controls properly during assembly. It started on the first kick, which was good, but the throttle was wide open, and with an ear shattering roar, it tore off down the driveway, throwing snow at least 50 feet in the air. It hung a hard left after it chewed up the mailbox and its 4X4 post then proceeded to chew up the row of white pines along the road. It shredded the oak tree, turned the shed and its contents into mulch. When it finished eating the shed, the damn monster did a 180 and came after Speed and me.

As we ran the high hurdles over fences, porches and dogs, Speed yelled, "It shouldn't be long now, Jimmy!"

"Till we get eaten," I yelled back. Just then, the engine sputtered, backfired, and died.

Speed replied, "No, it's a Harley, it'll run out of gas or oil any minute now."

In a way, being unemployed was a blessing because I had the time to rebuild the shed and plant new trees."

Steve began laughing at me, "You're so full of shit, your eyes are brown!"

Doc Gul gave me a hairy eyeball, "I think we've heard enough from Mr. Nunzio for one day. We'll gather again on

Monday, but Dr. Fitzpatrick will lead the discussion if she feels up to it.

Fitz gave me a vicious glare before growling, "I will definitely be ready to lead the group by then!"

CHAPTER THIRTEEN

The rest of the weekend was quiet except for a brief altercation between Steve and Yates. It seems the ex-jarhead had a hard-on for Army veterans, and he made the mistake of grabbing Steve from behind to put him in a headlock. Steve reached back, and grabbed Yates by the balls, squeezed as hard as he could, which caused Yates to let go and drop to the floor writhing in agony. No one had any sympathy for the bully, so we left him in the hallway as we snuck out for pizza and beer.

While downing the artery clogging meal, Steve and Vic sidled over to me. While Vic kept an eye open for undercover officers, Steve whispered, "I'll be at Salisbury airport no later than six on Monday morning. I'll flash the headlights three times fast and once long from the downwind end of the runway. That will be your signal to start taxiing to the main runway. Just make sure you open the door before you reach the end of the taxiway so I can jump in. The tower can't see the port side of the plane from there, so just take your time running through your pre-takeoff checklist."

Vic leaned closer, "I'll be coming along, too. We'll be using my car and Steve has a buddy who will make sure it crashes so it will look like I died in the wreck."

I raised my eyebrows at his revelation before I asked, "I think they'll need a body in the wreck before they declare you dead, Vic. And they'll be able to tell from the corpse's DNA if it's you or someone else."

"When the car goes over the side of the Bay Bridge Tunnel late at night, they'll eventually find the car with the driver's door open, and assume I got out, drowned and my body was washed out to sea."

"I guess you checked the tide charts and all that shit?"

"Fucking right I did! And my buddy is an ex-Navy SEAL! He claims he's done exactly this sort of thing before at least a dozen times, and he's positive we'll get away with it."

"What's he charging you for it? I know the guy ain't risking his life out of the goodness of his heart. And how is he going to survive? That's a hell of a drop from the bridge?"

Vic laughed, "He's going off the level section from the Eastern Shore, where it's only about fifteen feet above the water. He'll be wearing a wetsuit and my car has an airbag so it will cushion his impact when it hits the water. He'll have a buddy under the bridge in a fishing boat to pull him out, plus there will be an empty beer cans and a slider of whiskey in the passenger compartment to make it more believable."

"What are you paying him?"

"I'm leaving him my collection of five antique Harleys, a 32-foot fishing boat, and my antique muzzleloaders."

"But won't your ex supersede who you have in your will?"

"It's all spelled out and notarized by my attorney, who assured me she won't get shit! Doug, the guy who will fake my demise, has been a long-time friend, and since the bitch hates cycles, fishing, and guns, she won't bitch about it. Besides, he already has the titles; the Harleys are in his garage, plus I had him pick up the guns a couple weeks ago." He grinned, "It's all taken care of, Vinny. My accountant and attorneys will transfer every dime out of our bank accounts, in addition to my personal and business accounts by midnight tonight!"

We were in the process of deciding whether to sneak out and see a movie at the mall when Don signaled for me to meet him by the door.

"Vinny, I was speaking with Vic and Steve earlier and was wondering if you have room for one more on your plane."

"We have the room, but I can't say when we'll be back, Don. I know Steve won't be coming back, and I doubt if Vic will either. As far as I'm concerned, I can use a few months or even years in the tropics, although I won't be on anyone's wanted list and won't need to hide."

"I won't break any laws by going with you, but I really need to get the hell away from this country since that asshole Trump and the GOP are going to trash our economy and turn this place into a fascist state."

"You're welcome to come with us, Don, but like I said, you'll be on your own once you get off the plane. I'm thinking about heading for the Bahamas after Steve completes his business in Panama and Brazil. My plane will continue to its next charter from there, so if I decide to go anywhere else, I'll be flying commercial. But one way or the other, you'll be smart to bring your passport if you don't stay in the States."

The remainder of the weekend was uneventful, and Monday morning we held another group therapy session.

Doc Fitz appeared to be primed and had both barrels loaded and aimed right at me when she walked into the day room. Almost everyone noticed her glaring at me and as they shifted in their seats, someone muttered, "Don't sit too close to Nunzio or you're likely to get wounded by the stray rounds and shrapnel!"

Fitz stared at me for a few long moments before growling, "Your friends Dr. K and Dr. Gul won't be here to protect you today, Nunzio, so you're going to pay for all the slanderous remarks you made about me!"

"I didn't slander you, Doc," I replied calmly, "I just related our history, and I'm sure Fuzzy and the Philly cops would vouch for every word."

"Well, I managed to speak to your soon to be ex-wife over the weekend, and she gave me your sick and perverted history as far back as when she first met you. However, she also gave me the final straw that broke the camel's back and caused her to have you committed."

I just stared at her for a second before stating, "Yeah, she looked at her bank account, and then saw mine was much larger, so the greedy bitch decided she wanted all of it!"

Fitz raised her eyebrows as if she'd caught me in a lie before asking, "If that's so, then why don't you tell everyone about how you potty trained her nephew Jake and caused the poor boy all kinds of trauma in the process!"

I laughed at the memory, and as I glanced around at the men giving me really strange looks, began recounting the incident.

"I'd heard my wife's sister was having problems potty training her young son Jake. I called her and said she should drop him off at our place for the long 4th of July weekend. In addition, while I was working on the little rug-rat, she could take off for her brother's party with my old lady. I'd have him fully trained by the time she returned on Monday. I've learned there is a very common problem with most children since kids and "potties" were first invented. However, I think we need to clear up a few misconceptions before we get into the corrective action for the problem at hand."

"What the hell do you know about raising kids, Nunzio? You never had children, but you still felt qualified to help potty train your nephew!"

"I didn't have to have kids of my own, Doc! I came from a family with seven kids, and I was the second oldest, so I saw all my younger brothers and sisters go through all the stages of early childhood development, in addition to my cousins and the neighbors' kids. Plus, I was a very acute observer while growing up, and I learned a lot more from life than you can ever get out of a college textbook."

Several vets snorted their agreement before I took a sip from my coffee and began. "You see, kids don't think there is a problem with having a loaded diaper. They are much smarter and more down to earth than adults give them credit for. Studies have shown the odor emanating from a loaded diaper isn't unpleasant to a young kid, much as the smell of a skunk is not considered offensive by a dog. Just check out the look on your dog's mug after he tangled with a skunk; he'll appear to be proud of himself."

"Since kids have no real skills at this age and really can't do much in a productive sense, they are proud of the little they can do. In addition, being as small and lightweight as toddlers are, they are very reluctant to lose any ballast they accumulate on their back side, which helps counterbalance the milk-gut they've so laboriously built up on their front end. It also aids greatly in their initial attempts at standing and walking. They feel the extra weight will help keep them from becoming airborne in a high wind."

"Contrary to popular belief, most kids don't like to be held by strangers, aunts, uncles, and others not prepared to feed them, so they prefer to use their heavily laden and odiferous poop depository as a natural defense mechanism against unnecessary handling."

After the guffaws died down, I smiled at Fitz, winked, and continued. "There are also the artistic and tactile sensations so important to developing minds. The use of their self-produced wall coloring material aids greatly in the development of their artistic talents. They see nothing wrong with reaching into their back pocket to secure some contrasting burnt sienna with which to paint an abstract mural on the dining room wall or give the family car a new paint job. They may even use it to provide the dog or cat with an artistic hairdo, so a parent shouldn't be too quick to criticize their child for his actions without first admiring the potential talent displayed on their expensive wallpaper. I know of one kid who kept stuffing the family VCR with his diaper ammo as his way of making a statement on the choice of entertainment his parents were providing. It was discovered he preferred Clint Eastwood to Sesame Street, and who could blame him? The kid was way ahead of other kids his age.

"As far as the tactile pleasures, most kids love the sensation of extruding the stuff and then squishing it between their toes and fingers, not to mention the joy they get from watching the reaction on adults' faces when they're discovered decorating the house with the play-dough they made all on their own!"

Everyone except Fitz was grinning wildly by this time, so I went on. "Now to the question at hand: Potty training! It really is easy. Kids are creatures of habit, whether you know it or not. They eat on a regular schedule, and of course, process and eliminate on a schedule too. During the course of the day, keep close tabs on the condition of their diapers. Record the time they pinch off a loaf or soak their nappies. Keep accurate time records for about 48 hours, so once you've got their schedule down to where you can predict when they will be unloading within 15-30 minutes, grab the little sucker and sit them on the potty. Try to have it located someplace where they won't get bored and walk away, like in front of the TV, in the sand box, the front seat of Dads car, or wherever they seem to like it the most."

"Make it fun for them also. Boys are proud of their marksmanship, so you may want to paint a bull's-eye in the bottom of the potty or put a picture of someone they don't like there; such as Donald Trump, George Bush, Paul Ryan, an aunt who likes to pinch their cheeks, Daddy's boss, your boss, and weird in-laws; you get my drift! Then when he hits the target, praise the hell out of the little guy, "Oooh, look at how you crapped all over Uncle Charlie's face! What a good shot you are! Mommy, or Daddy is so proud of her little brown bomber!" And then give him a reward."

"It won't be long before he starts trying trick shots from the couch, long shots from the dining room, or firing one out of the car window as you drive to the mall.

"However, if you are using pictures of someone for target practice, be sure you hide them if the person is scheduled to visit. Also, you may want to lock the kid away during the visit or it may trigger some embarrassing events."

"I told my sister-in-law, 'If this doesn't work, just let me know, I have a few more ideas that may or may not work; such as paper training him first, using a large litter box, and my favorite, "Let's put a surprise in daddy's lunch pail!"

"Nunzio, you are absolutely insane, and if I have my way, you'll never see daylight again…"

I cut her off, "For your information, Doc; my sister-in-law dropped her kid off on Friday afternoon and he was voluntarily using his potty by Sunday afternoon! I discovered he hated his Uncle Paul! His was the first picture I put in the bottom of the potty bucket, and the kid went right on it, and the little bugger was laughing the entire time, too! Therefore, to celebrate this momentous occasion in the kid's life, I took him out for pizza Monday afternoon. His mother was some kind of vegan, so I made sure we had lots of pepperoni and sausage. On the way home, we stopped at my friend's tattoo parlor for a souvenir he could show off to his friends in day care. I had Ralph draw a full color beauty of an American eagle on his chest and stomach with "Uncle Jim" on the scrollwork. It was done in henna so it would wash off after a few baths."

"You filthy bastard! You scarred that poor young boy for life!" Fitz threw her pen and a file folder at me and was on her way to assault me when a couple guys grabbed her and held the screaming shrink down until Steve pulled Merri from her office to give Fitz a shot of something. As the tranquilizer was sending her to never-never land, I explained, "Henna is just painted on the skin's surface with an airbrush. It's not a real tattoo and definitely not permanent."

She was still awake when the guys propped her up in a chair as I went back to my story. "My sister-in-law was somewhat skeptical to hear I'd potty trained her recalcitrant son in only two days, but as she was giving me the evil eye, the pizza he had earlier was on its way out. Little Jake ran to the stack of his uncle's pictures, snatched one, placed it in the bottom of his potty, then dropped his drawers and sat on the thunder mug with a big smile. His mom stared quizzically at Jake and then me for a moment before she looked at the stack of photos. Her eyes suddenly went wide with shock just as the kid ripped off a tremendous fart a second before we heard semi-solid matter splash into the bowl. He let go with a few less impressive bursts before he stood, spun around, stared into the bowl, pointed and laughed, "I got him good this time, Uncle Jim!"

"After his mother cleaned Jake's behind, we sat for a snack before they left for their home in Pittsburgh, and that's when my nephew told his mother what a great time he had with his favorite uncle. Then he said, "Look at what Uncle Jim gave me for going in the potty!" He lifted his shirt completely over his head so his mom could see his really neat "tattoo".

"My sister-in-law went wide-eyed with shock before she passed out and fell off her chair. My wife damn near had a stroke, but after staring at my friend's artwork for a few seconds, she rushed into her room, and returned with her Bible in hand then immediately proceeded to beat me with it. I eventually seized her Bible, tossed it into the fireplace before I wet a finger and showed her the tattoo would wash off. She eventually laughed at my joke and said she wouldn't tell her sister what I'd really done before I went out for a steak sandwich."

The men were roaring with laughter when the sedative finally hit Fitz full force. She nodded out before slowly falling off her chair. Jimmy was kind enough to place her on a sofa before declaring the day's therapy at an end. We left for the patio when Barb and Merri stopped me in the hall and said Dr. K needed to speak with me in his office.

"Vincente, I have some good news for you," the good doctor stated with an enormous grin. He held up a handful of papers and continued, "I have your discharge papers, all signed by the powers in charge of this puzzle palace. All I need is for you to sign at the little red x and you're free to go, my friend!"

"I didn't think I'd get my discharge until Friday, Doc," I stated as I inked the appropriate lines.

Dr. K smiled, "I conducted my own investigation into your commitment with some friends at the Department of Health and Mental Hygiene. We discovered the alleged psychiatrists and psychologists who declared you to be a violent manic depressive do not exist! Their office addresses also do not exist, so there was no legal reason for you to be sent here! However, I've contacted the state's attorney general and asked them to file charges against your wife's attorneys for at least ten felonies, including fraud, falsifying state documents, false imprisonment, and forgery."

Barb laughed before rushing to give me an impassioned embrace and warm kiss. "I'm so glad to see you're getting out of here, Vinny! I just hope this won't be the last time I'll be seeing you again."

I gave Barb a long embrace before I kissed her passionately and whispered, "You'll see me tonight for dinner, then tomorrow for breakfast, lunch and dinner..."

Merri separated us long enough for a hug and kiss before Doc K asked, "Where are you going to live now that your soon-to-be ex has taken everything you have?"

"I still own the house and she hasn't sold it yet, so I'll..."

"He'll be staying with me until he can straighten out his finances, Dr. K," Barb said softly as she stroked my back. "I'm retiring next month, so we'll have lots of time to figure out where we're going spend the rest of our lives."

Merri and Dr. K laughed before K asked, "Are you sure you want to spend the rest of your life with a man that has a history of mental illness?"

Barb smiled, "I wouldn't want to spend it with anyone else!"

I gave everyone the good news as I was gathering my few meager possessions. Steve was wide-eyed with shock, but I told him, "I didn't need your lawyer; Doctor K was able to have me released when he and DHMH found out the shrinks my ex used don't exist, but I'll still see you Monday morning as planned."

"That's great news, Vinny. I'll be sure Don and Vic are there too." He grinned and added, "I'll have a little bonus for you since I won't have to pay my shyster to spring you. However, do you still want him to handle your divorce? I promised you he'd take care of it at my expense and the offer still stands."

"I appreciate the offer, buddy, but all I have to do is hand these papers to my attorney and I'm pretty sure the old lady and her shysters are going to be more worried about staying out of jail for all the laws they broke than trying to rip me off."

"Good enough, Vinny," He slapped my back, gave me a hug then walked me to the door where he reminded me, "Monday morning between 06:30 and 07:00."

Barb pulled her car up to the curb as I walked from the building, and she immediately drove us to a very nice restaurant for our celebratory dinner. Since I was now homeless, she invited me to move in with her until I found my own place or decided to move in with her.

"I have to take a trip starting Monday morning, but I'll be back as soon as I get my head straightened out, Barb."

"You take as much time as you need, Vinny. I'll be here waiting for you, and after I retire, we can do some serious traveling, lover." She grinned, kissed me, and then led me into her house for a night of passionate lovemaking.

Thankfully, Barb left early the following morning. I needed the alone time to recover from Barb's extremely physical sexual gymnastics that left me thoroughly exhausted. After spending the afternoon on the phone with my attorney and accountants, I called for a rental car. I drove to my house to see what was left of my personal possessions and had to kick the door open to find the house empty of furniture, and kitchen supplies. There were several boxes of my clothing stacked in the garage marked, Goodwill. I searched all my secret hiding places and retrieved my checkbook, pistols, ammo, house and car keys, extra credit cards, and important legal documents.

The shed housing my power tools for gardening and lawn care was also empty, so she'd sold or gave away every hand and power tool I owned. Her day will come when the court learns she and her shysters falsified the documents used to have me committed. Although I was pissed as hell over the shit she pulled on me, I couldn't help but smile knowing paybacks were going to be a screaming bitch.

The rest of the week was spent buying a new car, securing checks and ATM cards from my new banks, visiting the hangar at the airport to ensure my collection of muscle cars and bikes were still there, and reviewing the details of upcoming trip with my pilots.

I've had a nagging feeling Steve Hamm shouldn't be trusted ever since I'd met him. His history of lying, embezzling and stabbing his friends and co-workers in the back just might have contributed to my doubts about him. Just to cover my own ass, I disassembled two .45 automatics and hid them in the plane, along with 200 rounds of ammo.

CHAPTER FOURTEEN

Sunday evening was rainy, windy, and cold for this time of year. I called the hangar where one of the crewmembers stated, "It will be clear by the time we take off, and according to the national weather service, it should be smooth sailing all the way to Panama."

"Do we still have the six AM take off slot?"

"Yes sir, but it's no big deal since Salisbury doesn't have much traffic, especially that early in the morning, so we can actually take off anytime within an hour or so."

I breathed a sigh of relief, "Okay; I'll be there at five with our passengers, but we'll pick up one or more passengers at the end of the runway."

The co-pilot laughed, "I think this is going to be a flight for the record books, Vinny, but we'll be ready."

After packing my bag, I told Barb, "I have to get up very early tomorrow morning, so I'll sleep in your guest bedroom."

"It's okay, Vinny, you can sleep anywhere you want, but I'd feel much better if you slept with me since I have to get up early tomorrow for a seminar in Baltimore."

"I'd love to, Barb, but I was dead tired from last night's activities and had a hell of a time getting out of bed; plus, I have to be up on time tomorrow!" We both laughed before I said, "If you'd do me a favor sometime this week, I'm leaving my car at Salisbury Airport and I'd appreciate it if you'd bring it back here for me. I'll call the day before I return so you can pick me up, but it will be several weeks, at least." She agreed, I gave her the spare set of keys and a copy of the registration and proof of insurance. I planned to leave my keys in the car along with all the papers just in case things got hairy, and I needed to relocate in a hurry.

I called the numbers Don and Vic gave me, and surprisingly both answered on the first ring. Both claimed they'd be at the hangar no later than five AM, and neither would have a car to park there, where someone might trace them to my plane. I was already facing charges of conspiracy, aiding and abetting in several felonies, harboring a fugitive, and a host of other charges as soon as Steve stepped foot on my plane. However, I made several contingency plans in the event any number of concerned law enforcement agencies caught us.

I knocked back a stiff shot of brandy then hit the sack. I awoke with a start when the clock radio went off, playing and old sixties tune, "I Fought the Law and the Law Won." Hoping it wasn't an omen of things to come, I quickly showered, wrote a two-page note to Barb. Then made a phone call to an old friend working for the feds protect my ass, and headed out the door after carefully checking my bag and pockets for necessities, such as cash, passport, wallet, credit cards and phone numbers, including Barb's three numbers. My new car was a light blue, plain-Jane, Chevy Malibu that looked just like all the other cars on the road. After checking several times to see if I was being followed, I went to the airport, parked it on the far side of the long-term lot, and then hoofed it to the hangar.

I walked in through the door at exactly five, surprised to find Don and Vic seated on a bench just inside the hangar. Seated next to Don was Tommy Hewitt.

Don raised his arm, pointed to his watch and said, "Damn good thing you made it on time, Vinny, or we would have left without you!"

I gave Tommy a raised eyebrow rather than ask the obvious questions. He shrugged his shoulders and replied, "I need a vacation away from everyone, and a trip to the beach just ain't gonna do it for me. So, if you don't mind, I'd like to tag along and see what kind of trouble we can get into."

"We could end up in any number of jails, both foreign and domestic, buddy."

He laughed, "Better than sitting in the damn loony bin listening to that idiot Fitz!"

"Did you bring baggage?"

"Just one bag and I gave mine to the crew with Don and Vic."

"Of course, you know we'll probably have to find our own way back here, or at least back to the States after we drop off Steve."

"I've got my passport and plenty of credit cards with almost zero balances, so I'll be good, buddy." He stood, smiled and reached into his pocket and then handed me a thin wad of hundred-dollar bills. "This should cover my airfare to wherever we end up, Vinny."

"You don't have to pay your way, Tommy," I replied, "Steve is picking up our travel expenses, or at least he'd better…"

Don laughed, "Don't sweat it Vinny! Tommy had us stop at a convenience store in Annapolis where he ran to a group of people hanging around outside. He flashed a fake police badge and relieved them of their day's drug sales." While we were laughing our asses off at Tom's sheer guts and ingenuity, he pulled out another, much thicker wad of bills and remarked, "Those crack heads never even hesitated when I flashed the tin and held out my hand. They just reached into their pockets and gave me all their cash and dope! Then they took off like their asses were on fire. We sold the dope at bargain basement prices within fifteen minutes and here we are!"

The flight crew was busy with their pre-flight inspection, but George, the pilot shouted, "There's coffee and donuts in the office and we'll have a micro-waved breakfast as soon as we reach cruising altitude."

Just as we finished the last of the pastries, George entered the office, sat with me and went over the flight plan. "I've logged our plan as far as Brownsville, Texas, but I haven't received anything back from the Mexicans yet. This is not unusual for a charter like ours, but I'll re-file again from Brownsville to make sure." He gave me a hairy eyeball, "I sure hope like hell we're not going to wind up in a Mexican or Panamanian jail, boss."

"Me too, George," I replied quietly as Gary, the co-pilot sat and cast a wary look at Don, Tom, and Vic.

"Vinny, I hope you know I have a wife and kids at home," Gary growled, "and I sure as hell would like to see them again as soon as we finish this run."

I whispered to the two men, "Did you get the special equipment I told you to secure?"

George replied with a frown, "Yeah, we did, and I double checked them last night to make sure they'd work if we need them." He checked his watch and stated loud enough for everyone to hear, "Time to get everyone aboard and light up the engines, Vinny. Have your friends help Gary load the bags in the cargo bay."

The pilot stood by the door and checked IDs, and then recorded everyone's name and address in the manifest. "Just a precaution in the event we go down hard, and they can't identify our bodies," he laughed after Vic asked why he needed to provide identification.

As soon as George and Gary finished the cabin checklist, I stated, "Don't lock the door. We have another passenger to pick up at the end of the runway." I pointed to the area where I expected to see Steve waiting for us before continuing. "As soon as you begin to taxi to the runway, flash your lights several times and watch for a car's headlight flashing back. He'll flash a couple short and then a long one, which means he'll be going over the fence and will meet us where you'll turn onto the runway. Just stop for a few seconds, and I'll let him in."

George gave me a strange look before he asked, "This guy isn't going to have contraband on him, like drugs or guns, is he?"

"No, nothing like that, but he is probably a fugitive by now. He won't be coming back with us, so it shouldn't be a problem unless we're stopped en route." Just as George released the brakes and turned to begin taxiing, he flashed his landing lights several times, and a moment later, we saw headlights flashing from the far end of the runway. "Take your time taxiing to the end of the taxiway, then stop for a few seconds as soon as you begin to turn. I'll let you know when to get rolling again."

I was standing by the partially open door when I felt the plane slow and then stop. I lowered the door and as soon as it reached its limit, Steve dove through it in a rush, then turned to help me close and seal the door. While he was thanking me for keeping my promise, I shouted to the cockpit, "Let's get this show in the air, George!"

I pointed to an empty seat for Steve to occupy, and we were still strapping in when the pilot applied full power for his takeoff run. Just as we rotated, I glanced out my window, and I swore there were several people standing along the access road staring at us through binoculars, but we were moving too fast for a second look to verify what I glimpsed.

Turning to Steve, who was still breathing heavy from his run for the roses, I asked, "Are you sure you weren't followed to the airport?"

He managed to take a deep breath before he stated, "I left the hospital at three, and made sure my bed looked like it was still occupied with pillows and blankets. As you know, the night shift won't wake up until about now, and they won't check the beds for late sleepers until 7:30." He glanced at his watch, "So we still have an hour and a half before they'll realize I'm gone."

"Besides Don, Tom, Vic, and me, who else knows you're going over the fence?"

"Just my lawyer, but he thinks I'm driving to the border." He gave me a grin shortly before he grew concerned, "Why would you ask that?"

"I thought I saw a group of people with binoculars on the access road watching us take off."

He paled for a few seconds and stared at me with wide eyes and gaping mouth, but then shook it off, "You were probably imaging things, Vinny. You know how desperate situations can affect your imagination."

"Let's hope so, buddy, because I ain't too keen on spending time in the slammer for you or anyone else."

Hamm laughed, "In it for a penny, in it for a pound, buddy!"

I had slowly developed an aversion and deep-seated mistrust of Hamm ever since I learned he'd ripped off his company and fellow employees of their retirement money. Veteran or not, I was never one to tolerate thieves and knew he'd get what was coming to him sometime in the near future. We spent the rest of the flight to Brownsville sleeping fitfully. George woke us to make sure we were strapped in before he began his descent, and that was when I developed a case of nerves. Would the law be waiting for us, or would we be denied permission to fly on to Mexico?

I didn't see any police cars waiting while we parked by a hangar. A refueling truck pulled up to fill our tanks. Steve, along with the rest of our crowd and the crew, deplaned for the refueling process.

"I'm going into the terminal to buy something to eat and a bottle of Scotch, "Steve called over his shoulder as he walked away.

I replied, "Sounds like a good idea," and a second later, everyone, including the flight crew joined him. I held the pilot back for a moment, "George, call the office and see if he paid at least half for the flight yet. If he hasn't, let me know right away because we may have to change our plans!"

George walked off to the side to make his call while I trotted up to Vic, who waited for me. "How long will we be here, Vinny? I'd like to call my barrister and have him transfer some cash into my Barclay's account and prepare a few documents I'll need when I return to Sidney."

"We won't be here for more than an hour or so, Vic. If you're planning to stay in Brownsville, we can part company now, so you won't have to worry…"

"Actually, I was going to stay with you until you reach your final destination. Then I thought we might head for a place I own in Oz after we tire of wherever you intend to go. But I'll need an address where we'll be camping out."

"I won't know till we get there, buddy! There're a few nice places I know in the Bahamas, but I don't know their physical addresses, and I can't decide where I'll end up until Steve goes his own way. However, I'm assuming he's not going to stiff me for the charter or try skip out on me once we get to Panama."

"If we get that far, Vinny," George interjected. "Excuse my rudeness, but he hasn't paid a dime yet. So, do we confront him here and demand the fee in full or have him pay after we cross the border; if that's possible."

Ten minutes later, I found Steve speaking on his phone. He nodded to me as we sat at his table, but he was speaking Spanish to whoever was on the other end. While we waited for him to finish, Tom turned in his chair, and gave me a hairy eyeball before pointing to the counter and said, "I need a refill."

Standing next to him as we edged along the counter, he whispered, "I understand Spanish, and I overheard him asking someone if they could find two people who can fly a Cessna Citation."

"Golly gee, and our next stop is in Cancun! I wonder why he'd ask that."

"What are you going to do? That sneaky thieving prick is going to highjack your plane when we get to Mexico. And I don't doubt he plans to kill you and the rest of us in the process!"

"He may have a lot of plans, but I'm not stupid, Tommy. I know his history of embezzling money from his employers, in addition to stealing the pension and 401K money from his friends and coworkers. If he thinks I'm so naïve and dumb to fall for his bullshit, then he's in for a very unpleasant surprise!"

While waiting to pay for my meal, George sidled next to me, "What are you going to do, Vinny?"

"I need you to call the office again and make sure they have any money that's been transferred into our account, transferred out to our account in the Caymans as fast as possible and leave just enough money in it to keep the account open. I think he may transfer the money to us after I confront him, but he'll transfer his payment and anything else in our account out to one of his banks within the hour. Moreover, I don't think he's working alone. Tom said he called someone a few minutes ago and was speaking Spanish when he asked if they could find two people to fly a Citation."

"You've got to be kidding me, Vince! You're not seriously thinking about having us fly him any farther; are you? Listen' buddy, I really like flying for you! You pay well, give us great benefits' and don't try to micro-manage the company, but as much as I like it, this job ain't worth dying for!"

"Don't worry about it, George! I won't let anything happen to you or anyone else in our group. I only agreed to his charter because I thought he'd pay as he promised and then go his own way after we drop him off in Panama, but now I'm having serious doubts if he ever meant what he said. I'm going to confront him over the money as soon as we sit down.

I slid my tray next to Steve's as I sat and gave him a hard stare. He raised his eyebrows in response as I stated, "You haven't transferred the funds into my charter company's account, buddy. I told you while we were in the hospital, you had to pay at least half before you got on the plane, but it hasn't happened as of ten minutes ago."

"Sorry, Vinny," He replied with a grin. I intended to do it last night, but every time I pulled out my phone, one of the DCAs came close. I'll do it right now, and even pay it in full for you, Vince, since we're more than halfway there."

I nodded to George, who sat next to Steve and gave him our bank's name and payable account numbers. Steve put his phone on speaker before he punched what seemed like a hundred numbers into his phone before he held it up for George and the rest of the table to hear a synthesized voice proclaim, "Transaction completed!"

"Thanks, Steve, it's a pleasure doing business with you!" George rose from his seat and mentioned he had to check on the status of our refueling and see if the Mexican government approved our flight to Cancun.

Steve gave me a quizzical look, "I thought we were going to Acapulco?"

"We don't have the fuel to fly there in one hop. As it is, we barely had the gas to fly here with the people we carried. You have to understand this is a Citation Sovereign, and it normally has a 3,000-mile range, but it was modified with more comfortable seats, a full galley, and head, so it's only capable of 2,500 miles with favorable winds. In addition, we always maintain a good fuel reserve in case there's an unexpected problem."

Steve appeared to be lost in thought for a few moments before I saw the wheels in his head begin turning. I thought he must have his people in Acapulco on a tight timeline, but if he reached for his phone, I'd beat the shit out of him and leave him here. If he called while we were in the air again, I'd turn the plane around and dump him at the first airport where we could land, if I bothered to land at all. However, before he replied, George waved to me from the door. He grinned, gave me a thumbs up sign, and pointed back toward the outside door.

"Okay, everyone; let's get on the bus," I called to my friends and rose to my feet. While walking to the plane, George stated, "He paid the twenty-five grand in full, and Chris at the office transferred it to your other account right away, so the money is safe. She also said we have a return charter from Panama City to Washington, D.C., but the party won't be ready for departure until the day after tomorrow."

"How are you and Gary for flying hours?"

"We'll need to get at least 16 hours off duty to be legal for tomorrow, but if we make Panama City today before 10:00 PM we'll be good for the return trip." George grinned and added, "But we have you with us and I brought your logbook. You haven't logged any flying hours in over three months, so if we need to, you can take the command seat."

After we reached cruising altitude, I turned to Steve, "Why do we need to fly to Acapulco, buddy? I thought you stashed your money in Panama!"

He smiled, "I have a couple condos and a garage in Acapulco." He laughed and added, "Actually the garage is a hangar where I have my own Citation stashed, but I can't fly it, and unlike you, I don't charter it out and don't have a regular crew to fly it. So, in the event my contact there can't find me a qualified crew, I'd like to have you, or one of your pilots fly it to Panama City for me where I know I can find a pilot and co-pilot to fly me to Recife Brazil."

"Do we terminate the charter in Cancun if you have a crew there waiting?"

"No, I'll still need your plane to fly there in addition to mine, but you'll be carrying some cargo for me."

"Hey, Steve," I growled, "I don't carry drugs or contraband, buddy. Ain't no way I want to wind up in prison, and I especially don't want my crew and friends imprisoned in some Mexican or Panamanian shithole either!"

"Don't worry, Vinny; I wouldn't ask you to carry anything illegal. I have some furniture, artwork, and collectible glass to transport to a buyer there. I have papers for it all and I'll be paying import taxes on it when we land, so there won't be any trouble. I just don't trust common carriers to get it there without them stealing or damaging my goods."

We landed at Cancun, passed a very thorough customs inspection, and immediately after refueling, took off for Acapulco, only an hour and a half after landing. Steve fell asleep before we reached cruising altitude, so I used the opportunity to assemble the two .45s I'd previously stashed in the cabin. As good as he made his story sound, I wasn't about to trust a fucking thief, especially with the lives of my friends and employees, not to mention my pride and joy.

While hiding my weapons, Don and Vic glanced at me with raised eyebrows. Don whispered, "Expecting trouble, Vinny?"

"I believe in hoping for the best and preparing for the worst, buddy."

Vic leaned over and very quietly stated, "Let's hope they're not needed, but if they are, I was on my country's Olympic pistol team in 68 and 72."

"If it comes to that, you know where they are."

I sat back but kept a wary eye on Hamm until Don moved next to me.

"I'm getting off in Panama, Vinny. I'd like to catch a freighter or cruise ship heading west if it's at all possible."

"I don't know if they take on passengers there, Don. Did you check any of the travel sites to see if you can?"

"Yeah, I just finished and there's several due to arrive there next week. I've always wanted to cruise the South Pacific and if I don't go now, I'll never get another chance." He grinned and added, "Vic and Tommy are coming with me, so why don't you join us? You're a free man now, so there's nothing and no one holding you back."

"I'm kinda looking forward to doing something like that, but I need to wait to see how my business transaction with Steve turns out."

Something wasn't right! My stomach gave a lurch as I considered Steve and his plan to escape with his money. I reached down between the cushions on my seat to ensure my Colt was there and ready for action.

CHAPTER FIFTEEN

Acapulco looked very inviting from the air. The azure Pacific was almost too much to resist as we descended to land. I was half-tempted to tell Steve we'd be spending the next few days there, but the customers waiting for us in Panama could not be denied. I could always swing back here on my way home.

Mexican customs gave us another thorough search, but they ignored the interior and concentrated on the cargo bay looking for cash, per one of the officers. "The narcos need to get their money into Mexico one way of the other, senor, and they're willing to spend some to get their hands on it."

We had a quick dinner in the terminal before Steve led us to the hangar where he stored his business jet. It appeared to be in pristine condition. The fuselage, wings and engine nacelles gleamed in the light. The manufacturers ID tag on the doorframe indicated it was an X+ model. I was impressed his jet was a step up from mine, but then I noticed it was manufactured only two years ago. It meant he managed to buy it while he was in prison or at Crownsville, so he had access to a considerable amount of money; much more than the 15 million he stole from his employer. I began wondering just how much he embezzled from his employer and the company's 401K along with who else he ripped off, when Gary coughed behind me.

"Vinny, this is one hell of a bird. It's 250 mph faster than yours, and it has a cruising altitude five grand higher, too!" He grinned as he slipped into the cockpit, whistled and motioned me into the right seat. "I'll fly this down with you, while George will take our bird with your friends." He hit a few switches on the control panel and the LED screens flashed to life before he began running down the ship's self-diagnostic systems. After twenty minutes, he rose and gently pulled me after him. "We need to do a very thorough pre-flight inspection, Vinny. This thing hasn't been flown in almost six months!"

While we were inspecting the craft, a straight-truck pulled up with two men in it. Steve spoke to the driver for a few minutes before they began loading various pieces of wrapped furniture and corrugated cartons of differing sizes. They didn't appear to be heavy, but just to play it safe, Gary and I opened and inspected a few to be sure they weren't loaded with drugs. We found a variety of crystal goblets, small statues made from what appeared to be ivory, silver, marble, and gold. There were small paintings, several cartons filled with old books, Persian rugs, and wall hangings. I was about to ask about the value of one old book, when Gary pointed to his watch to emphasize we were on a tight schedule.

"I don't think we have more than three or four hundred pounds of freight, Vinny," Gary remarked as we finished our preflight, "So, we shouldn't be overloaded with me, you, and Steve on board. I'll take on a full load of fuel to be safe." We climbed back into the cockpit and while he ran calculations on the plane's computer, I watched the truck transfer the rest of its cargo into my jet.

"I think our buddy is dealing in stolen antiques and artwork, Gary."

"He shrink-wrapped all those books to keep them dry, and the paintings were all sealed in waterproof containers, so you're probably right." He grinned, "I'll bet he used most of the money he stole to buy that stuff, and now he's going to sell it. The man seems to be thinking ahead all the time. The Feds are looking for the money in bank accounts and safe deposit boxes, but they ain't gonna find it!"

"I'm wondering how he could not only afford to buy this plane but do it while he was in the slammer." I glanced out my window to see a fuel truck pulling up to the wing. "I'll go out and watch them refuel." Just as I rose from my seat I turned, "Did you bring the chutes?"

"Yeah, I have both stashed in the locker right behind you, boss. Do you really think we'll need them?"

"Let's hope not, but the more I think about it, the less sure I am that we'll land in Panama in his plane."

I checked the flow meter on the tank truck before they hooked their hose to the fuel inlet coupling, and again after, they finished. During the fueling process, Dave kept a close eye on the gauges and shifted fuel from one tank to another to keep the plane balanced and ensure all tanks were full.

While they refueled my own plane, I walked around Steve's ship to observe control surface functions while Gary operated the controls. Everything was operating as designed, and just to play it safe, I double checked various components for hydraulic and fuel leaks but found none. The longer I thought about what we were doing, the more hinky things seemed to be. Something wasn't right! This was all too easy, and I just knew Hamm and his deal were going to head south very soon. I must have been crazy to go along with him; but then, I was locked up in a nut house at the time we made our agreement! However, it didn't excuse my failure to think things through, and now I was going to pay for it. How much, I had no idea, but I needed to do something to limit my losses.

I called my plane to speak with George. "Hey, buddy, do you feel something just ain't right about this trip?"

"Vinny; if I were you, I'd grab Gary and hustle right over here! Don went to the cargo compartment and checked a couple boxes for me. He looked scared shitless when he came back! Donny swears he saw two shoulder-fired anti-aircraft missiles buried under and wrapped with Persian rugs."

I saw Hamm exit a pick-up truck with a Hispanic man and point him to my plane as he walked to our boarding ladder. "George, it looks like Hamm is placing his security man on your plane while he rides shotgun on mine. I suggest you neutralize the fucker as soon as we get in the air."

"Roger that, boss. I'll let the boys know before he gets here."

Hamm entered the cockpit, gave us a big smile, then slapped our shoulders and said, "Let's get these birds in the air! Times-a-wastin and we're burning daylight!"

"Get strapped in while Gary and George call for take-off instructions, buddy," I replied before switching the radio back to the traffic control frequency from our private one so George could hear my exchange with Hamm. I rose, walked back into the cabin to make sure everything was secure before take-off, and while passing Steve, I couldn't help but notice a bulge under his armpit that wasn't there before we landed. I didn't say anything or look twice at it as I entered the cockpit, buckled up and began running down the pre-flight checklist with Gary.

Traffic control assigned George to take-off first and we were right behind him as we taxied to the main runway.

Gary gave George a few extra seconds after he lifted off before he applied power and our jet rocketed down the runway with alarming speed.

"You gotta buy us one of these babies, Vinny!" Gary shouted as the enormous thrust and accompanying G-forces pinned us back in our seats. "This thing has some balls!"

I was impressed with the plane's performance as we continued to accelerate during the climb out to our assigned altitude of 35,000 feet. However, I noticed my own plane hadn't gained much altitude as it swung over the ocean, but as it turned south, I saw its wings level, the nose rise, and it rolled slightly to the port side. I heard George state to somebody on the plane, "OK, toss him out!"

Gary and I observed a human body fall from the ship; his arms and legs flailing away in a useless attempt to slow or control his fall. "Son of a bitch!" Gary glanced at me with wide eyes and slack jaw as we watched the man fall from about eight thousand feet to the deep blue sea. "What the fuck was that about?"

Someone in the background kept up a running commentary as the man fell. "He started with a pike, now he's going into a somersault and transitioning into a tuck! But wait, he's gone into a triple gainer and looks like he's setting up for another twist with a hell of a rotation and now he's transitioning into a beautifully executed swan dive from another tuck and OOOOOOOHHHH that's gotta hurt like hell! He didn't quite make a clean entry and belly flopped into the ocean! Man, you gotta hate it when that happens!"

Another voice added, "Who knew the guy was an accomplished diver?!"

"Maybe he used to dive off the cliffs in Acapulco and wanted to go in style!"

I gave my pilot a wink, "That man was carrying a gun, and I think Hamm put him on my plane to divert it someplace other than Panama. And you should know; Hamm is packing a weapon, too!" I frowned and asked, "Didn't you hear what George said a few minutes before we took off?" After he shook his head no, I filled him in on what Don found in the cargo bay.

We received a call from George on our private frequency, "Vinny, that fucker walked into the cockpit with an automatic visible in a shoulder holster and said there was a change in plans. He was explaining we were going to fly to Columbia where we'd land on a private strip, before he suddenly passed out. Vic and Don found another weapon on him while searching him for a medic-alert tag. They didn't find one and they also didn't find any kind of ID before he got to his feet and accidentally fell out of the plane through that defective door."

"We'll have to get that door looked at when we get home. Did you manage to secure it, so it won't blow open at altitude?" I was beginning to wonder just how soon Hamm was going to make his move, when George replied.

"Yeah, we secured it with duct tape and bungie-cords. So, what do we do now, Vinny?"

I knew Hamm didn't see his henchman make the world record high-dive due to his position in the plane, but I didn't know if they had satellite phones. "George, did you find a sat-phone on that guy?"

He required a moment or two before replying, "Nope; no phones of any kind! So, what do we do?"

"We'll continue on per the plan, but I want you positioned behind and below us by a thousand feet. In the meantime, I need to make a few phone calls."

I went back to the lavatory to take a leak and on the way, I saw Steve was sleeping. His seat was fully reclined, his eyes closed, and head was gently rocking from side to side with the motion of the ship. He had a chrome plated revolver in a shoulder holster. I reached down and after carefully unsnapping the safety strap, removed it. "That was too easy," I chuckled to myself while continuing to the john. With the lav door closed, I sat on the thunder mug and examined the Colt, .44 magnum. The damn thing was brand new and appeared to have never been fired! The cylinder was loaded with soft-hollow points, so he meant to use it on someone, probably me.

I slipped it under my belt, pulled my shirt over it and returned to the cockpit. Steve was still sleeping soundly as I passed him, and just for a moment I had an urge to club him over the head a few times, just on general principles.

"Did everything come out okay, Vinny?" Gary gave me a snicker as I strapped in.

"Yeah, it sure did…"

"I knew you had it in you, Boss. I tell everyone you're full of shit and you just proved my point!"

I pulled out the magnum to show him, "And I found this piece of hardware on our passenger!" His eyes went wide for a moment before he broke out in a sweat. "Something tells me he ain't exactly on the up and up, pilgrim. I'd even be willing to bet that fucker has some nefarious plans for us, too! Should we toss his ass out for the sharks?"

"Hell no! There are a few people waiting for him in Panama, and they're willing to pay me one point five million for him, alive!"

Gary raised his eyebrows with the obvious question on his startled face.

"The who, is our trusty FBI and IRS; the why is a reward for securing the money he stole from his employer and the employees' 401K. I don't have the money, but I think what we're carrying will lead them to the embezzled money, along with some bad dudes in Columbia."

"When did you set this up, Vinny?"

"I left a note with my girlfriend before I left the house, and it specifies exactly what we're doing today and where we're going. She's to call the appropriate agencies and then leave me a message on my phone." I pulled out my cell and sure enough, I had a text message from Barb. She sent, "DONE!" and that was all. I turned to Gary, showed him the text then asked him to call the office and make sure Hamm's payment was transferred out of our accounts receivable account.

He eventually got through to the office and was assured the money was received and then moved to my other bank account, so it was safe from withdrawal. He gave me a grin, "You're a smart son-of-a-bitch, Vinny. So, all we have to do now is fly into Panama City, drop your buddy into the waiting arms of the feds, collect the money, and enjoy a nice long vacation!"

"What do you mean, *we,* Kemo Sabe," I replied with a smile. "You and George are flying out tomorrow with a paying customer! However, once I tie up the loose ends with the feds, I'll take off for someplace exotic and warm where they serve ice cold tropical drinks with those little umbrellas. After you drop off your customer waiting in Panama, you and your brother can join me if we don't have anything on your flight schedule for the next two weeks or so."

Just as I was about to go back to the galley for coffees, I heard Gary gasp, "SHIT" just as George reported over the radio, "We've got company!"

I turned to Gary, "What the hell are you..." I saw an F-16 suddenly pull up alongside our port side. "What the fuck!" The fighter edged his plane close enough to see his hand pointing to their helmet. "Gary…"

"I got it, Boss!" He tuned the radio to the emergency frequency, and we heard the clipped military voice of the pilot, "Cessna 270, this is Raptor 30. Is anyone holding a gun on you two?"

Gary replied, "Raptor 30; not anymore. My co-pilot took it from him a few minutes ago."

"Roger that, 270. We had a report you may be under duress. Our orders are to escort you and Cessna 49er to the air force base in Panama where a reception committee is waiting for you. Don't do anything stupid or make any sudden moves. If you have a situation in your cockpit, notify me by using the call sign, Eagle 101."

"Roger copy," Gary replied before the fighter pulled away and kept station with us about 300 yards away and slightly ahead. Gary turned to me, "I'll bet George is shitting little green apples about now!"

"I hope he doesn't feel like the Lone Ranger! Do you see those Sidewinders on his wingtips?" I coughed, "One of those bastards would blow us out of the sky in a heartbeat, buddy, but if he misses with them, he still has a 20-millimeter Gatling gun that will shred the plane and us."

"Hey, man, we still have that magnum and your .45s, so I ain't worried." He laughed before we heard the fighter calling us to following him down to 20,000 feet. After we reached our designated altitude, Gary gave me a conspirator's grin, "Let's call George and ask if he dumped the drugs and guns yet."

A quick dope slap quieted my pilot before I went back to the galley and fixed a fresh pot of coffee. On the way back, I saw Steve was still snoring away, so I very carefully searched him and his seat for more weapons. I found a .38 two inch strapped to his leg, a large switchblade in his sock, and a box of ammo for each pistol in his jacket pockets. "Son of a bitch," I muttered as I pocketed his ammo and knife, "Who the fuck do you think you're going to use these on; you two-faced bastard?" A quick search of his gym bag produced a satellite phone, which I also appropriated.

I handed Gary his coffee and then strapped in just as we received instructions to drop down to 10,000 feet. "I don't think we're landing in Panama, boss," Gary said quietly as he pointed to the GPS screen. "I think we're going to land in San Jose, Costa Rica."

I checked the screen and saw it was the only place with a long runway, when our sat-phone rang, "Hey, Vinny," George stated rather tersely, "We ain't going to Panama…"

"It looks like San Jose, George. Are you going to have a problem with that?"

"No, sir, I can land this in your driveway, but our customer is in Panama, and I don't know how long we'll be delayed in Costa Rica."

"Figure we'll be there anywhere from 2 hours to 20 years, depending on who's waiting for us and the mood they're in."

We let George land first, and as we circled overhead, I saw several trucks with .50 caliber machineguns mounted on the cargo beds charge out of a hangar and surround my jet.

"Well, buddy," I said to Gary, "It looks like we're not going to have a friendly reception after we land. Be extremely careful and don't make any sudden moves once we deplane. And remember this was all your idea!" I slipped the magnum and .38 onto his lap before I ran down the landing checklist.

CHAPTER SIXTEEN

Gary lined up on the runway as I began reading off our airspeed and altitude. He wanted the lowest possible speed before we touched down because the runway was a little on the short side. The stall warning went off just as our main gear squealed contact, and I immediately engaged the reverse thrusters while Gary stood on the brakes.

We were both cursing and swearing when I activated the reverse thrusters twice more before we slowed enough to make the turn at the end of the runway where we met an escort of two machine gun-equipped jeeps.

"I sure hope like hell these fuckers got your message Vinny," Gary growled as he opened his window and tossed the two pistols into the overgrown grass alongside the taxiway. The soldiers or policemen in the jeeps were looking where they were going and not watching us as they should have been, so at least they wouldn't bust us for transporting weapons. But then, we probably had a shitload of contraband in the cargo hold and those two stinking pistols wouldn't do more than shave a few years off our life sentences.

My own plane was parked with all doors and hatches wide open. The passengers were lined up on the tarmac, on their knees, their hands held high, while the police aimed their heavy machine guns at them. There was a small crowd of people standing alongside the parking ramp, most in colorful civilian clothes, with a few police and military uniforms mixed in with them.

The ground guide waved us to park directly behind my Cessna. As soon as we shut down the engines and completed the post flight checklist, the door was opened from the outside, and two burly men in camo uniforms climbed in and held automatics on us as we unbuckled and rose from our seats. They tried to shake Steve awake, but had no luck.

"Let me help you out, officer," I stated and waved them back. "I spent the last month in the hospital with this fucker and I gotta tell you, he's a sound sleeper!" I hauled off and slapped him as hard as I could. When he didn't wake, I nailed him again hard enough to make my hand sting and his nose bleed.

One of the officers remarked in English, "I think he's on drugs!" He looked at me and said, "I assume you're Mr. Nunzio?"

"Yes, I am, and I left instructions for my friend Barb to call the FBI about this turd, in addition to making my own calls with information about what we're doing." I pointed to his automatic, "Can you point that somewhere else? I present no threat to you or anyone else; plus, I have a serious allergic reaction to lead." I introduced Gary before he waved us off the plane where we were thoroughly searched and then made to kneel while two other men held M-4 rifles on us.

My knees were killing me after five minutes, so I sat back on my ass to take the pressure off, but one fucker started screaming at me to kneel, so I turned and said, "I'm not the religious type, you peckerwood! I'm not about to go anywhere, so calm the fuck down before I have Gary here kick the shit out of you!"

"Fuck you, Vinny!" Gary shoved me on my side and while I was laughing, I heard a familiar female voice shout as she approached.

"Let them up, Agent Jankowski, you idiot! He's the man who supplied all the information about Hamm's escape!" Doc Malanai trotted up and helped me to my feet while she scowled at the junior agent, still pointing his rifle at Gary. "And put that damn rifle down before I stick the barrel up your ass and pull the trigger! These men are all innocent, except for Hamm, and he doesn't appear like he'll be causing us any trouble for a while."

Two agents were dragging the still unconscious Hamm from the plane; his body as limp as any I've seen, alive or dead. One remarked to the lady I'd thought was Gul, "Special Agent Carrera, this man has been heavily drugged. I don't know if he did it himself or someone slipped him something, but his pulse is slow and he's breathing a little ragged. Should we take him to a hospital?"

Gul, or Carrera, smiled at me, winked and replied, "Cuff him first and get him to the hospital right away. I'll join you as soon as we debrief Vinny and his friends." She waved away the men guarding my friends as she led us toward a hangar. "What happened to the Narco-Trafficante on your personal plane, Vinny?"

"He fell out over the ocean. The crew failed to properly secure the door and he fell against it while they were turning to port after taking off. The damn thing just popped open, and he made the world's best high-dive immediately afterwards."

"You're a lying sack of shit, Vinny! We monitored every word transmitted from your planes. That guy was one of the leaders of the Sinaloa drug cartel and was on his way to negotiate a deal to supply the Columbian drug gangs and FARC guerillas with shoulder-fired anti-aircraft missiles and weapons like mortars, TOW anti-tank rockets and heavy machineguns. And I can assure you, they won't be happy to learn you had a hand in his death!"

"How are they going to know? It isn't like we announced he was flying down with us!"

"Your friend Hamm told them everything before they left." She slowly shook her head and added, "They'll have people waiting in Panama to take over the planes, in addition to dumping your body and your friends' bodies in the swamps."

Christ almighty, I thought, I really outsmarted myself this time. Turning to Carrera, "What if we just dump everything here and hammer down for the border?"

"They know where you live and they're aware you're shacking up with Barb. But don't you worry your pretty little head about it, Vinny!" She grabbed my arm and pointed to a small group of heavily armed men in civilian clothes seated around a table. These men will land about ten minutes before you and will be ready to take out the bad guys there as soon as you land. Then we'll fly your birds to the rendezvous point along with a flight of F-18s loaded for bear. Those people won't know what hit them!"

"Who is flying my plane down there and what if it gets shot full of holes?"

"We have several government people who can handle your plane along with the big Cessna. They'll approach the strip as if they're going to land, but they'll split just before the fighters bomb the bad guys into oblivion."

"And what if the people who have my information aren't there?"

Carrera smiled, "We have them under constant observation in Miami, and as soon as they receive word your planes have taken off from Panama, we'll wait until they pass on the information to their friends in Columbia, then we'll pick them up." She patted my back and whispered, "We have every possibility covered, Vinny! And with the FBI, DEA, ATF and CIA working together on this operation, what could possibly go wrong?"

My life began passing in front of my eyes.

My friends, who heard every word she said, stated almost in unison, "I think I'll end my trip right here, Vinny!"

Don leaned over and asked Carrera, "Do you think we'll be OK as far as Panama?"

"I'm sure you and your friends have nothing to worry about, Don."

I was about to advise my friend to stick with the rest of our crew when one of the "civilian" men approached and stated, "Mr. Nunzio, I just got off the horn with my bosses. They said they'll cover any damages to your planes, right up to full replacement, so I wouldn't worry about them."

"I hate to say this, buddy, but only one of them belongs to me, and it has an appointment to pick up a paying customer tomorrow at noon. The other plane, the larger one, was somehow stolen by Hamm..."

"Hamm's people stole that plane from a drug-runner, who stole it from another narco after they killed him, so as soon as the operation is over, we'll have the title and ownership transferred to you, but we reserve the right to use your charter when needed."

Stunned at the government's generosity, I asked the only question I could think of, "Why?"

"That plane has a unique paint job and history. We want it seen flying around the country on legal business before we use it to move our people. Believe me, we know what we're doing!"

I was about to reply to him with the obvious sarcastic statement when another shouted, "Your planes are fully fueled, and we neutralized the weapons, so let's get this show on the road!"

Carrera grabbed my arm and said, "I'll ride with you, Vinny. I'd hate to see you get lost on the way to Panama!" She smiled sweetly, raised her sweater to show me she was packing a .380 automatic, then wrapped both arms around mine as she walked me to the plane. "We have so much to discuss on the way, Vinny! But first I must fill you in on what will happen after we land at Panama, then we'll have a heart-to-heart talk about our future."

I stopped dead in my tracks, "What do you mean, our future?"

"We'll discuss it after we're in the air, Vinny!" She gave me a one-armed hug and a warm smile before we climbed the boarding stairs.

There were two strange men strapping into the pilot and co-pilot seats. "Who the hell are those two?"

"They're our men and fully qualified to fly this plane, Vinny," an agent stated from behind me as Carrera led me to a seat in the rear of the cabin while more heavily armed men occupied the rest of the cabin. "There might be trouble when we land, and we want to be ready for it, so we brought along reinforcements." The agent gave me a wink and a nod before he pointed to my seatmate and said, "She'll fill you in on everything you need to know."

I glanced at my Citation and watched six armed men quickly climb aboard. Glancing at Carrera with my eyes wide open, I asked, "Want to fill me in now or wait until we're up in the air?"

Without hesitation, she stated, "We have reasonably reliable intelligence indicating the Columbian narcos and FARC guerillas will hijack both planes in Panama, kill you, your friends and Hamm. Your buddy thinks he had a foolproof deal with those people, but he failed to take into consideration he is dealing with cold-blooded killers who believe the only good deal is one that leaves a trail of dead bodies.' She sighed, gave me a long look and continued, "Hamm thinks the head of the Columbian family he's dealing with is an avid collector of antique French furniture and artwork, which he is. However, he also thinks the man will just pay him for the antiques while the FARC will do the same for the weapons, especially the Stingers, and then let him go to secure more weapons and antiques. However, the FARC know how sensitive those missiles are and realize as soon as they use one, it won't take long to trace them back to their origins. But then, they only need two of the four in your holds because they want to shoot down the president of Columbia and the head of their armed forces."

I interrupted, "How will that help their cause? The Columbians have succession plans in place…"

"Once the military learns the FARC have sophisticated anti-aircraft weapons, they'll have to change their tactics and significantly reduce their use of airpower when attacking them. The FARC are particularly effective when fighting in the jungles, and if not hindered by air attacks, they can control a great deal of real estate, which in turn, will provide more land to produce cocaine."

"And our buddy Hamm actually thought he could outsmart those bastards?"

"Too many people thought they could and are now occupying unmarked shallow graves," Carrera replied with a grim smile. She quieted as the pilot applied full power for takeoff then resumed her narrative after we leveled off at altitude. "Now, your part in all this is relatively simple and safe. You, your friends, and pilots will deplane in Panama. Your pilots will take your charter customers to where they want to go in one of our confiscated Lear jets since they aren't expecting to see either of your Citations. Your remaining friends will be provided transportation to wherever they desire in Panama or back to the U.S. You and I will wait in Panama for your aircraft to return from their appointment in Columbia and after the mission is closed, we'll fly back to the U.S. to settle accounts."

"I was planning to head to a tropical island someplace..."

"You need to provide written statements about your part in this mission and then sign off on your new Citation..."

"What about the reward money? I was promised ten percent..."

Carrera grinned, "How much did you expect as a reward for helping us? If my math is correct, you would be due one point five million, but we're not recovering all the cash he embezzled, so be glad you're receiving an executive jet worth over twelve million, even if it has strings attached."

"I guess I'm receiving more than I bargained for, so I should be grateful..."

"Not to mention I'm taking a thirty day leave as soon as we clean up the paperwork, so we'll have lots of time to get to know each other, Vinny." She gave me a very warm smile as she snuggled against me.

"Excuse me, Agent Carrera, but there is a certain young lady waiting for my return in Maryland..."

She nudged me with her elbow and grinned, "Call me Gul, and your friend Barbara will have a long wait before she sees you again!"

"What the hell are you talking about?"

"Barbara Wilson was about to be arrested when she called with the information about your trip with Hamm..."

"What the hell for? She is one of the nicest and hardest working nurses I've ever met!"

"She and her two sisters are charged with defrauding the state and federal governments for over eight million dollars in a welfare, Medicaid and Medicare scam. We're sure of that amount so far, plus what they stole from private insurance companies and their patients.

They were billing for home health care plus physical and occupational therapy they weren't performing as well as billing for people who died or didn't exist. In addition, they're being charged with income tax evasion and at least 20 other felonies."

"How did you find out?"

"One of the women they were supposed to be caring for was found dead in an abandoned building in Baltimore. The police said she died at least seven months ago. They contacted the family with the bad news, and they in turn called to complain to the department of welfare, because the woman who died was supposed to be under the care of the Wilson sisters in one of their adult care homes. Then during the investigation by one particularly honest and dedicated employee, they discovered one of the sisters was a social worker who arranged for the woman, among many others, were assigned to one of her sister's homes, which, by the way, do not exist as such. They owned a number of run down and dilapidated row-homes they claimed to be homes for their patients."

"Holy shit! I can't believe she's that cold and greedy! How long was she defrauding everyone?"

"As far as we've been able to determine, at least eight years, but that's a conservative estimate. I'm sure we'll discover exactly how long with a more accurate financial accounting before we go to trial."

I was stunned to say the least. Barb always impressed me as being a caring and honest health care worker, in addition to having the highest ethical standards. For the life of me, I couldn't think of a single incident or clue that would have me believe she would not only steal but allow vulnerable people to wander the streets and die in horrible conditions. She just did not seem like the kind of person…"

Gul shook my arm, "Vinny, you never know about some people. Just look at your soon to be ex-wife and how she turned on you!"

Shaking my head over the realization the woman I thought was my friend was also a thief. I rose, went to the head, then pulled a TV dinner out of the little fridge, nuked it and placed it on the tray next to Gul. "Want one?" She shook her head, so I sat and began chowing down on the tasteless mess.

Just as I finished, the pilot announced, "Our team in Panama reported they landed and didn't find anything out of the ordinary.

They're going to search the hangars near where we're going to park to make sure. In addition, be sure you're strapped in because we'll be landing in ten minutes."

He let-down somewhat faster than my pilots would, but then, the plane was full of government agents, so their comfort wasn't his prime concern. At least he greased the landing to save the tires and landing gear, before he passed on the situation report from the security team. "Everything on the ground seems to be OK as far the men are concerned. As soon as we stop, I want everyone to deplane and proceed directly to the hangar for a final mission briefing before we take off for Columbia."

"I thought we were going to get hit as soon as we touched down," I stated to Gul and one of the agents staring out our portal.

"That's why we sent a strike team out first," he replied with a grim smile. "They probably hit them before they knew what was happening…"

"OK, everyone," the pilot announced, "Welcome to sunny Panama; now get your asses into the hangar ASAP so we can get this circus on the road!"

I should have grabbed my personal belongings, especially my jacket as we were rushing from the plane, but I mistakenly thought I'd have time to return and retrieve everything. Gul had me by the elbow as we trotted toward the hangar. "I need my wallet and personal stuff like my bags, passport and…"

"They'll bring all that out to you as soon as they begin boarding the other agents, Vinny," she stated as we entered the big grey hangar. "They'll be back in a couple hours with both jets and as long as you're with me and my team, you won't need them."

I was surprised to find three dozen black-clad and heavily armed men waiting for us in the hangar. Most of their vests were stenciled in white with DEA, FBI, and ATF, but ten men in dark camo had no ID on their vests. I turned to one of our agents and pointed to them with raised eyebrows.

"They ain't here, Mr. Nunzio. You aren't seeing them, they aren't here, and you never saw them if you're asked."

As we walked to a table loaded with coffee urns and various snacks, I nodded to a few hard-eyed men staring at me with more than a little suspicion. Then one of them sidled next to me and gave me a gentle nudge as I was loading my plate.

I turned, and was surprised to be staring into the bearded, smiling face of my nephew, Cosmo, or Gus as we called him. My brother Al told me his oldest son was joining the Army against my best and most emphatic advice, but I never thought the kid would go this far. He grinned and whispered, "Well, if it isn't my favorite uncle Vinny! Fancy meeting you here!"

"And if it isn't my long-lost nephew, Cosmo!" I said, using the name I knew he hated, "What stupid shit did you get yourself into; you crazy bastard? Don't tell me you went Special Forces on me!"

He grinned, "Since the old man never went in, I couldn't let your side of the family hog all the glory. And I'm not exactly what you'd call Special Forces," he replied as he placed his index finger against the side of his nose.

"You obviously inherited your idiot old man's crazy streak, but not your mother's common sense or you would never have signed on with…Delta?"

"I can neither confirm nor deny your allegations, Uncle Vinny, but just know you'll be safe as long as we're here!"

"Did you guys search the area before we landed? You know those two jets out there are mine, and I'd hate like hell to have them shot full of holes."

"Yeah, we searched this entire area and didn't find a damn thing, so don't get your nuts all twisted about it!" He followed me to a table and after we sat to eat, he asked, quietly, "What's this I hear about you and Aunt Cheryl getting divorced?"

Gul sat next to me and was about to say something when there was a huge explosion just outside the hangar. A moment later someone screamed, "Condition Red! Here they come! Four trucks with at least thirty narcos and they're armed for bear!"

"Yeah, real safe, Gus," I shouted while rolling onto the floor with my coffee and plate.

CHAPTER SEVENTEEN

It sounded like someone was beating the hangar doors with many huge hammers, and as I pulled Gul off her chair and rolled on top of her, one of the big doors blew in with a tremendous blast of wood, steel, and glass splinters rocketing though the big hangar.

Gul was screaming for me to get off her and shoved me to the side while automatic weapons fire erupted from our group. I rose to a crouch and was just in time to see several of our black-suited men go down, including one standing at the end of our table. I crawled over to him, checked his pulse and was surprised to find a strong one in his neck. Then I checked him for bleeding but found none, so I assumed he was wearing good body armor. Hesitating for a moment, I grabbed and unclipped his M-4 rifle and ammo vest then scuttled over to Gul who was peering from behind our overturned table in an attempt to see what was going on.

"This stinking Masonite tabletop won't stop a thrown rock, so I suggest you get prone before you come down with an acute lead overdose, kid."

"I can take care of myself, Vinny, so…What the hell are you doing with a weapon?"

"The FBI guy over there decided to take a nap and being the nice guy that I am, I decided to warm it up for him before he wakes." I then noticed rounds coming in through the corrugated metal side wall of the hangar behind us. Don and my friends had taken cover behind an old tow-motor and row of machine tools, so I pointed Gul to them and then dragged the still unconscious FBI agent to the safety of the heavy steel equipment.

"Looks like we have nothing to worry about, Vinny," Don shouted, "Our federal law enforcement agencies have everything under control!"

"Oh yeah! We'll be perfectly safe with them, Don," Vic yelled sarcastically, just as a dozen or more rounds slammed into the opposite side of the tow-motor and knocked a few tools off the nearby machine lathe.

Don pulled Gul down as she stood to get a better look around, only a millisecond before an RPG round screamed by, right where her head had been. The RPG exploded against the opposite wall, opening a three-foot-wide hole in the thin sheet metal.

I was staring at the hole for a few seconds trying to figure out how the hell we were going to get out of here when a man wearing a green bandana around his head leaned in to get a look around. I brought up the rifle, made sure it was on semi, took careful aim and put a round in his face just as we made eye contact. A moment later, another man did the same and he too was given a third eye. The next narco stuck his AK-47 in and began spraying the room, but I got in a lucky shot and blew it out of his hands.

"That's some mighty fine shooting there, son," I heard Don state, "but that's only three out of how many bad guys?"

"I ain't the only one in here, Donny!" Turning back to watch our flank, a man in dark camo crawled to the hole, jumped up, gave the outside a quick glance then dropped to his knees off to the side. He removed a grenade from a vest pocket, pulled the pin, then glanced at me, smiled and let go of the spoon. My stupid nephew Gus nodded his head a few times before he tossed the grenade through the hole and went prone while shouting, "Grenade out!" After it detonated, we could just barely hear men outside screaming.

"I better get over there and cover that stupid bastard," I told Don. Then, I noticed the wounded FBI agent beginning to stir.

Vic leaned over and said, "He was saved by his body armor, but the round knocked him down and he hit his head pretty hard on the ground. Must have cracked his skull and knocked him out."

"Give me his ammo belt so I can help these guys."

"I have his pistol and extra mags. Do you need me to provide supporting fire?"

"Sure, Vic, but stay low and behind something that will stop incoming rounds. That corrugated-tin won't stop shit!"

While crawling across the debris-strewn floor of the hangar, I noticed our team was returning fire in a more controlled manner and seemed to have made some hits on the bad guys since their fire had slackened noticeably.

Gus grinned as I settled next to him, "It's about time you got your lazy ass over here, Uncle Vinny!"

"You guys did a hell of a job searching the area, Cosmo!" A shadow moved by the blasted hole. I rose to a crouch, fired several rounds at a short, dark complexioned man as he pulled the pin on a grenade. He staggered backward while the grenade went flying off to his left. I hit the ground shouting "Grenade!"

As soon as it detonated, Vic hopped up and emptied his pistol at several targets of opportunity, then dove to the ground before a long burst of automatic weapons fire perforated the wall where he had been crouched.

"Son of a bitch!" Vic shouted at the hole, "This is no way to treat tourists to your country, you nasty bastards!"

Someone outside replied in a growling voice, "You fucking Yankee dogs should have stayed at home, because we're going to kill all of you!"

I could tell the man was crouched next to the hole, but opposite our location, so I turned and emptied my magazine into the wall while Gus crawled to the far side and lobbed another grenade through the hole in the general direction of the voices. We were reward with the sound of several men screaming in agony a split second after the blast.

Vic shouted back, "Excuse me, but you must be sadly mistaken about who the hell is going to die, you narco asshole!" Someone outside replied in Spanish and Vic responded with, "You should at least have the courtesy to learn English, but I can see you ain't got no upbringings!"

I glanced past Gus at the far end of the hangar and was surprised to see unguarded man-doors on either side of the closed sliding hangar doors. "Hey Gus, do you have anyone watching the back doors?"

He gave the area a quick glance before his eyes went wide and he spoke into his radio. A few seconds later he said, "Everyone is kind of busy welcoming the people at the front door. The boss suggested we keep an eye on it until he can send a few men back there."

I looked back at where I had been to see Don wrestling with Gul while my pilots were doing their best to find targets out on the apron. I caught Don's and George's attention, pointed to my eyes then toward the rear of the hangar. A momentary lull in the fighting was enough for Gary, Tom, and George to low-crawl over to my position before I explained, "No one is watching the back doors, and I don't think it will take much longer for the banditos to try to cut us off..."

"Gotcha, boss," Gary replied as he slapped Tom's shoulder and began crawling to the far end of the hangar. A moment later Don arrived with someone's pistol in hand and a very angry FBI agent attempting to take it away from him. "That's my weapon, you ignorant son of a bitch! Give it back before I arrest you for…"

Don elbowed her off his back and shouted, "This is no place for a lady! Now go find a safe place to lay down and I'll bring it back as soon as we eliminate the bad guys!"

George rushed to shove Gul down as a line of tracers ripped right over her head. "I got an M-4 from one of the wounded feds along with his pistol and ammo vest. I'll take Don to the far side and smoke anyone who tries to force their way in."

I suddenly saw a man carrying a shortened AK, wearing a black T-shirt with ammo bandoleers across his chest and a shoulder holster, stick his entire upper body through the hole in the wall. We briefly made eye contact. He gave me what appeared to be a friendly smile. He shouted, "Buenos dias, Yankee pigs," before four of us ventilated his chest and head. He slumped forward and remained there, effectively blocking the hole. I heard Vic reply, "Buenos nachos, you idiot!"

Gul quickly seized the dead man's weapons and bandoleers then ran after Don and George at the far corner of the hangar; muttering something about taking her pistol back from the big bully.

"Jesus Palomino, Gus," I laughed, "It don't get no easier than that!

He held up his index finger for me to wait a second before he stated, "We've got the upper hand on those fuckers and the Panamanian police and army are on the way. The bad guys are trying to use their pickups to get away, but they won't start with a hundred bullet holes in them. They want me and few other guys to go out and sweep around the hangar…"

Gunfire suddenly erupted from the rear of the hangar. We both spun to see pinholes of light perforating the back doors as the narcos fired through them before charging into the hangar. Gul dove for the floor to take cover, but she slipped and landed on her pistol hand first. When it slammed onto the floor, the automatic accidentally fired once, the round just barely skinning across Don's buttocks. Gus and I saw the 9mm slug rip through the seat of his pants, leaving a thin spray of blood in passing. With all the gunfire echoing through the hangar, we still heard Don bellow, "Son of a bitch!" He rolled on his side, dropped his weapon and seized his butt-cheeks with both hands as he screamed every curse in his vocabulary.

Gul wasn't fazed in the least and immediately dove over Don's writhing body to repossess her .380 automatic. "You got what you deserved for taking this away from me, you asshole!" She rolled to her stomach, extended her arms and pistol, then shot the first three narcos running through the man-door. She dropped the empty magazine, inserted a fresh one she pulled from her pocket, then nailed two more before she rolled back to Don, "You know it's a felony to seize a firearm from an FBI agent! If I wasn't busy right now, I'd arrest you!"

Don was incredulous at her actions and statement but had the wherewithal to pick up the M-4 rifle and join the back-door team in eliminating six more narcos as they too made an unsuccessful attempt to ruin our day.

It suddenly grew quiet while the bad guys regrouped to decide what to do next. I yelled over to my buddy, "Hey, Donny, you know you just proved my point that some women are nothing but a royal pain in the ass!"

"Fuck you, Vinny," he shouted back before he turned to give Gul a piece of his mind, but she was already up and running toward the door with Vic and George.

Gus grabbed my arm and pulled me to the front door. "Me, you, and two of my guys will sweep around the left side while some others will move around the right. Now move your ass, you old fart, or do I have to carry you?"

"It will be a cold day in hell when a young whippersnapper like you needs to carry me, Cosmo!" Two Delta men were just turning the front corner of the hangar when we arrived. There were a few quick shots when several voices shouted, "Clear, Clear!"

I had to step over a at least a dozen bodies as we made our way to the rear of the hangar where I saw Gul and George frisking two men spread eagle on the ground. Both were bleeding and cursing a blue streak in Spanish as George was none too gentle with his search.

Don limped out of the hangar, holding his butt with both hands as blood leaked out between his fingers. "You shot me, Gul! I'm filing a complaint with your superiors for shooting an innocent man and doing it right in the middle of a firefight!"

Gul glanced at Don, gave him an embarrassed grim and replied, "It was an accident, Donald. The gun went off when I fell, and it struck the ground."

One of the Delta men ambled over to Don, pulled his hands away and gave his ass a quick glance before he stated, "It's only a minor flesh wound, buddy. I'll fix you up right here." He yanked Don's pants down to his ankles then forced him to lie on his stomach. After he washed the blood off his ass cheeks using water from his canteen, he asked Cosmo for his medical kit. Cosmo handed his buddy the kit then pulled out a spray can and emptied it on Don's wounds.

"Holy shit! What the hell is that stuff? It burns like hell?"

"It's just antiseptic," Gus replied with a laugh, "It's supposed to burn, you wimp!"

Gul wandered over, stood and watched while the medic worked on Don's wounded ass cheeks. She smiled and said loud enough for Don and everyone to hear, "I've seen better butts on dead bodies pulled from the bottom of a river after being there a month."

When the laughter died down, I got up and went around to the front of the hangar to check on my planes. I was stunned to find both gone. A Delta guy walked past as I was about to start crying the narcos had stolen my planes. He glanced at where I was staring gap-mouthed then turned back to me, "Those two jets took off for the other side of the airport as soon as the narcos drove onto the airport. I think they got away clean, but I'll call and check for you, buddy."

A moment later he reported, "They made it to the far side of a hangar way over there on the other side of the airport. Our man said they got away without a scratch and will come back as soon as we have the area cleared of all the bad guys."

"Have them wait until the local cops and army guys have left the area. I don't want them searching the plane and finding all that contraband we have in them."

"Good idea! You never know whose side those bastards are on."

"As I think about the whole situation, I think I'll hide out in the hangar over there until they're gone, buddy." I trotted to the hangar next to ours and found a door unlocked. As quickly as I could, I found a place to stay out of sight but still observe events next door until the local constabulary left the area.

A voice from nowhere scared the shit out of me, "Hey, Uncle Vinny, got a smoke?" Another voice, "Yeah, I need one too!"

"What the hell are you guys doing in here? Don't you have clearance to be in Panama?"

Gus replied, "Hell no! That asshole buddy of yours and the narcos own the local cops and the National Guard here. After they see what we did to their buddies, they'll kill us and feed our bodies to the sharks."

"What about my friends and the FBI agents? Don't you think it would be a good idea to get them the hell out of that hangar?"

Gus's partner had been speaking into his radio while I was arguing with my nephew. He turned to me, "They're either on the way over here or they're shagging ass for the far side of the airport."

Just then the back door swung open and angry voices were growling about the situation as several pickup trucks and a black step-van marked "Policia" came racing into view from the far side of the airport. Gul rushed up to me and breathlessly gasped, "We've got to be very quiet! If they search this hangar and find us, we're..."

"I know! My nephew just told me!" I glanced at the small crowd and asked, "Did everyone make it out, including our wounded?"

"Yes, we all got out, but we had three men severely wounded and judging from what I saw, they won't live much longer." Gul was obviously saddened by the outcome of our firefight, but then she added, "They weren't FBI or any of your friends. I think they were some of the military people..."

Gus spoke into his radio before turning to me and Gul, "Everyone from my Delta team are accounted for, so they must be DEA or..."

I exhaled slowly while wondering out loud how we were going to get the hell out of here alive.

Vic piped up, "We sure as hell can't do anything until the Federales leave! And even then, unless we take your planes, we aren't flying out by commercial planes either. You know those bastards will be watching the airport passenger terminals."

Gus coughed, gave me a baleful glance and pointed to the runway. "We ain't taking my uncle's planes either. The locals sent two trucks full of cops to search the rest of the airport for your planes, and the pilots decided to cap up and split on us rather than spend the rest of their lives in a Panamanian slammer." We all turned to the window just in time to see both my jets roar into the sky from a taxiway. They obviously didn't ask permission from the tower, and they were almost nose to tail as they lifted off and kept low until they were out of sight. Gus laughed for a few moments before stating, "According to the pilots, our mission has been aborted and we're to make it back to the States on our own!"

"That's just great," I growled. "They have all my documentation, like passport, driver's license, my wallet, credit cards and money on the plane! What the hell am I going to do now?" Don, Vic, and everyone else from my group echoed my statement rather angrily.

Gus and his buddy just laughed, "Remember your escape and evasion training from your days in the army? Now is the perfect time to put it into practice!"

CHAPTER EIGHTEEN

There was nothing else for us to do, so we made ourselves as comfortable as possible while we waited for the police to leave. We took turns standing watch with the understanding there would be no lights, smoking or noise in our hangar.

Gus and I were locking and bracing the back the door as quietly as possible to prevent the locals from searching the building. The front doors were already locked, and the windows could only be opened from inside, so we were relatively safe. As long as the cops found the doors locked, we hoped they'd figure we didn't get in and move on to search the next building.

It was almost one in the morning when my turn to stand watch came up. I peered out the filthy window and saw the police were wrapping up their investigation. They picked up all the bodies, tossed them into the back of several dump trucks and had them hauled away. They probably didn't bother with expensive body bags or toe tags to save the Panamanian taxpayers the expense, and I doubted the dead had any identification anyway. The shot-up trucks the narcos used were towed away and then several airport workers swept up all the expended brass to prevent the shell casing from being blown around by aircraft exhausts or sucked into their engines.

Just as I was about to call everyone together for a strategy session, a hand lightly touched my shoulder, causing me to jump at least three feet off the ground.

"I'm sorry, Vinny," Gul's soft voice whispered.

"Geez, Gul, you should have made some noise before you touched me!"

"I thought we were maintaining silence so we wouldn't attract the locals. I'm sorry to bother you, but while you were moving around the hangar, did you happen to see a lady's room? I have to go really bad and can't hold it much longer."

The thought of her needing a bathroom never occurred to me. Gus and I used a gallon anti-freeze jug while we were working on the back door. I didn't recall seeing any signs for a bathroom. "I didn't see any, Gul. We used a plastic jug half full of anti-freeze, but we can't turn on lights or use a flashlight to find you a toilet until the bad guys leave."

"Vinny, I have to go, like right now!"

"I'll find you a jug or a bottle you can use…"

"That won't work for I need to do!"

Gus approached from out of the darkness, "Can't sleep, Uncle Vinny. I'll take your watch if you want to catch some sleep."

"It looks like they're getting ready to go, Gus, and soon. Quietly wake up everyone while I help Gul find a potty." I felt a hard slap on my shoulder, but she didn't say anything.

"I think there's an office over there where that little red light is, and if there's a latrine in the building, it should be there. But this is why we don't allow women in Delta; in case you were wondering." He gave us a short, quiet laugh before he turned and moved away.

Gul muttered, "I'll shoot him on purpose next chance I get, and it won't be in the ass!"

We quietly made our way past several partially dismantled aircraft to the office, but the door was locked. A sizeable twin-engine plane was parked nearby, so I climbed inside and found it had a small bathroom. I whispered to Gul, who was now doing the female potty dance at the foot of the ladder. "PSST, come on up! I found a bathroom and it even has toilet paper!" As she rushed past me, I added, "Watch your step, the deck is missing some floorboards." After giving the interior a quick flash with my penlight for her, I climbed down and stood under the nose, so I could guide her down the ladder.

I could just hear men's voices quietly discussing something when there was the distinct sound of a liquid stream splashing on the cement floor. As I suddenly realized the aircraft probably had the plumbing for its head removed, several loud, wet farts erupted from the ass end of the plane a split second before a series of heavy splats hit the floor, accompanied by more tinkling that seemed to go on forever. Just as I was thinking, "That woman has a hell of a bladder," more wet farts echoed through the hangar along with the sound of more shit plops on the concrete floor.

Voices from the front of the hangar whispered forcefully, "Vinny, will you keep it quiet! Your farts are loud enough to wake the dead!"

Unable to contain myself as the sound of Gul emptying her bladder and bowels continued unabated, I began to giggle and was forced to bite down hard on my tongue to keep from roaring with laughter. I couldn't believe a beautiful, dainty little woman like her could produce so much...

"Hey, Vinny," my nephew's buddy Gene whispered as he approached, "There's a big step van on the other side of the hangar and it looks new. If I can get it started, we'll use it to make our escape."

"Sounds like a plan, Gene," I replied as he moved under the plane toward the van. "Hey, be careful where you walk! "Geez..." thump. The sound of his body hitting the floor came just as I finished, "Don't walk directly under the plane."

He growled, "Goddam, I slipped on some...AW Shit! Who the hell took a dump right in the middle of the..."

"Did you get any on ya?"

Just then Gul began climbing down the ladder, "Vinny, I didn't flush the toilet because I didn't want to make any noise... What's so funny?"

Gene was slipping and sliding while getting to his feet when he fell again, letting out a long, but very quiet stream of invectives. I pointed to him and said, "They must have torn apart the entire undersides of the plane, including the toilet plumbing for a complete rebuild and Gene is now slipping and sliding on everything you've been holding." Even in the almost complete darkness of the hangar, I could see her eyes and mouth open wide as she considered the implications of my statement.

Several men came by to investigate the disturbance but stopped short when the aroma of Gul's deposit struck them. While they gagged and choked, I advised, "Stay to the right on your way to the van. I don't think Gene is going to be much help until he cleans up a little."

Gus choked, "The locals have gone, and we have to get the hell out of here as soon as possible. They'll probably be back as soon as the sun comes up to continue their search. I'll see what I can do about the van. What the hell is that stink? Geez, it smells like someone died here, last week!"

I was still trying to keep from laughing out loud when I choked out, "I'm going to break into the office to see if they have the keys for the van and something Gene can wear." The office door had a good lock on it, but a large screwdriver worked as a master key. Since there were no exterior windows, I turned on the light and was pleasantly surprised to find a long rack of coveralls, flight suits and best of all, a clean bathroom, complete with a shower.

Gul stared daggers at me the entire time Gene bathed. We discovered the coveralls were marked with, "Panamanian Customs" emblems and the flight suits had Panamanian Coast Guard patches.

"Just what the doctor ordered," Vic commented as he tried one on for size. "I suggest we all put these things on before we take off. It might just give the local police pause if we're stopped."

"And here are several sets of keys!" Gul rushed them out to the van while the rest of us suited up.

A few moments later, Gene stepped out of the shower, donned a flight suit with Major's oak leaves on the shoulders. "I can't believe such a tiny little woman had that much shit in her! Hey, George, did you see the pile of crap she left on the floor? I grew up on a farm and I'd swear only a huge fucking horse would dump something like that! Damn, and it really smelled bad too!" George turned to me for an explanation when Gene spotted a desk phone, grinned then picked it up and dialed. A few moments later, he said, "It's Sgt. Gallagher: team Sigma…" he listened a moment then stated, "Fuck you too! We're stuck here in Panama and need to be extracted immediately! Our mission was aborted after the narcos ambushed us, and our aircraft split without waiting for us…"

He listened for a few minutes before he asked, "Will it have room for all of us? There's fifteen in our group: six from our team, a couple FBI, two DEA and some civilians, one of which is Gus's uncle. You know, the crazy one he's always talking about..." He listened for a moment before replying, "We ain't leaving anyone behind, so find us another mode of transportation and do it quick! We only have a few more hours of dark left, and we don't want to be found wandering around here…"

I turned to Don just as an engine started in the hangar, "Think your desire to take a long, relaxing ocean cruise has been put on hold, buddy. How about a highly exciting overland excursion up through Central America and Mexico?"

Gene hung up the phone and held up his hands, "OK, they're trying to set up our extraction by boat. They said to get down to the canal and wait at the Gatun locks where we'll be picked up by an eastbound ship or something."

"Like no one will be watching for a bunch of strange Yankees climbing aboard a ship?" Don was pissed as hell over the events of the past twelve hours or so, plus he was still sore as hell at Gul's marksmanship. "How the hell are we going to know which ship to board, and for your information, they don't let you just stand around as the ships are locking through, and did he happen to mention what color or kind of ship, boat, submarine or what the fuck…"

"That's all the asshole said. He said it will be obvious which boat we're supposed to take, but we have to be ready to move and move fast because the Panamanians are a little hot under the collar about the whole thing…"

Don was about to explode when George grabbed his arm, "Listen Don, we don't have much choice. We either go along with these idiots or end up in the hands of the narcos…"

Gus stuck his head in the door, "OK, everyone, the bus is leaving in two minutes! We have a full tank of gas and room for everyone. I just got off the radio with headquarters and they'll have our extraction at the Gatun locks at noon today, so we have to haul ass to get across this stinking shithole by then."

I turned to Gene, "How come he knows more than you do?"

"Gus must have made direct contact with our C.O. I talked to some dickhead chairborne ranger who couldn't find his ass with both hands if we put a light on it."

We hurried into the van while two other Delta men slid the hangar doors open. I grabbed my nephew and asked the question I knew Don was thinking, "What kind of boat?"

"He didn't say specifically. He just said he's been on the horn with the Navy ever since our pilots told him they had to boogey. But we'll know when the time comes."

"Fuck me!"

"He also said we'd have to get out of Panamanian waters as fast as possible, so their Navy won't arrest everyone. Anyway, Uncle Vinny, I would assume it will be a very fast boat."

Don had a hard time climbing into the van due to his wounds, and as I helped pull him in, he muttered, "There's a huge pile of shit and piss right under that plane. I wonder if it was all backed up in the plane's plumbing until they began dismantling it."

"You'd think they would have expected it and put a big barrel under it," Gene laughed as he nudged Gul, but she was not in the mood and replied with an elbow to his ribs. Then she turned to me with a glare that would kill a buffalo at a hundred yards.

The Delta men closed the doors behind us as we pulled out, then went back inside to lock the doors and jam the locks to slow down whoever tried to enter in the morning to give us just a little more time to make our getaway. "No sense letting them know we stole their truck right away," One of the Delta troopers stated then added, "That's if they can even see through the stink in there. That's the most gawd awful odor I've ever smelled!"

Gus and I just sat there and laughed while Don explained his theory on the origins of the feces.

I and the others who had never been to Panama before were pleasantly surprised at the road network. A very smooth multi-lane highway took us all the way across the country, and we ran into very little traffic along the way. "Damn, this ain't bad for a road trip," I opined while glancing at the speedometer over Gus's shoulder. "Sixty-five miles per hour on an interstate that's better than anything we have back home!"

"We'll need to buy some gas to get there, so let's stop at the next station, fill up, and have some food," Gus remarked.

Gene added, "And we can also hit the latrine too!"

"I just hope like hell they haven't put out an alert on us," Vic stated. "Because if they did, I'd expect the locals in the station to call the police before we even finish taking a leak!"

Gul spoke up, "I hate to ask, but does anyone have money or credit cards?"

Blank stares all around until Gene opened the glove compartment and pulled out a billfold. "I have an American Express card, and a Diner's Club made out to the Panamanian Government, along with a book of tickets that look like bridge passes."

"I wonder if we can buy food with them," Gus asked as we pulled into a rest stop with a gas station and a McDonalds."

"We're about to find out, buddy," Vic stated.

"If not," one of the Delta men added, "We'll also be wanted for armed robbery."

"I hate to ask, but does anyone speak Spanish?" A voice in the back asked.

One of the Delta men who appeared to be Hispanic grinned, "Si Senor, I can speak Spanish like a native. Just call me Habib!"

The gas pump accepted the American Express card with no problem, and when we pulled up to the drive through, the girl didn't hesitate with it, although we had to wait at in a designated parking spot until they filled our huge order. They needed three people to carry it all to the van, but we didn't hang around to eat and pulled out right away.

We experienced a bit of anxiety when we came up to a toll booth, but the toll taker just waved us through. We stayed on Route nine, or the Panama-Colon expressway until we were just outside Margarita where Gus pulled over.

"Hey, Phil, want to take over from here? You know this area better than any of us since you worked here a while back." Gus slid out of the seat and made his way to the back of the cargo area while Phil, his tight-lipped Delta buddy, climbed behind the wheel and Habib took the shotgun seat. He turned to us, "We'll be on a shitty two lane from here on. We'll drive as far as we can, but if we get stopped at Ft. Davis, we'll have to fight our way to the Gatun Locks." He frowned, "And we better hope like hell our extraction is on time, because we'll have nowhere else to go if they find us."

We weren't stopped. He parked the van on the south side of the new locks and turned to Gus. "Care to transmit our location for the extraction?"

Gus pulled out his Sat-phone and spoke quietly to someone for a few minutes before he turned it off and told his buddy, "Drive over to the old locks; the southern side and park as close as you can to the canal. They'll come for us. Just keep your eyes open, they should be here in fifteen to twenty minutes."

We sat and watched as a large container ship locked through before checking our watches again. I turned to Gene, "It's been fifteen minutes, buddy, and I don't see anything that looks like an extraction ship or vehicle of any kind."

"Shit, my battery is dead! Let's get out so they can see us, just in case," Gus suggested before we piled out and watched the container slowly move away. Several canal workers approached us, but once they saw the emblems on our coveralls, they moved away. "I guess these guys aren't that popular in these parts, eh, Uncle Vinny?"

An oceangoing tugboat pulling a large barge behind it slowly entered the lock, rubbing its right side against the lock wall. Just as the gates closed behind it, a group of ten men carrying various types of luggage tossed a ladder against the lock wall, scrambled up it and onto the deck. They immediately began running toward us. One of them grabbed Gus, "Hey, man, if you're looking for transport to the U.S., better get on board most Rikki-Tik before it pulls out!"

Without hesitation, Gus and his men ran for the tug while shouting for the rest of us to follow.

"What about our weapons?" I heard George shout.

"Leave them, we won't need them now," someone responded as they leapt onto the tug and ran through an open hatch to the interior of the boat.

I distinctly heard Don shout, "A fucking tugboat! You've got to be shitting me!"

Just as I was about to echo his statement, I was pulled inside along with Don a split second before a Delta man swung the hatch shut and locked it. "Don't ask questions at a time like this, buddy, or I'll throw your ass overboard and leave you to the locals!"

We all stood wide-eyed and gape-mouthed at each other as we heard and felt the engine throttle up a little while the tug shuddered and slowly began to move out of the lock.

"Now what?" I asked the Delta man who pulled me inside.

"We wait!"

"But a fucking tugboat!" Don was beet red in the face as he continued, "We need to get out of Panamanian waters as fast as possible! I can swim faster than a fucking tug, and I'm sure anyone with even one arm and one leg can swim faster than this tub while it's towing a huge barge!" He turned to me while waving his arms wildly about, "Oh sure! Everything will be cool! The FBI and these spooks have everything under control! What can possibly go wrong? Oh, we'll have a great time in the tropics sucking down drinks with little umbrellas in them!"

Gus shoved Don out his way, "I'm going upstairs to see what the hell is going on. Try to keep your temper under control before Gul here gives you another shot in the ass."

Gul growled at Gus, "There had better be something other than this boat to get us back home!"

Gus trotted up the stairs, and after thirty minutes returned, appearing rather stunned. He stared at me and his Delta buddies for a few seconds before quietly stating, "This isn't our means of extraction! Those guys we saw on the pier weren't sent for us; they jumped ship and were running away from this tub and that crazy bastard who I assume is the captain!"

A collective groan rose from our group, followed by Don and Vic muttering, "Yeah! Right! What could possibly go wrong?"

Gus added, "And to make things even more interesting, that damn barge is full of guano, or bird shit for those of you who can't speak Spanish. Once the wind shifts around, the stink will be enough to burn your sinuses out permanently!"

Gene coughed, "It can't be as bad as what I fell in back at the hangar."

I turned to Vic, "I guess that answers your question, buddy. I'm going upstairs to talk to that guy and see if he can't drop us off somewhere along the way."

"I'm coming with you, Vinny," Gul stated as she holstered her pistol. "Maybe if I ask him nicely…"

"The bastard is bat-shit crazy," Gus interjected, "He needs to be committed someplace with padded walls and bars on the windows!"

"We just came from a place like that," Everyone from my group volunteered simultaneously before we broke up laughing.

The bridge was kind of cramped with six people jammed in there, but the Captain, a short, stocky, powerfully built man with a shaved head seemed nice enough at first. "Call me Captain Ron," he requested and held out one hand, "Ron Roman, and I've been working these tugs for over fifty years. I'm glad you all joined my crew because the last suckers didn't want to work and expected to sit on their asses like this is some kind of holiday cruise ship."

CHAPTER NINETEEN

He had an iron grip from years of hard work on tugs, but my hands were much larger than his so he only crushed part of my hand. Capt. Ron was gentle with Gul, but I heard Vic's knuckles crack under the pressure.

"Thanks for the welcome, Cap, but we really didn't join your crew. We thought you were our extraction vehicle..."

"Yeah, I heard all about it from the other guy with the beard, Vince. However, I can't run this tug alone, and I need to get this barge to Houston as fast as possible, so once you stepped foot on *"Queeg's Revenge"*, you became part of the crew..."

"But none of us know a damn thing about boats, tugboats, or Navy shit," Vic stated. "We need to get back to the US as fast as possible, and this tug isn't going to do the job..."

"This tug is pulling a top-secret cargo!" He leaned closer and whispered, "It's the raw material for a powerful rocket fuel our space fleet needs! This stuff is going to power our newest fleet of starships when we attack Snarfeloficus." He went on a wild rant about the Snarfs lying in wait to ambush his tug and barge. I could see the gears churning in his eyes, and somehow, they weren't meshing with reality. I turned, made eye contact with Vic and Don, and it was immediately understood the Captain had spent too many years at sea.

Someone tugged my elbow. I turned to see Gus and one of the Delta guys waving me away from the bridge. "The cheese slid off his cracker a long time ago, Uncle Vinny," Gus whispered, "I think we ought to use his radio to contact someone out there and get the hell off this tub as soon as possible."

I turned back to Cappy Ron, "Hey, Captain, can I use your radio to contact some friends of ours? I think they'll not only get us off your tug, but also find you a crew experienced in operating tugs and fighting off alien invaders."

"Like hell you will! The friggin Snarfs are monitoring my frequencies and as soon as you hit the transmit button, those bastards will be all over us like stink on shit!" He spun around, raised his fist and brought it down on the radio with enough force to not only crack the chassis, but cause the device to spew a shower of sparks and flames. "No one transmits anything from my tug, you son of a bitch!

I'm not losing my cargo or my tug; plus, I don't want to end up on their dinner plate tonight!"

Before anyone else could move, Gul whipped out her pistol and gave the man several hard blows to his head. The man dropped like a sack of rocks before she turned to me, "Let's get this guy secured to a bed and see what we can do to contact someone."

It took four men to drag his body down the stairs and into the crew quarters where they tied him to a bunk with small ropes they found in a locker. "That ought to hold him for a while," Tom remarked as he wiped the sweat off his face. "That son of a bitch was heavier than any man I've ever met before!"

"Poor bastard hasn't been playing with a full deck for some time," Vic added. "Now what do we do? None of us knows a damn thing about these boats and until we can get in touch with someone to extract us..."

Just then, the sound of helicopters filled the cabin. We rushed out to see four grey Navy Blackhawk choppers roaring past in the direction of the canal. Gus shouted, "That's our goddam extraction team!" He and everyone else began shouting and waving their arms in a useless attempt to attract the pilot's attention. We watched as they slowed, circled over the end of the very lock where we'd boarded the tug and then dropped down to land. Less than a minute later, they rose, and swung out over the bay just as four F-18 fighters zoomed past no more than 100 feet overhead.

"That's their air cover in case the Panamanians want to put up a fight," one of the Delta men shouted. The fighters made a wide sweeping turn and flew back the way they came, with the choppers following less than a minute later. Again, we all went crazy trying to attract their attention, but they gave no indications they saw us as they zoomed directly overhead and flew due east.

"Those sons of bitches probably picked up the guys who jumped off this tug!" Gus screamed as he pointed to the last bird flying by with the doors open. I could just make out three smiling men in civilian clothes waving to us as they flew past.

"There must be a carrier out there if they have that many choppers and fighters," Tony shouted as he ran back inside and up the ladder to the bridge. "We need to head in their direction and let them know they picked up the wrong people!"

Don was steering the tub when I entered the wheelhouse and was turning the wheel to the right to correct our course. "Vinny, we need to get rid of that barge if we're going to make any headway! We're barely making five knots with that thing holding us back. Go down there on the ass end and see if you can cut it loose!"

Me and several others flew down the ladder and ran to a huge winch with thick cables wrapped around two drums. I was looking around for a release switch when one of the FBI agents said, "You can't just let go of the cable from here. You'll need to reel it in to the bridle and then unhook it. All you'll do is let out more cable from here which won't help at all!"

I glanced around, saw no controls on the side of the cable drums around and somehow knew he was right. "How do you know this shit?"

"I investigated a murder on one of these things and learned a little bit about them," he replied then shook his head at the barge.

One of the Delta guys shouted, "They have an oxy-acetylene torch just inside the door! Give me a hand dragging the tanks out here and I'll cut the cable."

Ten minutes later, we had the torch and tanks alongside the cable, and the Delta guy began cutting. I suddenly recalled a lesson learned back when I drove a tow truck for Triple-A in the 60s. I ran up the ladder and shouted for Don to back off on the power before the cable snapped back and cut everyone on the ass end of the boat in half. He immediately moved two big silver handles back and we heard the engines throttle down and the tug slow, just a moment or two before we felt a lurch and a voice yell, "We're free! Put the pedal to the metal and head for the fleet!"

Vic had been standing alongside Don, helping him figure the controls when he pointed to a video screen, "I believe this is our radar display, and if my best guess is correct, those symbols appear to be in some kind of formation. I'd bet my left nut it's an aircraft carrier and its escorts, like destroyers, frigates and supply ships."

We took turns peering into the scope and after a few minutes we all agreed the blips were probably the source of the helicopters and therefore our saviors.

"They're directly east of us, and I'd estimate their distance to be approximately twenty miles," Don stated with Vic in full agreement as he turned back to the wheel.

Just as Don began steering toward the blips, Gene and Tom rushed to the bottom of the ladder screaming, "WARP SPEED! Get to warp speed, you crazy bastards! We're about to be run over by the barge!

I glanced out the back window and saw the huge black barge we had been towing about three hundred yards behind us, was now only fifty yards behind and closing fast! Don turned to see what was going on and when he did, I noticed the throttles were still at idle. In a panic, I lunged for the two handles and my hands hit them instantaneously with Gul's and Vic's. The engines hesitated a second or two and then roared to life as we lurched forward. The barge was now about twenty feet behind us and still closing the distance, but a little slower than a second ago. We all stood wide-eyed with fear as the barge crept within ten feet of the fantail before we slowly began pulling away, engines roaring and more than a few of us screaming in terror.

When we'd pulled a sufficient distance away, everyone let out sighs of relief before someone stated, "From now on, we have two people on watch up here at all times! One guy steering the friggin' boat and someone else watching our ass end."

After a rush to the bathroom or head, most of us just hung our plumbing over the side to relieve our inner tensions. As we laughed at each other over our close call, Tommy yelled, "We almost got our asses drowned by a tub full of birdshit! Can you imagine what our friends would say when they found out?"

"No one knows where the hell we are, and if we had been sunk and drowned, they wouldn't be able to tell who the hell was on this tug!" Gene laughed and then said, "We should have a meeting inside where we could hear each other over the noise of the engine and wind."

"We need to set up a watch schedule for the bridge and another in the engine room," Tommy stated. "We have no idea what is going on in the engine room, but they must have an owner's manual for something as complicated as this thing; otherwise, we could seize an engine, burn out a transmission or whatever they use on this tub."

"I think we'll need to wake up the captain sooner or later," I added. "If anyone knows, he will, but I'll bet he'll be more than a little pissed to learn we cut his barge loose."

"We'll tell him the Snarfs caught up to us and stole the damn thing," Gerry laughed.

"Yeah, and they cut the tow cable with a laser weapon," Gus added with mock sincerity, "But we fought them off when they tried to take control of the tug!" He laughed and added, "He's just crazy enough to believe it, too!"

I was just about to ask if anyone checked for food when one of the Delta guys interjected, "I checked the food locker and all they have is baked beans, hot dogs and beer. The fresh water tank is still full, and according to what I saw on the fuel gauges, if they are fuel gauges, we have all tanks full, so we should have enough to get to the States, but if we run short, we can always fart down the air intakes because we'll be producing more methane than the entire state of Texas."

Don yelled down the stairs, "I need someone to take over up for a few minutes while I take a dump." I ran up with Gerry and Tom. "Just hold us so the compass is always on the E. And check the scope to make sure we're pointed right at those big blips on the screen." He turned and hopped down the ladder while Tom took the wheel.

Approximately thirty minutes later, Don was still screaming in the latrine when we spotted a group of large ships on the horizon. "I'll steer right at them, Vinny. Get the glasses and see if you can tell what they are."

I picked up the large binoculars and after focusing on the largest ship, I could clearly see it was a huge aircraft carrier. "Yup, that big one in the middle is a carrier and probably the one that sent the choppers and F-18s after those guys on the dock. There's another boat that looks like a destroyer or something and it's turning toward us. It looks like its picking up speed, too!"

"Maybe they figured out they picked up the wrong people, Vinny," Gerry replied before he called down to the group, "Hey, we're about to be saved by the Navy, everyone. It looks like they're sending a destroyer to pick us up!"

The entire group ran to the front of the boat and began cheering whooping and yelling they were finally going home, when I noticed the ship was flashing a light at us. "Hey, Gerry, Tom, do you see that light on the destroyer? Do you think they're trying to tell us something?"

"I haven't got the slightest idea," Tom replied, "But it looks like Morse code. Ask if anyone understands it." I shouted the question down to the group, but they just shrugged their shoulders and replied, "Never learned it! We used voice radios, not telegraph keys."

Tom called for someone, "Raise a white flag in case the Navy thinks we're terrorists, especially since most of the males in our group have bushy beards, long hair and wear bandanas on their heads."

Gus ran inside and emerged a few moments later with a sheet he stripped from a bed. He and Gerry clipped it to a rope leading to a tall pole and then raised it, but we all damn near vomited when we saw a huge brown stain in the center of the bedsheet."

"Aw geez! Couldn't you find a clean one, you idiot?" I shouted before gagging. "Take that one down and find a clean one!"

The destroyer was closing fast and was less than a mile away when someone shouted from inside, "Don can't get off the throne due to his wounds, but he wants to know what the flashing lights are saying, Vinny."

"OK, get ready to relay what I say," I replied while bringing up the glasses. I noticed the light was blinking furiously and the damn ship had rotated its front turret directly at us. "Here ya go," I yelled, "Blink blink blinkety blinkety blink blink blink, blinkety blinkety blinkety blink blinkety blink blinkety...." A flash of flame shot from the forward turret and a split second later, we heard a loud ripping noise just before the round impacted and exploded just a hundred feet in front of the tug.

"Tell Don they punctuated their message with five-inch naval gunfire!" I yelled to Tom, "Turn away from the fucking destroyer! They must have found out we're all Army guys and don't want to be sodomized!"

A second after Tom steered away, Don rushed up the ladder while holding up his pants, "What the fuck are you doing, you idiot? Blinkety blink blink, you dumb-ass, you almost got us killed! Give me those glasses!" A few moments later, he reported, "Stand off or we will fire on you! You will not be warned again!"

One of the guys handed him a flashlight and said, "See if you can signal with this." Fortunately, it worked, and Don had to think for a bit before he began transmitting.

The destroyer was headed in the same direction as we were and keeping pace with us but had ceased flashing its light. I was hoping they were able to read Don's message because he hadn't used his Morse code skills in close to fifty years, and after a few minutes of his efforts, the guys hoisted a reasonably clean sheet to let them know we were surrendering.

"You getting through to those squids, Don?"

"Don't know for sure. I never used a flashlight to send Morse before. I always used a key set, so they may be scratching their heads trying to figure out what I'm saying."

"Try sending an SOS; that should be easy enough for anyone to understand, and pull up your pants, too. The sight of your naked and bloody butt is enough to send anyone running in terror." I turned back to the destroyer to see the other ships were quickly disappearing over the horizon. "Hey, buddy, it looks like the Navy beat feet and are leaving us behind."

Tom stepped out on the wing, "Those carriers can do better than 40 miles per hour and the support ships can go about that fast. I'd be willing to bet they think we're terrorists or the next best thing," he added, pointed to Don's white legs, "and they ain't going to hang around here to find out. That destroyer was probably assigned to hold us back while they split for their home port, and with this thing capable of doing no better than twelve knots running downhill with a tailwind, there's no way in hell we're going to catch up to them."

Just then, the destroyer sent another series of flashes before it cut loose with another round that landed about one hundred feet off our ass end drenching everyone with the splash. It then put on a burst of power and sailed off over the horizon.

"What the hell was that all about?" I yelled to Don.

He had to think a couple seconds before he replied, "They obviously didn't care to read what I was trying to send them because that last message said, 'Eat shit and die, you scum-sucking pigs.'"

"Well, fuck them, too! I'll be damned if I ever pay another penny in taxes to support those squid assholes."

Tommy laughed, "Oh geez, what the hell can possibly go wrong? We'll fly down to Mexico, then we'll go to Panama where we'll fly a charter back to the U.S…"

"Shut the hell up, you idiot!" Gul growled, "You were given a choice in what you were going to do, so quit your complaining and find enough coffee for everyone." She turned me, "Vincent, we'll take that bedroom right by the stairs…"

"That bedroom belongs to the captain, Gul," Don stated quietly. "When he wakes up, he's going to want to use it, and I don't think he'll be in a mood to argue with you." He thought for a few moments, then turned back to her, winked and asked quietly, "Are you and Vinny developing a special relationship?"

"It's none of your business! And unless you want another set of scars on your ass, you'll keep your mouth shut and your opinions to yourself!" She grabbed my arm and whispered as she led me to the captain's quarters, "It's not what you think, but as the only woman on this tub, I am not about to use one of those filthy beds and have all these men stare at me while I get undressed or take a shower."

I closed the door to the small room behind us and asked, "So what are your intentions, young lady? You know I may be easy, but I'm not cheap! Besides I don't want everyone to think I'm allowing you to take advantage of me…"

A quick but reasonably hard slap to my face brought me back to reality as she pointed to the floor by the door, "You'll be sleeping right there, blocking the door while I use the bed. In the meantime, I want to wash the bedclothes and clean this pigsty while you get everyone organized to do housekeeping, cooking and…"

A hard knock at the door interrupted her. "Let me in my quarters, you crazy bitch! I'm the captain of this tug and these are my quarters! And you should know, while we're at sea my word is the law! Now get the hell out of there before I kick the door down!"

Gul opened the door and stuck her automatic in the captain's face, "If you ever call me bitch again, I will use your empty skull for a planter. I don't care what your position is because you're obviously having problems dealing with reality, especially our new reality. As I told everyone else, I am the only woman on this ship and will not sleep in the open crew quarters! I need my privacy and a level of cleanliness this tub has never seen before, so go back to whatever you were doing or are supposed to be doing and leave me alone!"

Something seemed to have clicked in Captain Ron's brain since he was knocked senseless, and after a moment's hesitation, he politely asked, "May I enter to retrieve my shower kit and a change of clothes? I haven't been able to take a shower in several days because I couldn't trust the crew to stand watch…and I want to apologize for insulting you a few minutes ago…"

Gul backed away from the door, lowered her pistol and watched as the man went to his small head, threw a few things in a leather bag, then pulled an assortment of clothes from a chest of drawers. He turned to Gul and me as he left the room, "The past couple of weeks have been hell on wheels for me, but that crack on the head you gave me, plus the following six hours sleep brought me around. Let me get cleaned up and put some food in my gut before we all have a long talk!"

Just as Cappy was turning to go, Tommy stuck his head in the door, "I found several large bags of coffee beans, but no grinder. How do you make coffee from whole beans?"

"Come with me and I'll show you," Cappy stated. "We picked up ten bags of roasted beans for free on the way here, but we don't have a grinder. We use an old crank pencil sharpener to grind them. It takes time, but it works."

Gul grabbed one of her agents, "Go find me a mop, a bucket full of hot soapy water and another with clean water. I also need something to clean the furniture and bathroom in here."

"I need to use the bathroom before I get everyone together to hear Ron's talk," I said quietly and walked to the bathroom. After closing the door, I noticed the latrine was reasonably clean. The toilet bowl and sink could use a dose of Clorox, but otherwise it was probably as clean as most single men's bathrooms. At least he kept a good supply of ass-wipe that didn't tear easily, and his bath towels were reasonably clean.

Our group was assembled in the big room where I assumed the crew ate their meals, among other things. Captain Ron was clean and just finishing a big bowl of hot dogs and baked beans. After letting out a loud belch, he looked at each man and asked, "Where is the barge?"

Tommy maintained a straight face when he replied, "The fucking aliens got it! They attacked the ship and cut the cable with a laser before they lifted it into their ship. They tried to seize your ship, but we fought them off..."

"Bullshit! You expect me to believe that crazy shit? Now tell me what happened to the barge I was towing."

"You even said it yourself; you were being followed by an alien spaceship and they wanted the bird shit on the barge to make fuel for..."

"Jesus H. Christ!" He lowered his head, raised his hand and said, "Okay, I kind of remember something about that..." He shook his head then began, "Those guys who jumped ship weren't real seamen. I think they were working for the drug lords in Columbia because my men went into town as soon as we tied up, and they never came back. Then those guys showed up and said my men took off for home and they'd take their place. There were about a dozen armed men guarding that barge when we tied up to it and they wouldn't let me on board to make sure it was properly secured, which is just insane."

"Sounds a little suspicious to me," Gus muttered.

"Yeah it was real suspicious to me too, fella, but what can you do with an AK-47 stuck in your face? I guess they did a decent job of tying up to the barge because it didn't break loose during the two thunderstorms we went through. I think they buried a shitload of cocaine under all that guano to keep it from being sniffed out by the DEA."

"That stuff would hide any odor from any sniffer in the world," Gene laughed, "And who the hell would want to go digging into it to see if there was anything hidden in under that shit."

"Those fuckers must have put something in my coffee or food a few days out because I started seeing and hearing all kinds of strange shit. I mean the hallucinations were hell on wheels, but at least I got us this far."

"If those guys were narcos, why did they bail on you at the Canal? They must have a fortune in dope buried in that barge!"

"They were watching the people on the Canal's aprons when we entered the last of the Gatun Locks and one of them started screaming about the DEA, Customs and Panamanian Military waiting for us. I guess they saw your uniforms…"

"And they thought we were going to bust them!" Gene gave me a wide-eyed glance before we all burst out roaring with laughter. "Of all the people in the world, they sure as hell got us mixed up! We're wanted by every law enforcement agency and military branch in Panama, not to mention the Narcos!"

"It took some balls to approach us while we were waiting for our extraction," Gus laughed.

"Those guys were high on something the entire time they were on board," Ron growled. If you search their bags, I'm sure you'll find whatever it is they took."

Don and I slipped out of the dining area and opened a leather overnight bag. I pulled out a plastic bag, held it out and whispered,

"Hey dude, they must really be into gardening because this guy was carrying a two-pound bag of compressed peat moss!"

Don grinned, "Ya think? There's only one way to determine what it really is. Let's head out to the fantail and test it under strict scientific standards. I have a PhD so I can ensure it's done properly."

CHAPTER TWENTY

"Hey, what the hell are you two guys doing with that bag of dope," One of the Delta men shouted as he and two of his buddies approached.

"Doctor Farmer and I are conducting an experiment to determine the exact nature of this vegetation we discovered in the baggage of the men who jumped ship." I replied while Don stuffed a handful of suspected peat moss into the huge bowl of a bong we found on a shelf.

Don turned to the wide-eyed Delta men, "I have a PhD, and therefore, as a doctor I am eminently qualified to conduct strict scientific field tests to determine the true nature, identity, and potency of this rather aromatic leafy substance."

"Hey, Doc, I think I can tell you without testing it; the stuff in the bag is grass, marijuana, shit or holy herb, as known in the vernacular," The more senior man, Steve replied with a smirk as he held a light to the bowl for me. "I took some courses in biology while I was in college, so I'll assist with the tests."

I inhaled the smoke, handed the bong to a Delta man, and after a prolonged coughing fit, stated, "I think it's Columbian Sphagnum."

Don took the bong, sucked his lungs full after Steve, a tall thin Delta trooper had a long hit, then passed it to his willing buddies who claimed to have taken science courses in college or high school. After my fourth turn on the pipe, I asked Red, one of the Delta guys, "Do you think the DEA sprayed this shit with herbicides? It has a slight chemical aftertaste."

Red took a long hit, stared at me as he held it in as long as he could, then after coughing out a huge cloud, choked out, "Roundup, it definitely has a Roundup flavor to it!"

"Let me try it again," Don muttered before he sucked in the last of the bowl. He glanced at each of us before he exhaled a long streamer of smoke. "Nope, it isn't Roundup. I can state that with certainty. Herbicides leave a distinct petroleum flavor. This stuff has been contaminated with coca leaves. They grow coca and peat moss on the same hillsides. The pickers often throw in any green leafy material into the bags they use when they harvest…"

"I think we need to test another bowl to verify Don's theory," I coughed out before refilling the bowl. Just as I was about to light it up, I turned to Red, "I think some food would go a long way to help with the test." He just nodded and staggered into the superstructure with Steve helping him along, although Steve was just as unsure on his feet.

"It will take a while before we get our sea-legs," Don laughed.

"But the ocean is as calm as a pond, buddy. I think this peat moss is definitely having its effect on those boys." I glanced over at the Doctor of English and Mass Communications then watched as he slowly slid down against the wall of the cabin until he was sitting with his legs splayed out.

"Aaahh yessss! It's definitely working wonders on the pain I should be experiencing from my gunshot wounds. However, I believe we should fire up that test tube right away. It may take Red an inordinate amount of time to return with some comestibles, and I'd hate to interrupt our test protocols and lose the analgesic effect of the peat moss before they do."

We'd just finished off our second bowlful when Red and the rest of the crew suddenly appeared in a rush. "What the fuck are you two doing?" An FBI agent shouted as Gus pulled the bong from my hands.

Although I was unable to stand, grasp the pipe, or even hold my head up, I muttered, "We're testing this stuff to see if it's real peat moss or just some cheap Chinese imitation they're trying to pawn off on us."

Another FBI agent shouted, "You're on a US registered ship and thus subject to all civil and criminal laws of the United States. I can arrest you for smuggling a controlled and dangerous substance into the United States…"

Red roughly pushed him aside, "He didn't smuggle it; Vinny found this shit in one of the bags left here by the men who jumped ship. He and Doctor Farmer, along with a few of our Delta men are testing it to see if it's peat moss, tea, oregano, cat-nip or something else, which he suspects to be marijuana, but we won't know until we finish the tests…"

Gus grabbed the bag containing the suspect matter, but rather than throw it overboard as I feared he would, he immediately walked away from the FBI men, stuffed the bowl full and lit it. After he let out a long, thick cloud of smoke, he stated, "Uncle Vinny, as you know, I also have a degree in science, so I think I should assist you and the good doctor conduct an in-depth examination of this stuff." He handed it off to the two remaining Delta men and patiently waited his turn as the bong was tested five times by me, Don and each of the men.

Steve returned with a huge steaming pot, placed in front of me and Don then handed us paper plates and forks. "It's all we have, so dig in, but leave enough for everyone else because you know we're all going to have a near-fatal case of the munchies."

The hot dogs and beans tasted wonderful, as would almost any food while the consumer was under the influence of high-grade sphagnum. Gus sat next to me to eat while Red and Steve loaded up the bong again. One of the two FBI agents picked that moment to give us another raft of shift. "You people are felons and as such, you will be prosecuted to the fullest extent of the law as soon as we reach the US!"

"Who the fuck are you to threaten us with arrest?" Gus staggered to his feet and glared down at them.

"I'm Special Agent Schoppy, FBI!" He whipped out his badge to intimidate my nephew, but he had no way of knowing he was dealing with a Nunzio. However, he quickly discovered my family was not known for being submissive or even respectful to anyone, especially feds.

Gus grinned, snatched the leather bifold out of his hand, turned to me and said, "I can buy one of these badges at K-Mart, Uncle Vinny." He then casually flipped it overboard and remarked to the stunned fed, "I'm not impressed; what else ya got there for me, pilgrim?"

The FBI agent was stunned at Gus's actions and was trying to make up his mind whether to jump overboard to retrieve his badge or seize my nephew when Tom grabbed him from behind in a chokehold. Tommy waited until the man was turning blue before he let him go, and as Schoppy inhaled to refill his lungs, Red blew a huge cloud of smoke in his face and croaked, "Don't knock it until you try it, asshole."

Gus turned to me, "Uncle Vinny, don't you have a science degree?"

"Yeah, I have a Masters in Political Science; International Relations."

"Shit! That definitely qualifies you to conduct this test."

While I was discussing my qualifications with Gus, a Delta man was busy choking and releasing the FBI asshole while Tommy made sure he inhaled enough smoke to at least get a good buzz on. The other FBI man saw what was happening and decided a good high was preferable to enforcing a silly law and joined in the bong rotation until he fell to the deck and crawled over to help himself to a large serving of hot dogs and beans.

Captain Ron rushed out to our crowd from the superstructure, took a long slow look at each of us, snatched the pipe from Don's hands and took a long hit. "This is just what I needed to clear the cobwebs from my head."

As he was taking a second toke, I asked, "If you're down here, who's steering the boat?"

"Your girlfriend Gul is up there and she's doing a fine job, so I thought I'd join you guys for a break." After handing the bong to Don, he picked up the pot, shoveled a few loads of beans and dogs into his mouth and remarked, "I need to contact my home office to see what they want me to do. Does anybody have a cell phone that works?"

Gus choked out, "You shouldn't have smashed the radio, you idiot! I have a Sat-phone, but the battery is dead. Do you have a charger?" Several others added, "I have a cell, but my battery is dead too." Gus gave me a blood-shot hairy eyeball, "Uncle Vinny, don't you have one?"

"It's on my plane along with all my other stuff, like my wallet and passport. But if those guys were guarding a barge full of dope, they might have brought phones in their bags, to stay in contact with their boss."

The crowd on the fantail, except for one FBI agent, were too high to do more than sit around slowly nodding out. Ron and the agent staggered into the superstructure to begin their search, and with a superhuman effort, I grabbed my nephew, "Come on, Gus, we have to make sure that fucking FBI turd doesn't toss any peat moss overboard and ruin our study."

"Yeah, there might be a Nobel prize for science in it for us if we do it right."

We were just in time to seize two large duffel bags full of the suspected vegetation before the Fed tossed them overboard. I hid mine under Gul's bed while Gus took his into the engine room.

Later, during what passed for a dinner of hot dogs and beans, Ron assigned the reasonably sober agent to take the wheel while he briefed the rest of us.

"Listen up, everyone. We found a couple different types of chargers; sadly, none of them fit anyone's cell phone or the Sat-phone, but Tommy and Red say they have experience with electronics and will try to rig them up, so they'll charge. In the meantime, you should learn some of the more important things about working on an ocean-going tug. For instance; there ain't no doors on this tug: they're hatches, and those little round windows are portholes. We are currently in the galley and up those stairs or what we shall call the ladder, is the bridge or wheelhouse." He went on to use a picture of the tug to teach us about the port side, starboard, the bow, aft, gunwales and main deck, in addition to our need to constantly keep an eye on the fuel tanks and how the boat will get catawampus and roll over if we didn't keep it balanced. I fell asleep about halfway through his lecture but whispered to Gus to take notes for his favorite uncle.

I slept soundly until I awoke with a start when I fell out of the chair.

Gul was laughing as she helped me to my feet whispering, "I think it's time for little Vinny to go to bed." Once in our room with the door closed, she gave me a long lingering kiss as she held me tight, then just as I thought I'd get lucky, she pointed to the made-up bed on the floor before she moved it to block the door. "Sleep well tonight, my sweetheart, and try not to snore." With a warm loving smile, she added, "You can take your shower while I get undressed and climb into MY bed!" She made a show of pulling out her automatic pistol, jacked a round into the chamber then slid it under her pillow and pointed to the bathroom; indicating I wouldn't even get to watch her undress.

Loud banging on the door suddenly woke me, and as I gathered my wits about me, I heard Gus shouting, "Time to get up, Uncle Vinny! It's 06:00 and we have to stand watch in 30 minutes." I turned toward Gul and saw her wide-eyed with surprise and pointing her pistol at the door.

"It's okay, Gul. That's my nephew..."

"I know who it is! Get cleaned up and then stand your watch. I'll bring your coffee and breakfast up to the bridge after I take my shower."

"I think you can put your gun away, dear. I don't think Gus or anyone else will try to break in and molest me."

Still holding her aim at the door, she muttered, "I don't trust any of those Army guys or the Delta people, and especially not someone related to you! Now get a move on and once you're cleaned up, I want you to guard my door while I shower, but do it from the outside."

While standing guard, Don passed by on the way to his bunk and handed me a hot cup of coffee. He winked and whispered, "Have a good night's sleep Vinny?"

I winked back, "Hell, yeah!"

"You lucky bastard!"

I wasn't about to tell him or anyone else the truth, but it wouldn't hurt to let them continue believing their misbegotten and obscene ideas, even if it did make me look cheap and easy. Don turned to me at the bottom of the ladder, "Ron wants us to slow down a little this morning. He has a supply of fishing rods and is going to try catching something to vary our diet. He'll call with the speed he wants in a couple minutes. I think he's rigging the fishing lines with some lures and hot dogs as bait."

Gus had the wheel and just as Gul exited her room, he asked her, "Can you bring us something to eat for breakfast?"

She gave him a hairy eyeball and replied, "I'm going to fix something for Vinny and me, and if there's enough left over, you can have that."

My nephew gave me a baleful look, "That wasn't very nice of her, Uncle Vinny. After all, we're going to be related sometime in the near future and you'd think she'd want to be on the good side of your favorite nephew!"

Gul gave him a derisive sneer then turned to climb down the stairs as she growled, "I don't think you should admit to anyone you're related to a fine man like Vincent. Talk about polluting the family gene pool!"

A few minutes later, Ron had us slow down to something like eight knots while he fed out line from the rods, but three hours later, just as our watch was ending, he came up and said he didn't get a single bite. "We'll keep our eyes open for signs of baitfish jumping and then cast into them. It's a surefire way to catch something big, or at least enough fish to feed the crew." After a quick glance at the compass and GPS, he stared off at the horizon for a moment, then grabbed the binoculars and reported, "There's a big container ship out there and it isn't moving. She's probably trying to reach us on the radio because she wouldn't just sit out there unless it's having engine trouble. Let me take the helm. We'll see if she needs help and maybe they'll have some good food to give us."

"And let us use their radio and battery chargers," Gus added.

"What if they were taken by pirates?" I asked.

"Doubtful in these waters, but if they were, they'd be headed for their own port..." He gave me a slap on the back, "See the light? They're sending an SOS, so they must figure our radio is out."

Thirty minutes later, we were alongside the huge containership. and Ron was scrambling up a rope ladder they lowered after he had a brief discussion with some of the ship's crew. "I'll be back in about a half hour. Keep us right against the ship's hull but don't try pushing it."

"I hope like hell we don't have to drag this big sucker to some port, because it will take us forever to get anywhere," Gus growled.

"If they have communications, they probably called for help as soon as they broke down, so another tug will be along shortly." Tommy replied, "But as long as we can charge the sat-phones, you can call for extraction and get us off this tub."

Just as I was about to add my two cents to the conversation, someone on the ship threw down a canvas bag attached to a line. He shouted, "Put your phones in the bag and we'll charge them for you!" Everyone grabbed their phones and tossed them in the bag. As he was hauling them up, he added, "We're going to lower a pallet full of food for you, too! Do you need anything else?"

Gul shouted up to the man, "I need some decent shampoo and a woman's soap and deodorant!"

The bag was hauled up and over the side a few moments before a woman leaned over the side, smiled and shouted for Gul to climb aboard. Gul was reaching for a rung when she turned to my nephew and Red, "You two had better not stare at my ass while I climb this stinking ladder!"

Gus, like his father, lacked all the social graces and even a trace of common sense. He replied, "Don't worry about it, little lady. I've seen better rear-ends on old pickup trucks."

Red was wise enough to keep his mouth shut and his face impassive, so he was able to help me drag my nephew into the crew quarters. "Listen, Cosmo, you should know better than to make smart remarks about any woman's ass, no matter what they say! Now just lay here on the bunk until the swelling in your nut-sack goes down and you can catch your breath. We'll be back as soon as we can find your front teeth. I think we can put them back in if I can locate some cotton balls and armature wire."

An hour later, I had his teeth back where they were before Gul gave him a hard and painful lesson in female sensitivities and proper responses to her statements. "Look, Cosmo, this is the best I can do with what I could find on this tub, plus what the container ship had. You'll have to avoid biting anything, but I don't think it will be a problem since I wired your jaw shut to keep pressure on the teeth and gums. The container sent down a couple dozen straws, so you'll at least be able to eat soup and drink."

Gus mumbled something, but I don't think he was expressing his thanks for my dental work. Red, the unit medic peered inside his teammate's mouth, looked at my handiwork and remarked, "Jesus H. Christ! It looks like a bird's nest in there! I sure hope it all holds together until we can get him to an oral surgeon."

"I asked if anyone wanted to handle the job and no one stepped forward, so if you think you can do a better job, have at it, dude!" I held out the needle-nose pliers and side-cutters for him, but he just shook his head and walked away.

Gus indicated he wanted a pen and paper since he couldn't speak. "I need painkillers!" And then he wrote, "You just wait till I tell my dad!"

"I'll beat your old man like a rented mule, Gus. Now listen; I did what I could to keep you from looking and sounding like a Trump supporter, so shut the hell up and live with it until we can get you ashore someplace. I'll load the bong for you to take care of your pain, but be damn careful when you get the munchies later on."

I went outside with Red to catch a smoke and was told Gul wanted to see me on the big boat. While climbing the ladder, somebody opened a hatch on the side of the ship, so I was able to gain entrance after climbing only ten rungs. A mate helped steady me as I swung off the ladder before he shouted to the rest of our people on the tug, "Our captain has invited your crew to join us for a fine dinner as a reward for coming to our rescue."

"What kind of food do your cooks prepare," I asked while watching our men rush past me, "Strictly Italian, sir. This ship has Italian cooks and they refuse to prepare anything other kind of food."

"Sounds good to me!"

Fifteen minutes later, we were seated at a long table set with fine china, gleaming silverware, and large servers filled with spaghetti, sausage, meatballs and other foods emitting fantastic aromas. The captain gave us a big smile and was about to launch into a speech when we all felt a shudder beneath our feet. A moment later, a wall phone rang and after he spoke briefly with the person on the other end, the captain grinned and shouted, "Our engine room crew have found and repaired the problem with our engines! Let's eat this fine meal before we bid our good friends a fond farewell! We shall be on our way in thirty minutes."

One of our people asked about our phones and the woman who asked Gul to come aboard replied, "They're being charged as we speak and should have a sufficient charge when we finish eating."

I noticed our Captain Ron had a serious frown on his face as he counted and recounted out people. Just as I was about to do the same, he stood and shouted, "We had twelve of you people on my ship and I count eleven! There should be one more person on the tug standing watch in the engine room or the bridge. One of you bastards had better get your ass back on the tug!"

Don gave me a sick look, "I was standing bridge watch when they invited us to come aboard, so I yelled down for Gus to take my place."

Gene stood, "I asked him to stand watch in the engine room!"

I shouted, "The guy is probably out like a light because I gave him a full bong to kill the pain in his mouth! There's no one at the wheel!"

We rushed out to the main deck just in time to see our tug slowly drifting away to the north.

CHAPTER TWENTY-ONE

Cappy Ron shoved me aside and stared at his tug, now approximately two hundred yards away. He turned to Don and slapped him so hard, he was knocked off his feet, then he nailed Gene right on the tip of his jaw as he screamed, "You stupid bastards! You never leave your duty stations unless I give you permission! I don't give a shit what the hell is going on, you never abandon your posts to anyone, especially someone doped up and out cold!" He spun to face the ship's captain, "I need to borrow a boat to get back to my tug."

The captain just laughed and turned to his executive officer, "Make the number two lifeboat ready for Captain Ron and his men. Gather their phones together for them and give them a charger that will fit their phones." He turned to Gul, "You are welcome to travel with us to our next port of call, Baltimore, Maryland."

"I accept your offer, Captain, as long as Vincent Nunzio can join me." She slid an arm under mine and gave me a warm, loving smile. "Would you prefer to travel with me in a rather luxurious and spacious cabin, or continue on alone in that floating pig-pen with your ignorant nephew and his crude friends?"

I shouldn't have hesitated to think about it, but as soon as she grabbed me by the throat, I choked out, "I have a few things on the tug, plus there's my friends, my pilot and co-pilot. Let me retrieve my duffel bag and tell the guys we'll meet them in Baltimore."

"You're a lot smarter than you look, Vincent. Come back with this ship's boat and no stopping along the way!" She gave me the evil eye when I swung my arm around to show her the vast, empty ocean. "You know what I mean!"

The ladder leading down to the captain's big Boston whaler was way too long for someone as old as me, but I made it and joined, Cappy Roman, Gene, Tommy and Don for the trip to the tug. We found Gus out cold on his bunk, and everyone decided to let him sleep since he was probably unaware he'd been asked to stand watch. I tucked his fully charged Sat-phone under his pillow without being seen then grabbed my duffel-bag, now only half-full of suspected peat-moss, threw in the few items of clothing I had; a T-shirt, a pair of undershorts and of course, the bong.

Cappy Ron put the engines in drive and motored back to the ship to pick up the rest of his crew while I jumped into the whaler and rode it with the ship's second mate, a burly Australian named Ian.

As we were hooking up the boat to the ship's davit, he said we could sit tight and let the davit lift us aboard. "No sense in doing all that ridiculous climbing, mate, and bedsides, it's damn dangerous!" He pointed to my bag, "Is that all you have?"

"It's all I need," I replied with a grin and a wink. Just a T-shirt, a pair of shorts and some peat moss. We were scientifically testing it on the tug to determine exactly what it is for the past couple days"

Ian grinned, "Let me take a look at that peat-moss, mate. You may need a second opinion." After he opened the bag and took a deep breath, he smiled, pulled out the bong and held it up. "Is this one of the test tubes you were using?"

I nodded with a grin.

"You know, this might not be peat-moss! If I may make a suggestion, I'd venture to say it could be rough cut tea, oregano, or even cheap pipe tobacco of some sort. I'll ask a few of my mates to help you conduct further testing on the fantail this evening after supper."

"You can do me a favor by finding a safe place to hide this stuff because my girlfriend does not approve of my scientific method or the material I'm testing."

"No problem, mate, I know just the place. I'll stop by your cabin before we begin our study session."

The rest of my friends, along with the FBI agents and Delta team were standing on the main deck with me and Gul. As they turned to me, Don shouted, "What's this shit we hear about you and Gul taking this back to Baltimore while the rest of us have to take the tug?"

Gul stood next to me, put her arm around my waist then smiled up at me with incredible warmth as she gave me a squeeze and replied, "The captain asked if I'd rather travel back to Baltimore in a luxury stateroom they have available and I gratefully accepted. Then I asked Vincent to accompany me on the long voyage as my personal bodyguard to protect me from the ship's crew, and Vincent felt obligated to…"

"You rotten bastard," the group shouted simultaneously. Then Gary angrily added, "You got us into this mess, Vinny, and now you're abandoning us to this stinking tub…"

"Shut the hell up," Cappy Ron yelled back. "You're all in my crew now, except the young lady, and that's all there is to it! You'll get paid as soon as we dock in Baltimore. I called the home office on the ship's radio and they said to bring *Queeg's Revenge* home for a refit after we make a stop in Miami to pick up a yacht for some rich guy in Annapolis. All of you have been on the payroll since Panama, and the boss said you'll all receive regular mate's pay plus a bonus of four grand each from the yacht's owner. So, every one of you will pocket at least six grand for the trip."

The men gave each other glances with raised eyebrows before one of the Delta guys mumbled, "That ain't bad money on top of our regular government pay!"

My friends stared at me for a few moments before Vic growled, "You're coming with us, Nunzio! Like Don said, you got us into this, and I have a good mind to hog tie you and make you…"

All eyes suddenly turned to my waistline and when I looked down, I saw Gul had wrapped her arm around my waist with a pistol in hand, which she was now pointing at the crowd. "Like I stated a moment ago, Vincent will be traveling with me! So, I suggest everyone should immediately get that tub moving. Have a pleasant voyage home." The men mumbled, grumbled, and swore up a storm as they disembarked to the tug.

Gul pulled me into a passageway, gave me a warm, passionate kiss and whispered, "I used the ship's satellite phone to speak with my office in D.C. They said Hamm regained consciousness several hours after he was brought to the hospital, and he's now safely ensconced at FBI headquarters in a holding cell. They said he's confessed to everything and told them where the money he embezzled can be found. It seems he's also been dealing in guns, drugs, and stolen artwork for the past ten years and that's how we came to be here. The A.G. said I should inform you there is a total of six million dollars in reward money waiting for you when you arrive home."

I raised my eyebrows at the amount she mentioned, then added, "I thought it would be one point five million."

"You received the extra money because they were also able to seize the bank accounts where he kept his drug money, which totaled over fifty million. It seems Hamm had a serious change of heart when he was informed his Columbian drug buddies were going to kill him after drugging his drink. They wanted to get rid of him and take his jet, but you and my agents were able to fight them off and get him to a hospital before he died of an overdose."

"That's kinda stretching the truth, isn't it? We shot it out with those guys *after* he was taken to the hospital…"

"It doesn't matter, Vincent. The government recovered the money he embezzled and it's going to be returned to the people he stole it from. You're now six million dollars richer and you also have two executive jets." She embraced me for a long moment then said, "And we have ten days alone on this ship in a beautiful cabin where we can get to know each other much, much better."

"Will I still have to sleep on the floor?"

"We'll discuss that matter during the trip home. I'm not looking for a short, fiery romance. I want a long-term relationship built on love, understanding, and trust."

"Even though I'm considered damaged goods?"

She laughed and replied, "Second-hand goods is more like it, Vinny, but I don't mind. I'll just consider you to be more experienced than most men."

Just then a crewman opened the door and said the tug was leaving and the men wanted to say goodbye. We walked out to the deck, looked down and saw half the men were giving me the finger while the others had bent over to moon us. They were shouting all kinds of epithets, curses, and obscene suggestions, in addition to questions about the location of the duffel bag and bong.

I waved my hands over my head until they quieted, then shouted back. "Have a nice trip, boys! Enjoy yourselves, have fun and just think of it as a working vacation! I don't think you'll have any trouble since you have a sturdy ship, a good captain, and fair weather. Plus, after all the shit you've been through, what else could possibly go wrong?"

If you have comments concerning this or any of my other books, please feel free to send them to tcwsauthor@yahoo.com I will be most appreciative to hear of your constructive criticism. If want to submit a story of your own, send it in; I'll even blame it on you when it's published.

If you need more twisted humor and wild stories, all my books, are available for download or in paperback at Amazon.com, and at Barnes & Noble.com.

Also available for your reading pleasure; "The Alien's Reward Trilogy," three books about a man who initially thought UFOs and ETs were no more than hallucinations of brain damaged rednecks. However, he's quickly and definitively proven wrong by a group of crazy, fun loving and hard fighting aliens. This is a Sci-Fi book for everyone since I've left out the endless technobabble, weird religions, strange languages, and complicated histories, plots and endless list of characters.

Alternate Earth is a combined sequel to "The Alien's Reward III" and "The Replacement Priests". What would happen if people from an alternate earth landed on our planet? How would they be received? Would the televangelists freak out and call them evil spawns of Satan? What would our military industrial complex do? And what about those ten nuclear warheads planted above the Yellowstone volcano in The Replacement Priests?

You'll also appreciate reading, "Legacies, an American Journey." It's a fictionalized account of my family's military and law enforcement history. Someone once said, the unofficial, verbal history of events is much more interesting than anything a historian could ever imagine. And the history handed down to me by family is truly incredible.

If you're into Para-normal stories, you definitely want to read, "Der Schatten Teufel: The Shadow Devil." After completing his tour of duty, the main character from Legacies, an American Journey, returns home to Philadelphia from Vietnam to learn his fiancé was murdered by a brutal serial killer. He vows to hunt down and kill the man responsible, and in the process, discovers his target is possessed by a demon. He also must deal with drug smugglers, gunrunners, the Mafia and an old enemy from his time in Alaska. It's one hell of a wild story with great action scenes, lots of humor, heartbreaking loss and incredible redemption.

My book, "Alaskan Paybacks", is about an avid outdoorsman living in Alaska with his giant mutant husky, Snarfles. It has yet to be determined which character is smarter, but you can decide for yourself, and it won't be an easy decision as they deal with mafia hit men, the Taliban and others during their journeys.

In addition, "Running Down Terror," is a thriller ripped right from today's headlines, and will have you wondering just how effective our security forces really are. The main character is enjoying a brew in a North-East Philly bar when he overhears Islamic terrorists planning a horrific attack on the United States. He learns many recent industrial and other disasters around the country were not accidents, but carefully calculated acts of terror designed to appear as accidents. When the FBI and CIA refuse to believe him, the man and his friends go after them, fully intent on bringing down the entire terror network, but things don't go quite as he planned.

"The Replacement Priests" tells the story of three Jesuits, normally assigned to provide coverage for parish priests who need vacations. When they uncover a conspiracy by the senior members of the archdiocese to enriched themselves after the violent murders of priests in a drug-infested parish, they take matters into their own hands. Christ taught you should turn the other cheek if assaulted, but He didn't say what to do next, and these three men act accordingly.

And finally, there is "Kathryn's Summer". A young adult novel about two shy kids who fall in love for the first time, but only after the hilarious actions and schemes one shy boy employs to meet the girl of his dreams.

Thanks again for taking the time to read my book. I truly appreciate it and look forward to hearing from you.

Connect with me online:

Facebook: https://www.facebook.com/jim.ricca.3

Smashwords: https://www.smashwords.com/profile/view/jricca

E-mail: tcwsauthor@yahoo.com

www.ingramcontent.com/pod-product-compliance
Lightning Source LLC
Chambersburg PA
CBHW032125170626
46808CB00006B/2109